# Good Samaritans

**The Brendan Cleary Series, Volume 3**

P.M. Heron and Dexter Bradgate

Published by Sirani Publishing Limited, 2019.

GOOD SAMARITANS

**First edition. May 11, 2019.**

Written by P.M. Heron and Dexter Bradgate.

# Chapter One

'WHAT ARE WE DOING HERE?' Lorna shivered, side-stepping from her left foot to her right in a bid to keep herself warm.

'Will you stop that pacing; you're making me cold just watching you,' Brendan complained, pulling his hands inside his cuffs. His eyes scanned the road on the other side of Adelaide Street, a central street directly behind Belfast City Hall. He gestured to the gym that was directly facing them. The lights came on. 'I'm waiting for my mate to open up.'

'Brendan, now's not the time to be trusting people.'

'I don't trust him.' Brendan looked at Lorna, then looked back as an athletically built man opened the doors to the gym. 'That's him.' Before Brendan had a chance to say another word, a high-pitched scream cut through his ears.

He stepped out from the shelter he was taking below the block of apartments to see a lady being tossed out of a car. She stumbled and fell sideways, tripping over the kerb and landing in a puddle. The car she was in – a black VW Passat – took off.

Brendan and Lorna went over to help the lady out. She lay on the ground covering up her face. Crying into her arms.

Brendan reached down to give her a hand. He grabbed her by her left arm and pulled her up. 'Are you okay, love?'

'Brendan, look at the fucking state of her; she needs a hospital,' Lorna said.

'No, no...please no hospital. I can't go to the hospital.' The lady looked at Brendan, then Lorna, as if pleading for her life. She spoke with an accent. 'If I go to hospital, people will ask questions. Then they will ask for police. If police come, I will lose my son. Please. He's all I have.'

'Where is your baby?' Lorna asked, taking a tissue from her handbag and giving it to the lady.

'He's with him; he gives us shelter and food.' She gestured towards the car she'd just been thrown out of.

'He also gives you a busted nose and a fat lip,' Brendan said. 'What did you do wrong?'

'I don't want to talk about it.' She pinched her nose to stop the bleeding. 'I've got to go.'

Lorna grabbed her arm. 'Where are you in such a rush to get to at this time of the day?'

'It doesn't matter, I've got to go, now please...'

'Let us buy you breakfast,' Brendan said. 'What's your name?'

She didn't resist the offer. 'Diana.'

'You're Polish?' Brendan asked.

'Romanian,' she said, calming down.

'Come on, I know a nice café that opens soon,' Brendan said. 'We'll buy you breakfast and help you get cleaned up.'

'We'll even get you some new clothes.' Lorna said. 'I'm Lorna, and this is Brendan.'

'Just call us the good Samaritans,' Brendan laughed.

'WHAT DO YOU WANT?' Lorna asked Diana as the three sat at the window staring at the menus.

'Full Ulster Fry, large,' Diana said, an expression of hope written across her face. 'And a cup of coffee, too?' she asked with uncertainty in her voice, as if they would have said no.

'Is that it? Anything else?' Brendan asked. 'Think I'll have the same.' He looked at Lorna. Lorna kept her eyes fixed on the menu, her face serious as if she was struggling to make the best decision.

'Christ, you're not deciding whether or not to donate an organ,' Brendan joked.

'I'll have the same as you pair.' She looked up as the waiter came over.

'We're all up early today,' the tall slim guy said, sounding as if he'd just rolled out of his bed.

'We've got a busy day ahead,' Lorna said. 'Can't start the day without three large coffees and three large Ulster breakfasts.'

'Give us about fifteen minutes. We've just got the fryers on.'

'We're in no rush,' Brendan said, looking out the window of the shop as people started making their daily commute to their jobs.

'So,' Lorna said, ready to address Diana's morning. 'You want to tell us what really happened this morning when that twat bowled you out of the car?'

Diana looked down at her hands, which were clenched into fists.

'Whatever it is, it can't be any worse than stories I've heard before,' Brendan said.

'I came here from Romania five years ago. The guy in the car is somebody I knew in Romania. He promised me a better life here in the UK. First we started in London, then we came here.'

'And what work are you in?' Lorna asked. 'And what's his name?'

'His name is Dimitru, and he's very dangerous. Trust me, he is very much feared in both Romania and here in Belfast. His organisation in Romania has close ties to the UDA in Belfast. The UDA allow him to bring women, men and children here for many purposes, and the UDA turns a blind eye to his operations as long as he pays them a cut.'

'Makes good business sense,' Brendan laughed sarcastically. 'What's that on your wrist?' He gestured to a scar.

'That was a day when I wasn't feeling so good. He was beating me and took pleasure in it.' She looked at Lorna, her eyes filling up like glasses of water. She wiped her nose on her sleeve. 'Anyway, what do you two do, apart from being good Samaritans that hang around in the rain in the morning?'

Brendan and Lorna looked at each other.

'We take it upon ourselves to fight crime, in a way the police don't!'

'I'd prefer to think of it as being more like Robin Hood, except we rob from the crooks so that we can fund our profession.'

Lorna laughed. 'Yeah, so we should all be grateful for the breakfast. It's on your boss Dimitru.'

'You've got his money?' Diana sounded confused.

'We will,' Brendan said. 'With your help.'

'I don't understand.' She looked confused. Her eyes narrowed and mouth dropped as if she'd been told a bad joke.

'You want to go back to him later, and, forgive me for being rude, continuing in this depressing excuse for a life?' Lorna looked at Brendan, then back at Diana. 'Or do you want to help us two put an end to his operations?'

'And a foot in his ass?' Brendan added.

Diana's eyes darted from Brendan to Lorna. She shook her head, then fixed her eyes on the table. 'I don't think you should be talking like this. Dimitru is a very dangerous man and you should not talk about him...'

'Fuck Dimitru and the UDA he's working with,' Brendan hissed below his breath to ensure only the three at the table could hear what was being said. 'He's getting what's coming to him.'

'Look,' Lorna said. 'You show all the signs of someone who's been programmed. That bastard's instilled that much fear in you; he thinks he's your master. And the sorry thing is, you're starting to believe it.' She looked at Brendan, nodding in agreement. 'I've worked with scum like him many times before, back when I actually worked for the government. And all the tell tale signs are there, Diana.'

'I don't know,' she said as the breakfast was brought over.

'Eat your breakfast, then make up your mind.' Brendan rubbed his hands, grinning. 'Enjoy some good Irish food.'

# Chapter Two

'SO, WHERE CAN WE FIND prince charming today, then?' Brendan asked as they stepped out of the shop into the sea of people, adding to the pedestrian rush hour. He put his hood up as the rain began, and by the look of the clouds, it wasn't going to be a short spell.

'When I text him, he's picking me up from the location he left me. He said he's got business to take care of over in the Shankill first, so he said not to be any sooner than midday.'

'Okay, if he's going to be out of the house for a while, perhaps we'll take you home and we can snoop around to see if there's anything there that we can find useful.'

'I'm not sure that's such a good idea,' Diana said.

'Look, it'll be okay, don't worry,' Lorna said. 'We can set you and your son up somewhere safe.'

'Where does he live?' Brendan sounded more like he was telling Diana to give him the answer. It was like a game of good cop bad cop and it was obvious who was who.

'Okay,' Diana gave in. 'But we need to get Teodoro first. He's priority number one.'

'Okay, where is he?' Lorna asked as they turned the corner to arrive back on Adelaide Street again where they'd met.

'He's at his grandparents' house. It's not far, in a small town called Ballymena.'

'Great, as if I haven't been there enough,' Brendan laughed, opening the driver's side door of the black Audi A8 that his backstabbing uncle Bobby had so kindly gifted him.

'It's Dimitru's parent's house.'

'Will they ask questions if you just turn up and take Teodoro?' Lorna jumped into the passenger seat; Diana got into the back. 'I mean, they're not going to smell trouble and call their son, are they?'

Diana shook her head. 'They dislike his activities more than I do. They love me and Teodoro. They've always told me to take him away from him and his life because they don't want Teodoro becoming...'

'Like his father?' Brendan looked at her in the mirror. She was looking down at the floor, her face red, full of shame. 'Look, you shouldn't feel ashamed of your past. Today's a new day.'

'Yeah, and you should have seen the state of him.' Lorna gestured to Brendan, who'd started the engine and was making his way past a marked PSNI vehicle. 'This charming devil here was lying in a heap on the dirty mattress of a cell in Musgrave Park station with the worst hangover I'd ever seen.'

Brendan just continued to drive the car, an awkward grin on his face.

'You mean, you arrested him?' Diana asked.

'No, I was in Belfast with my superior, we were investigating Brendan and his infamous family. One of the most feared and notorious families in Belfast.'

'Bunch of dicks, if you ask me,' Brendan said.

'Wait one minute.' Diana took her phone out and flicked through it, looking up at Brendan's reflection in the mirror and back down at the phone. 'It's him, you...' Her jaw dropped open. 'Oh my god, why didn't I notice this earlier? You're Brendan Cleary, *the* Brendan Cleary.'

'No autograph requests please,' Lorna joked. 'His head is already fat enough.'

'You know I could hand you in and get a massive reward,' Diana laughed. 'Wait a second, on the news it said you had a female...'

'Accomplice,' Lorna finished. 'Again, no autographs. But for what it's worth, those things we were supposed to have done weren't true.'

'I don't give a shit if you did them or not. I don't trust half of what I hear on the news. And I certainly don't feel bad for those MPs that were shot.' Diana said.

'You know it wasn't actually them that were shot?' Brendan said. 'Those two bastards were laughing all the way to the beach...'

'And the bank.' Lorna added.

'You're right in not believing everything you hear in the news,' Brendan said. 'It's a load of bollocks, most of it.' He stopped at a red light, number four in the queue behind three taxis. Switching on the radio, there was a story saying the bodies of Brendan and Lorna had been found. Unrecognisable. It took their dental records to identify them. Case closed. They were now dead.

Brendan looked at Lorna and laughed. 'Looks like we're free.' He grabbed Lorna's hand, but she reached over to him and gave him a kiss.

'At least we've got the authorities off our backs.'

Diana was stunned. She had no idea what this meant. 'This means you can both go and do whatever you want.' She paused, momentarily pondering. 'I don't know if I'd like that to be my life or not.'

'We've had to make the best of a terrible situation,' Lorna said. 'We've turned the tables on the very government I'd dedicated my life to and who had no problem having me shot in Belfast, too. But when we got away, the very people I thought would protect me right to the end were the ones who'd betrayed me in the first instance.'

'And you?' Diana looked at Brendan.

'If I'm going to go down, I'm taking as many of these dirty bastards as I can. We've negotiated with the British government that we'll keep their secret as long as they let us go and don't come looking for us.'

'So, what, you're just going to go around taking the law into your own hands?'

'Well, after the British state proved it's as crooked as any criminal empire, we're going to do what they should be doing.'

'What makes you want to do this?'

'Let's just say we've both seen things that have opened our eyes.' Lorna said.

Driving along the duel carriage way towards Ballymena, the chatter died away, leaving only the thumping sound of the wind beating against the window. Brendan was focusing on the personalised registration plate on the black Mercedes directly in front of them. It had P35HRN on it. Lorna was staring absentmindedly out the window, watching the trees whizz past. Diana was staring at her phone.

'Wow, he's such an asshole,' Diana laughed without humour in her voice. 'Dimitru has just texted me saying he wants me to go and buy him a large gym bag from Sports Direct.'

'He goes to the gym? Lorna said.

'He's a steroid monster, but he needs it to move some "stash" this evening for his mate.'

'So, drugs or money, then.' Lorna said.

'How many others are there that he's using to do all his dirty work? Brendan added.

'There are a few houses full of Romanian women and children throughout the city. Because we have Teodoro together, he sees me as his own. He doesn't put me out on the street for sex trade, but he treats me like shit anyway.'

'How much does he tell you about his operations?' Brendan asked, his tone lifted as if a light bulb moment had arrived.

'I do anything, from weighing the dope to weighing the underweight prostitutes. If it wasn't for Teodoro, I'm sure I'd be one of those underweight girls, out sucking off random strangers who are unhappy in their marriages.'

'Okay, change of plan,' Brendan said as he indicated to pull into an Apple Go petrol station. 'We can help you today. Get you and Teodoro away from this scumbag, or you can help us find out about his operations. We'll make sure the evidence falls into the right hands and his whole operation comes to an end.'

'Half of his operations come from Romania. It's not just Belfast.'

'Well, it looks like our entrepreneurial friend will be shutting down his multinational enterprise, then!' Brendan said.

'What will you need me to do?'

Lorna looked over her shoulder. 'We can give you a private mobile to contact us on. And for god's sake, don't let him find it. Do you have a private email, one he couldn't possibly get his hands on?'

'Yes.'

'Okay, I'm going to email you a list of suspects we have on file. If you can identify any of them as being his current associates, we can bring them down, too.'

'So, I just act normal for now?'

'Yes. And I'd love to know what's going into that sports bag you're buying for him today.'

'If it's laundered money, we'll make some use if it.' Brendan looked at Lorna. 'Perhaps we can use it to become a pain in their ass.'

Brendan and Lorna had now become ghosts in a world where they'd been made public enemies number one and two. For Brendan, his life was never one he enjoyed or embraced; growing up in a family where there was always police around, British army raids, guns and bombs were in his house. He'd been moulded into the person he was. His father had disappeared and returned at the moment he'd needed him the most. Dying in Brendan's arms had sealed the deal for Brendan. Not only had his life dealt him a hand that would serve to create a pissed-off human being with a hate-the-world mentality, but the world had given Brendan the one person his life was missing, just to take him away again.

It was as if it was a tease - bringing his father into his life for a matter of hours, only to have him die in his arms. At least Brendan's father had chosen his last words before he died. Those words were: 'Help as many people as you can, Brendan. You're not a bad person. Don't let the bad things that have happened to you define you.'

# Chapter Three

AT THREE THIRTY IN the afternoon, while in their suite in Lurgan's Premier Inn Hotel, Lorna entered the bathroom to tell Brendan that they'd received a text from Diana. Brendan was in the middle of shaving his head – a new look for himself in contrast to the long-haired and bearded Brendan that was notorious on the streets of Belfast.

He quickly jumped into the shower to wash off the loose hair that would have otherwise plagued him with an itchy back for the rest of the evening. Stepping into his boxer shorts, he followed the smell of freshly-brewed Lavazza into the room.

'What's she said?' He dropped himself down on the bed beside Lorna, who was fixed on her phone.

'Well, there are going to be guns in that bag,' she said. 'But she doesn't know what for, yet.'

'Did she say anything else?' Brendan downed the espresso and lay back down on the bed. 'I mean, anything that we can use before getting out of here.' He paused for a second. 'I've to get out of this place. It's driving me crazy.'

'From my experience, to get close to Dimitru, we need to get close to his friends. And not his UDA bum buddies, but his Romanian friends who he brought to Belfast.'

'The best way we can get close to his friends, without raising too many suspicions, is to use their services.'

'Okay, well you can pick. Which service do you want to purchase: you want to get high, or you want to get laid?'

'You know you're the only lady I want to be with.' He sat up quickly and kissed Lorna on the cheek. 'I only have eyes for you.'

Lorna grunted in mock agreement.

'But I think if I must choose,' he paused for a second, 'screw it, let's do both.'

Lorna looked at him, eyes narrowed. Confused. 'You're being greedy now.' She laughed, but there was a serious tone coming through her words.

'I want to know who operates the "shops" and where they store their stash. We're not just going to cripple these fuckers financially. I want to remove their resources as well. And I won't lose any sleep over punishing them physically.'

'I only care about setting those hookers free and bringing anyone who's been exploiting them to justice.' She now lay back down on the bed. 'But you can do what you feel's best.'

Brendan lay back down beside her. He knew Lorna was still scarred by seeing her mentor's brains spread all over the windscreen of their car; the car in which Brendan had been taken out of the police station in. No matter what each other's different motives were, they both had the other's back.

Lorna texted Diana to inform her what they were planning. With the Romanian lady and her son both in immediate danger, both Brendan and Lorna had to ensure they were careful in their pursuit to bring these criminals to justice.

'There's a guy called Loan Ungur; Diana's recognised him from the file of suspects I sent her,' Lorna said. 'She said he runs the drugs out to the street corners. He fancies himself a bit of a hard man and...' she laughed. 'She even said the bastard stood as one of Teodoro's godparents.'

'Where does he live?'

'A quiet little estate over in the Holywood part of the city. But Diana said he goes to a gym on the street we found her this morning. He goes there with Dimitru.'

'Wouldn't be surprised if the two of them hand out a few needles while they're training.'

Lorna replied to Diana's update, thanking her for putting her trust in them, especially when trust was perhaps the last thing she was capable of. As both Brendan and Lorna knew first-hand, trust was fragile, taking a long time to build and can be dismantled in a moment.

'I know that gym well,' Brendan said. 'I used to train there once upon a time. It's still being run by a fat fuck called Stephen Henning. He's another steroid injecting wannabe hard man.'

'God, they all are, Brendan.'

'Tell Diana to text us the second her old man gets back for his dinner. Then, we'll just borrow his training partner for the evening. Are you coming for a gym session?'

'Why not? Don't want to get fat now that I'm no longer working for Her Majesty's services.'

At five twenty-five, Brendan and Lorna met in the lobby of the hotel. Brendan was dressed in black tracksuit bottoms and a matching hoodie, looking more like he was on his way to the gym rather than having just been in one. He put a cap on to hide the face that had been plastered all over the TV.

'What are you gawking at?' Lorna asked him as she sat down on the cream leather sofa beside him. A queue of customers was growing impatient at the new guy on reception taking so long to check them in.

'The message my father sent me.'

'Brendan, it's understandable that you want to hold on to that, and you're not going to like to hear this, but it's better if you shut your mind off from it, at least until we get out of this depressing city.'

He locked his phone and dropped it in his pocket again. He sighed and looked around the lobby area. 'You said you've been to Paris. What's it like?'

'Like any city, I suppose,' Lorna said. 'Got it's good parts and bad parts. Just on a much larger scale.'

'Which part of London are you from?'

'Croydon.' Her usual high-pitched upbeat tone fell.

'Why the voice?'

'Unlike you, I actually like where I come from. And I miss being able to just go home and see my family and friends.'

'You're only realising this now?'

'No, but talking about it brings it all back again.'

'Okay, well, just as I shouldn't think about my father, you shouldn't think about home.'

'You asked, knob head.'

'You should have told me to drop it, you knob head.' Brendan tapped her foot with his.

'Somebody should give that poor guy a hand.' Lorna gestured at the guy facing the ever-increasing line of customers. 'Come on, let's go and fuel the car while we wait for Diana's call.'

As they left the hotel, a light drizzle had started. Lorna was dressed in tight-fitting cream trousers and the damp was showing her underwear through. Her white blouse getting wet distracted Brendan and reminded him that this incredibly smart, insanely tough English lady was still a lady, a lady who'd get the attention of many people.

He got into the passenger seat of the car.

Lorna put the air conditioning on as they left the carpark. The swooshing sound of cars ploughing through the puddles that were forming on the roads were a sign of Irish weather at its best. The Cool FM news bulletin said the British Prime Minister was arriving at Stormont Estate later in the week for talks around the crisis which the six counties of Northern Ireland were in.

Joining a queue of vehicles merging onto the Westlink underpass towards the M2 motorway northbound, they took the left exit just before leaving the city and pulled into the Cityside shopping complex.

'You want anything to eat?' Brendan asked as he jumped out. 'I'm starving.'

'Grab me a chicken sandwich and a bottle of Pepsi.'

After filling the car, they pulled into the carpark to wait for Diana's call. The call didn't come until six thirty-five.

Loran answered, then looked at Brendan. 'Diana, why are you whispering?'

'I'm in the garage. Dimitru is in the kitchen. I've got to be quick; he wants me to join him. He told me he's meeting his training partner for a "drink" this evening at the Red Brick on Elmwood Avenue of the city centre. He's too trusting of me.' She laughed. 'I know the passcode to his phone.

I've checked Google Maps, as he told me he's to go to this guy's house for the first time today to pick him up as his car's getting fixed.'

'You've got this guy's address in Holywood?' Brendan sounded impressed.

'Yes, I will email it to the account you guys sent me the suspect file from.'

'Diana, can you find out the addresses where they're keeping the slaves?' Lorna asked. 'If they're out tonight, we can go and check out the place out.'

'I already know what conditions they're living under. Terrible. They're crammed into very small spaces. Bunk beds on top of bunk beds. The houses are worse than pigsties. I've got to go. I'll send you the addresses later.'

# Chapter Four

BACK AT THE HOTEL, Brendan and Lorna went back to their rooms, patiently waiting for Diana's text. A message that didn't come. Lorna grew worried.

'Screw this,' she said, 'we can't just sit around here waiting for her to text back. You fancy a night out at the city's nightclubs?'

'Dressed like this?' He laughed. 'We can go and get you something from the supermarket. It's only across the road.' He smirked. 'I've always dreamed of being asked out on a date by a beautiful lady. But never in my life would I imagine being asked out by a sexy ex-British agent turned enemy of the state.'

'This is strictly business, and your charm might work on the girls you've hooked up with before, but not with me.' She blew him a kiss.

She was right. Lorna was a lady of exceptional class. And Brendan knew it. That didn't stop them from teasing each other. And after what happened in Italy, they both seemed to have a newfound attraction for the other. The old *you don't know what you've got until you've lost it* had smacked them both like playing chicken with a bus.

As they left the hotel, Lorna continued to check her phone. Still nothing from Diana. 'Hope she's okay. God hope nothing's happened.'

Brendan nodded as he pulled his hood up over his head. Exiting the hotel's entrance, they turned left and proceeded to walk towards Tesco twenty-four supermarket. Seeing the homeless people lying under the shutters of closed shops caused a feeling of gratitude to sweep over them like a winter chill. Grateful for their own, far from perfect, lives. They were far from perfect, but they weren't sleeping on the streets, like many others in Belfast.

Inside the shop, they strolled along the limited isle of men's supermarket branded fine evening wear. Brendan wasn't really bothered by what he wore. He would have been happy with a pair of dark-coloured jeans and a checked shirt. But Lorna, on the other hand, had a different idea. She went straight for the suits.

'Here.' She snatched a pair of pinstripe grey suit trousers and a plain purple shirt off the rack and handed them to him. 'Go and try these on.' She gestured towards the cubicles in the corner of the clothing area, a member of staff stood staring at her fingernails, probably more worried about what time she finished than how well Brendan's clothes would fit. This wasn't a high-end shop on London's Oxford Street.

Brendan let Lorna take charge, perhaps like most men would have. When shopping for clothes, food, or any other form of commodity that didn't require an internal combustion engine to power, women were in charge. Most men would go on auto-pilot mode and let the finer sex naturally take the lead.

Brendan stepped out of the cubicle. Lorna was sitting cross-legged on a seat in the shoe fitting area, fixed on her phone.

'Well?' Brendan said. 'Feel like a twat.'

She looked up from her phone, smiled, and whistled. 'I'd date that.' Being flirtatious, she stood up. 'You like this?' She pulled a cream-coloured silk dress off the for-sale rack and held it up against her.

'I'd date that,' Brendan said.

'Maybe you will, one day.'

'That ship's already sailed.' He smirked. 'Right, are we done shopping? I'm beginning to itch.'

Making their way towards the self-service checkout, Brendan looked at the ground, almost aligning it with the ground, as he noticed his ex-girlfriend marching in with a pram and two toddlers chasing each other. Lorna looked at him, knowing something had caused him to start acting weird.

He swiftly turned his body in the opposite direction of the lady and children in question. Then Lorna understood.

She grinned at him. 'Old flame?' She nudged him as she proceeded to the till. 'Hope those kids aren't yours?'

'Me, too.'

Lorna looked at him, her eyes wide in shock.

'I'm joking,' he reassured her.

But it was a reminder of how much they needed to stay away from watchful eyes.

'Still no word from Diana?' Brendan asked as they exited the shop.

'No,' Lorna said. 'I hope we haven't gotten her into trouble.'

Brendan nodded, a serious expression on his face.

They got into the car and went back to the hotel. After a cup of tea and a quick shower, they both got ready to leave. Parking three streets away from the club, they walked along Shaftsbury Square, which was being overtaken by rowdy students acting boisterous. Of course, there was always one who'd drink too much during their pre-drink session, and this one was now fit for nothing more than hugging a lamppost. He even decided to throw up on his shoes.

Brendan looked at Lorna. She looked at him.

'There's a guy for you.' Brendan grinned. The guy was being laughed at by his mates, who were trying to help him. He managed to throw up his dinner from the evening. 'Pure class. Hope they don't expect to get in the club now.'

'I'm more interested in this guy, here.' Lorna gestured to a group of men chatting to the door security. They were obviously not getting in and were not happy about it. Brendan led the way up to the door. One of the doormen looked at them both and held the door open for them.

'Have a good night, guys,' the guy said. He had an accent similar to Diana's.

Lorna thanked him in Romanian to see if he'd respond. He did. He thanked her back in Romanian and told her to give him a shout if she needed something extra to have a good time.

'Romanian?' Brendan shouted in Lorna's ear as they entered the club to the sound of Run DMC's collaboration with Aerosmith.

She nodded her head. 'He told me to come see him if I wanted an extra kick, you know, make my night more enjoyable. Think we've found a member of Dimitru's crew.'

They went to the bar and yelled for two cokes. Taking a seat in the corner, they had a good view of the entire area. Especially the door.

Sitting under the colourful lights of the club, listening to a collection of nineties and noughties music, they both grew bored. The time was eight forty-five and the venue still had only a handful of people, most of whom were in their late teens and early twenties. About to go out for some fresh air, Lorna finally received a text from Diana.

*Sorry for the late reply, he's left the house now. He's going to pick up his training buddy and they're meeting another mate at the entrance to the M Club at nine-thirty. I've sent a link to their Facebook profiles. Look through these for recent photos of them. Dimitru also has a profile picture.*

'Let's go and grab a chippy. We've got an hour to kill anyway,' Lorna said. 'I want to see what I can get off this guy at the door, too, if he'll be so kind as to sort me out.' She forwarded Diana's message to Brendan.

He clicked on the link to Dimitru's Facebook profile. 'Nice car,' he said. 'Business is good for old Dimitru.'

'Not for long,' Lorna said as she approached the Romanian doorman. He watched as she strutted towards the door, running her fingers through her hair. 'What can you get for us?'

'Anything you want,' he said, grinning at Lorna and then at Brendan. Brendan grit his teeth, wanting to give the entire door team a bit of exercise. 'You are okay, my friend?' The door man shouted at Brendan, in an angrier tone than he offered Lorna.

Lorna looked at Brendan and answered for him. 'He's just got a sore head tonight.' She looked at Brendan, her eyes piercing him. 'He'll be better if we can get something to shake his mood.'

'Come back to me in about one hour, I am waiting for someone,' he answered Lorna while fixing his stare on Brendan.

'What's your number and I'll call you, we have to go.'

Lorna handed him her phone. He thumbed his mobile number in and shook her hand. 'I'm Andrei.'

# Chapter Five

SITTING IN THE MONTE Carlo fish and chip shop on the bustling Lisburn Road, a five-minute walk from the pub, Brendan recalled many years of staggering into the establishment for his end-of-night fish and chips. The memories flooded his mind like an amusing dream. A different time. He was a different person. Perhaps a more innocent person; but someone who had all that skill locked up in his bones. All that responsibility waiting for him. All it took was someone to walk into his life and draw it out.

'I'm not used to being in here sober,' Brendan laughed as he dipped a chip into the pot of mayonnaise. 'I would have stumbled through this door and fallen against the counter.'

'Well, you're a lot more attractive now,' Lorna said as she cut through her foot-long cod with a plastic knife and fork. 'I remember the morning we met, seeing you on your back sprawled across that mattress in a cell.' She laughed. 'I gotta be honest with you, Brendan.' She looked at him, biting into the golden batter the fish was wrapped in. 'I thought you were nothing more than a drunken twat then.'

'Ouch.' He laughed, dropping his head, paying more attention to his meal. 'Have you never been married? No kids?'

She shook her head while staring at her meal. 'No kids. No boyfriend. Never had time to think about it.' She put another chip in her mouth, her eyes glazed as she looked at him. She smiled then looked back down at her plate. Cutting into her fish again, she said, 'You?'

'My doctor thinks I have trust issues.' He laughed, as if mocking the question. 'I've never been in a relationship longer than three months.'

'Well, you can be hard to stick, if I'm honest with you.' Lorna looked at him.

'Piss off.' He lightly kicked her foot. 'What time is it?'

She pulled her phone out as it sounded in her bag. She opened a message. 'It's time for us to go and score some dope.' She grabbed her meal and stood up as if she were excited about getting some drugs.

Brendan wrapped the rest of his meal in it's paper and followed her.

As they stepped out into the cool air, Brendan looked at the car. 'Let's leave it here. We can come back for it. It's only five minutes away.'

Lorna linked her arm with his, and they crossed the street in between the few cars flying past in both directions.

'Don't be starting anything with this guy, Brendan. I saw the way you were looking at him.'

'Yeah, like I wanted to put his head through the bar's window.' Brendan threw the last few chips in his mouth and crumpled up the wrapper, dropping it into the roadside bin. He cleared his throat. 'And I know how to contain myself. Why would I risk an opportunity to cut the head off this entire organisation just so I could spread a doorman around the street?'

Approaching the pub, they noticed it was livelier than it had been when they left. Andrei now had a colleague to assist him, now there stood two threatening door men. Andrei spotted them coming; he whispered something in his colleague's ear. The two watched as Brendan and Lorna approached, but at around thirty yards from the door, Andrei shouted for them not to come any further. He'd be over to them in a second.

They stopped and watched as he disappeared inside the pub, then reappeared with a black bomber jacket on, his hands shoved in the pockets. He aimed his smug grin at Lorna, giving Brendan just a brief glance of recognition. It was obvious, the way the Romanian was acting, that he was never going to make it easy for Brendan to act friendly around him.

'What have you got for us?' Lorna said. Her question was abruptly interrupted by Andrei gesturing towards a silver BMW 5 series, parked directly under the street lighting on the other side of the road.

They followed him across. He opened the driver's door and indicated for them to get in. Lorna got in the front passenger seat. Brendan got in directly behind the driver's seat. If Andrei was to try something, Brendan would be in a better position to hide his hand movements.

'I don't usually give product to strangers,' Andrei said as he turned on the internal lighting. 'Especially a posh English lady who speaks as if she should be preparing lectures tomorrow for students instead of scoring dope on the streets.' He looked at Brendan in the rear-view mirror. It was almost as if each were trying to read the other's mind.

'Why did you, then?' Brendan said, holding Andrei's gaze.

Andrei grinned. 'Because, business is business. And it is none of my business who or what you do, Brendan Cleary.' He looked at Lorna. 'And you, Miss ex-MI5 agent—your facial features are still as striking and memorable even with a change of hair.'

Lorna didn't say a thing.

'So, you know my name.' Brendan spoke casually. Was he supposed to be worried? He knew no matter what their business was, criminals weren't in the business of calling the authorities on people who were wanted. 'Big deal. Now have you got what we want or not?'

Andrei sniggered, pulling a see-through plastic bag out of his coat pocket. 'Some ecstasy will lift your mood. But might I suggest you leave this country? If I can recognise you, anyone can.'

'Thanks for the advice.' Lorna snatched the bag and looked inside. 'How much?'

Andrei looked confused. 'For?'

'All of it?'

'You take all of these, and you'll not see tomorrow morning.'

'Let us worry about that,' Brendan said. 'And we'll not be back here again. If we want more, who can we get them off?'

'You come to me, my friend. You come to me and I'll get you your drugs. You don't need to deal with anyone else. Is that okay for you?'

'You're the boss,' Lorna said. 'Now how much for the bag?'

'For you, sexy British agent, five hundred.'

Lorna pulled out her purse. She counted five hundred crisp twenties into his hand. 'Pleasure doing business with you.' She blew him a sarcastic kiss and threw the door open as if she couldn't get away from him fast enough.

Brendan and Lorna made their way back to their car on the Lisburn Road. Lorna stopped just beyond the bus stop, looked at Brendan, and blew him a kiss. 'You don't need these to have a good time.' She produced the bag and forced it between the iron bars of a street drain.

'Waste of money,' Brendan said. 'Come on, we'll get a re-fund off him when we're done with them.'

'You want to go back and take the money off him?'

Brendan linked arms with her as they walked across the road. 'For five hundred quid? No. We'll tax the boss when Diana gives us more intel. Then we can take the cash and the stash. Everything.' He opened the passenger door for Lorna. She kissed him on the cheek as she lunged into the car.

As Brendan got behind the wheel, Lorna was gawking at her phone. 'What is it?'

She looked up at him. 'Diana.'

'What has she said?'

'That Dimitru is only going to the M Club briefly, then on to a late-night lock-in at the Red Brick.' She cleared her throat. 'Looks like tonight's going to be a busy night.'

Brendan started the engine and took off down the Lis-burn Road towards Shaftsbury Square, a bustling part of Belfast, with nightlife that could compete, be that on a smaller scale, with London.

'I want a shower,' Brendan said as he stopped at the red traffic lights outside the historic Europa Hotel. 'We'll park up and go sit in the hotel for a while. I don't know about you, but I'm starting to feel a little bit like a Robin Hood.'

'Dream on, handsome.'

'Except, I think we should rob from the criminals, and give to ourselves to fund our campaign to take out other gangsters.'

'Don't you want a peaceful life?' She squeezed his hand as he thrust the stick into first and took off.

'Maybe one day. But if my father's dying wish was for me to try and do something with all the bollocks that I've had to endure all those summer months, then screw it. I'm going to play with these good-for-nothing sons of bitches that are bringing misery to people.'

'You really turn me on when we you talk like that.' She squeezed his hand again. 'And you're right.'

'We just need to plan our operations properly.' He squeezed her hand. 'Let's start with these fools who think they can run the streets of Belfast.'

AFTER SHOWERING TOGETHER, Brendan took Lorna to bed and showed her his animalistic side. After two hours of sex, she fell asleep in his arms, with her head resting on his bare chest. Soon, he dozed off.

At twenty minutes past midnight, Brendan's alarm went off. He kissed Lorna on the forehead, and she rolled off him, reaching for his phone. After switching the alarm off, she turned around and lay back down on his chest again. Neither of them wanted to move.

'How about we skip what we'd planned tonight and just stay here?' she grunted, turning around to face him, smiling mischievously. 'I could think of something better to do.'

Brendan kissed her. 'I'd love to, but we've got some heads to crush. Don't worry, I'll take you back to bed afterwards and show you how beautiful you are.' He spotted a green light flashing on her phone at the foot of the bed between them. 'You've got a message.' He sat up and grabbed it. Handing it to her, he rotated his legs off the bed and placed his feet down on the ground. Reaching over towards the bed-side cabinet, he switched on the light and took a drink from the glass of water. He handed it to Lorna to finish. 'Who's the message from?'

She took the glass and finished the water, while still reading from her phone. 'Our Romanian friend.'

'Is she okay?'

'I'm not sure.' Lorna didn't sound as sure as she usually did. 'She's asking whether or not any of this is going to come back on her. She's terrified Dimitru will find out what she's done and kill her.' She paused momentarily. 'Christ Brendan, she's starting to panic. She's saying she's going to clear her stuff and get out of the house tonight. She's more afraid for her son than herself.' She paused as if reading another text. 'She said she's got to do what's best for Teodoro. She's about to do a runner, Brendan.'

'Fuck sake.' Brendan ran his hands across the top of his head. 'Tell her there's nothing we can do for her if she just disappears.'

'I'm calling her now.' Lorna got up off the bed and went to the wardrobe. She reached into the clothes and moved them across, tilting her head as if trying to work out what to wear. With her smartphone pressed to her ear she finally got an answer. 'Look, don't panic,' She lifted out a pair of dark blue jeans and a black polo neck. 'I promise you, neither of you will come to any harm. I'll cut the bastard's balls off first.' She put the phone on loudspeaker and set it on the dressing table.

'How do you know he's not already suspicious?'

'Because there is no reason why he should be,' Lorna spoke loudly at the phone as she stepped her right leg into her jeans and followed with her left. 'Why would he be suspicious?'

'He asked me this evening if was something wrong. He was acting like he was trying to get information out of me. Being too inquisitive.'

'Look,' Brendan said. 'Don't panic. He doesn't know anything is wrong. By the time he does, he'll be nursing the wounds I deal him with my hands.'

There was silence. She didn't respond.

'Listen.' Brendan adopted a more encouraging tone, softer. 'The only way we can hurt this organisation is if we remove all of its moneymaking schemes and send him and anyone else in his crew to prison. Or back to Romania. We need your help. You can get closer to him than anyone else. While you're doing that, Lorna and I will start destroying the bastard's merchandise. His prostitution rackets and his drugs.'

She didn't respond.

'Are you there?' Lorna shouted as she pulled her top over her head.

'I'm here.'

'Listen, we're on our way to the Red Brick. We're going to get involved with them tonight.' Lorna looked at Brendan, a rebellious smile on her face was mirrored by him. He walked over her and gave her a kiss. 'And when we find out where all his merchandise is, tomorrow night,' she pulled Brendan in close and gave him another kiss, 'we're going to destroy everything in one night.'

'Two of you can't bring down everything in his organisation.' Diana sounded defeated. 'It's a huge organisation and it will take a long time to bring it down.'

'What you don't understand is,' Brendan grabbed his backpack that hung on the back of the desk chair, 'we don't have the luxury of time. If we start messing with their business one night, then by the second night they'll have their guard up and it'll be much harder for us. They'll have their merchandise protected and it would take us going in all guns blazing.' He opened the backpack and shuffled through the selection of firearms. 'And as attractive as the thought of sending a few of these bastards to their maker is,' he zipped the bag closed. 'It's better not to.' He flung the bag over his shoulder. 'Can you just keep it together a little while longer?'

'Okay.'

'Do you know if he'll be home tonight?' Lorna asked.

'It's a birthday party they're celebrating, so they'll probably go and get themselves a few girls.' She laughed sarcastically. 'Without paying of course.'

'Perks of the business, I suppose.' Brendan pulled open the bedroom door, holding it open for Lorna.

'Don't worry, we've got it under control. It'll all work out for the best. Get some rest.' Lorna hung up and dropped the phone into her jeans pocket.

# Chapter Six

THE TIME WAS ONE-FIFTEEN in the morning. The city had all but gone to sleep. Belfast was quiet, like a sleeping baby. The odd taxi could be seen chasing the money, taking advantage of the quiet, lifeless streets. Brendan drove. He left the car at the same location, they had earlier in the evening. Lorna was almost as tempted as Brendan to get their second Monty Carlo chippy, but they'd decided against it. The Red Brick would be closing it's doors at one-thirty, and they didn't want to lose their mark, or their opportunity to get through the doors.

'What do you think?' Brendan said as they crossed the tree-lined street, passing Andrei's BMW. 'Will they be using this place for their party or will they head somewhere else?'

'It's hard to say,' she said. 'Depends on how much influence they have on this place.'

The front door was closed. The security team had retreated into the heat. Lorna led the way, considering she'd already won the affection of Andrei. As she knocked, he greeted her with the same smile and look of excitement as earlier.

'As much as I'd like to let such a beautiful lady in, I'm sorry. We've closed our doors. We're not letting anyone else in.'

Lorna fell into him, wrapping her arms around his neck, giving him a sloppy hug and kiss on the cheek. 'How about a dance?'

Brendan stood back, hands in his pockets, realising what she was doing.

'I see you're enjoying the stuff you got earlier.' Andrei laughed. He looked at Brendan over Lorna's shoulder as she clung to him.

Brendan started swaying his jaw, as if feeling the effects of the ecstasy. 'Yeah, they're good, mate. Haven't had these in years. I'm buzzing.'

Andrei laughed as Brendan approached him and did everything but beg to have a handshake. He shook Brendan's hand. Brendan almost stopped the blood flow in the Romanian's oversized paw.

'Okay, I'll let you both in, but we shouldn't really. Only because I like you guys.'

Brendan continued acting as if he was experiencing the effects. Lorna was in more of a playful mood and gave Andrei another kiss on the cheek.

They made their way towards the bar.

Brendan looked at Lorna, grinning. 'You may as well be a high school girl with her first crush, blowing bubbles with your gum, twirling your hair.'

'You can talk, Mr swinging jaw.' She looked at him in the reflection of the mirror that ran the entire way along the back of the bar. 'Anyway, we're in.' She smiled at the barman as he approached them.

'Last orders, folks. We're closing.' He looked at Lorna, not paying much attention to Brendan. 'What can I get you?'

'I'll have a coke,' Brendan said.

'Vodka and coke for me,' Lorna said. She pulled her credit card out of her phone wallet, noticing the green light flashing on her device, alerting her that she'd received a message. She opened it. 'Diana said Dimitru's planning a trip home to meet with the boss.' She looked at Brendan. 'Fancy a trip to the Romania?'

'Not if I can help it. Maybe we can mess things up while they're away.'

'You afraid to go and meet with the big boys?' Lorna knew how to tease him.

'Okay, I tell you what.' Brendan looked at her, then over his shoulder, scanning the room. A group of men sat in the corner by the windows. One of the bouncers, Dimitru, and a few others, including his gym buddy, all huddled together around the small wooden table. 'We get an introduction tonight, tomorrow night we carry on as planned, then once we've shut down their operations over here, we'll take a trip across Europe and meet the big boss head on. Unless we bump into better options here.'

The barman came back with their drinks. Lifting their glasses, they made their way towards the table beside Dimitru and his crew. The group didn't take any notice of them, too busy egging each other on in a drinking competition, trying to see who'd finished their pint the fastest.

Brendan watched as their mark erupted into a fit of laughter; his gym buddy spilling half of his pint down his face. Lorna tried not to laugh, but the expression on her face was one of sheer entertainment.

'In Russia they wrestle bears; here the bears are men and wrestle with their drinks,' Lorna said. She put her lips to her glass, ready to drink it, but paused as she noticed something floating in it. 'What the hell is this?'

'What?' Brendan shouted. He took the glass from her and looked inside. 'Fucking pills?' He turned and looked in the direction of the barman, who'd quickly shifted his gaze from their direction. 'Have you got your pistol? We may need it.'

She tapped on her handbag.

Brendan stood up and brought their drinks back to the bar just as the venue's music shut off. The chinks of glass and roars from the crowd in the corner would have been a distraction to most. Brendan, however, had his hawk eyes on the guy who'd just served them their drinks.

'Everything okay with your drinks, mate?' The barman approached Brendan, grinning falsely.

'Aye, apart from this.' He held the glass up under the light. The pill was all but dissolved, a tiny spec swimming around inside the glass.

The barman squinted and looked closer at it. He shook his head, acting dumb. 'Sorry mate, I don't see anything.' He looked at Brendan, staring into Brendan's eyes. It was as if he was trying to read his mind. Then his eyes broke their stare and looked beyond Brendan, in the direction of where he came. Dimitru's muscle-bound gym buddy approached the bar. Through his side eye, Brendan glanced in the mirror; the guy was looking directly at Brendan.

'Can I have another drink?' Dimitru's buddy shouted, leaning against the bar, looking at Brendan. 'Do I know you from somewhere?'

Brendan didn't respond. He just shook his head.

'I do, I never forget a face,' he pressed for a response. 'You're...'

'Someone you don't want to fuck with.' Brendan turned and looked directly into the guy's eyes. The guy's breath stank of cider. Brendan turned and looked back at the barman. 'Now tell me why the fuck you spiked our drinks?'

The barman stood up and made his way towards the pump. 'That's a serious accusation, mate.' He looked at Dimitru's mate again. 'Same again?'

'Who the fuck do you think you are, hard man?' The gym head was oblivious to the barman's question and now had his focus purely on Brendan. He squared up to Brendan. His nose tip almost touched the tip of Brendan's. 'Do you know who I am?'

'I don't give a shit who you are; this piece of shit just spiked our drinks.'

The gym head looked over Brendan's shoulder at the barman. 'Did you spike their drink?' he shouted, as if the animosity he felt towards Brendan had now been re-directed at the barman. The barman didn't respond, but he looked in the direction of the doorman. The gym head turned and looked at the table where Dimitru and the others were now sitting quietly watching, then he looked back at the barman. 'Are you at it again? You prick. What did I tell you about that, you stupid...'

Brendan snatched up the two drinks from the bar and made his way towards the table.

The doorman stood to meet Brendan, but before he could say a word, Brendan rammed the glass into the side of the doorman's head. Bits of glass flew everywhere. The second bouncer came running at Brendan, but he got the second glass to the side of his head.

Dimitru jumped from his seat. He shouted for the barman to lock the door. Lorna produced her pistol. The two doormen were on the ground, both bleeding from their wounds. Dimitru looked at Brendan, then Lorna. 'Do you know who I am?'

'A scumbag Romanian who makes money off the exploitation of others,' Lorna said as she pressed her pistol into his back.

'And who are you, Mother Teresa?' Dimitru shouted in Romanian.

'She wishes,' Brendan spoke in Romanian, much to the surprise of everyone in the pub.

'You, Brendan Cleary...'

'That's right,' Brendan said.

'You've got some balls coming back here again. I don't know who wants you dead more, the Catholics or Protestants.'

Brendan smiled falsely. 'I'll choose door number three and say it's the government.'

'You're probably right. So what, you've just decided to come in here and start wrecking the place?' Dimitru said.

'No, we've come here to make you a business proposition,' Lorna said.

'Our business is doing just fine.'

'Yes, but it could be much better,' Brendan said. 'Ireland is one tiny country. I want you to imagine how much your organisation would grow with our contacts across the water.'

'Why don't we just give you up to the authorities?'

'Because, even though you may not be the smartest person in the world, you're not a rat. And in this world, you wouldn't last a week without someone putting a bullet in your head if you were.'

Dimitru looked at his mate, the gym head. 'Get a round of drinks in, I want to know more about this proposition.' He gestured for Lorna and Brendan to take a seat and ordered the two bouncers to clean themselves up and go get their heads checked out.

Brendan sat down at the table. Lorna stood, keeping her pistol pointed at Dimitru.

'What makes you think I'm interested in growing my business?' Dimitru said. 'I'm doing fine.'

'No you're not,' Brendan said. 'I've heard you're still handling your own merchandise. You're still on the ground, with all your little scumbag dealers. Your business isn't so good that you can put your feet up and count all the money that comes in. Whatever you're making in Belfast, we can quadruple the amount in the next six months.'

'How? You've spotted a gap in the market somewhere?' He looked at the gym head and laughed as four shots of whiskey were set down on the table.

'No, not a gap in the market,' Lorna said. 'But being in my former line of work, I know where to find all the drugs, guns and prostitution rackets. You want to take over the British market, if you've got the balls, we can give you the information needed.'

'*If* you've got the balls,' Brendan said.

'What's in it for you?'

'We get a cut of any money made from business across the water.' Brendan pushed his whiskey away. 'After the mess the British and Irish governments made a few months ago, it's not as if we can just go get a job in the local restaurants.'

Dimitru sniggered. 'This seems a bit too good to be true.' He knocked back one of the shots and offered one each to Brendan and Lorna. Both refused. 'Why don't you both take over the trade in England? What do you need us for?'

'You're already a big outfit,' Lorna said. 'You have the numbers and the resources to get the job done. We've got the intel that can make it happen.'

Brendan stood up. 'Mull it over. If you're interested. Give us a call. If not, no hard feelings.' He pulled a receipt out of his wallet and asked the barman for his pen. He scribbled his mobile number down and handed it to Dimitru.

They both exited the bar and made their way towards the car.

'What do you think?' Lorna said, out of earshot from the pub.

'I think they're a bunch of scumbags.'

'I mean...'

'I know,' Brendan laughed as he looked over his shoulder. 'But, I think Dimitru's as greedy as the average person. Meaning he's going to really think about how he can grow his business.' Brendan put his arm around Lorna as a gust of wind whipped around them. 'We'll see tomorrow. If we get a call.' He looked at Lorna as they approached the car. 'Fancy another chippy?'

She grinned. 'Go on then, but we'll need to join a gym to burn off all this shite we've been eating.' They went into the shop just as they were switching off the ovens. 'Are we too late?'

The same girl that had served them earlier smiled. 'I should say yes, eating this food twice in one day isn't good for your health. But you both look like you don't use this of place often. What can I get you?'

'Same as earlier?' Lorna looked at Brendan. He nodded and sat down on one of the metal seats that accompanied the three tables that ran along the window.

After grabbing their dinner, they took it to the car, not wanting to remain on the streets of Belfast for too long. Both were under no illusions, after what had happened at Stormont; they couldn't afford to be seen and caught.

Brendan habitually locked the doors once he got behind the wheel. After taking his first chip, his phone vibrated in his pocket. He pulled it out.

'Hello.' Brendan looked at Lorna, who was looking at him while making mincemeat out of her takeaway.

'We're having a late-night party for a friend's birthday.' It was Dimitru. 'We'd like to invite you. If we're going to be going into business, we'd like to know more about you.'

'So you're saying you want to go into business?'

'We can't say yes, now. We've only met you, Brendan. But we are interested in what you've got to offer. Of course, we'd like to grow our business. But, we'd certainly like to know more about you and the beautiful Agent Lorna Woodward.'

'Send us the address.' Brendan said.

'You know the Rathcoole estate?'

'What do you think?' Brendan laughed sarcastically.

'Drive to the takeaway shop. You will see it as soon as you enter the estate. Someone will be waiting for you.' Dimitru hung up the phone.

Brendan looked at Lorna. 'We've been invited to a party tonight.'

Lorna's brows furrowed. 'I don't know, Brendan.'

'We can't back out now.' He put two chips into his mouth. 'Tell you what, I'll go into the party. You can wait in the car.'

'What if there are loyalists in there?'

'That's why you're going to stay in the car. You can watch the house.' He started the car. 'These guys are businessmen; if they think we can make them more money, then that's what they'll be more interested in. Besides, do you think they'd want to consult the loyalists about other business ventures that have nothing more to do with them?' He put the car into first and pulled out onto the Lisburn Road.

# Chapter Seven

THEY PULLED INTO THE typical Irish housing estate of Rathcoole, which was mostly fields and trees with sporadically-placed rows of grey plastered houses. As they entered the estate, they regarded the first row of houses to the left, portraying a mural of an armed UDA man touting an automatic rifle. In most other places in the civilised world, images such as this would have been nothing less than unacceptable and would have been removed. But the organisation whom the mural glorified still ran the neighbourhood with an iron fist. Although Northern Ireland had experienced much peace in recent times, it was still plagued by the paramilitaries who saw themselves as protectors of their communities. Now drugs, weapons, and intimidation were what the groups were more interested in. Money. A business.

As Brendan pulled the car into the takeaway car park, he shut the engine off and looked at Lorna. 'I'll not be long. It'll be a simple meet and greet, kiss each other's ass for a while and then be done with it.'

'You've got your weapon?' She didn't look as enthusiastic about the situation as he did. But this was his city and he knew the score. 'I don't like this, Brendan. But if it gets us anywhere, then I've got your back.'

He took her hand and raised it to his lips. He looked into her eyes and kissed her knuckles. 'I won't be long.'

Just as he said this, a piercing whistle brought their attention to the other end of the carpark. Under the orange glow of street-lights, Dimitru walked towards them, smiling, his eyes wide. He certainly didn't seem like someone who felt under threat, but more like a man excited about a new business opportunity.

'If you sense anything wrong, get out of there, Brendan.'

'I'll be okay. I'm not meant to die in Rathcoole.' He smiled at her and got out of the car.

The night air bit him instantly. He slammed the car door closed and walked around to the other side towards Dimitru. The Romanian held his hand out to shake Brendan's. Brendan humoured him and greeted him in Romanian.

Dimitru followed the handshake with a pat on the shoulder and putting his arm around him. 'A bi-lingual Irishman,' he laughed. 'Most people over here can't even speak their own language.'

'Multi-lingual,' Brendan corrected. Then he said something in Gaelic.

'What was that?'

'I said I also speak my own language.' Brendan smiled, Dimitru erupted into a fit of laughter.

'An educated man. I like it. The beautiful lady?'

'She's not feeling that well. Think it had something to do with the drugs that twat sold her.'

'Yes, Andrei is also quite upset at what you did in the bar.' Dimitru laughed again. It was almost as if he'd taken something, or else he was just really happy to be in Brendan's company. 'I'm excited to learn more about what ideas you might have for our little business in Belfast. My business already makes me very happy.'

'Yet you choose to live in a little shithole estate like this.' Brendan spoke frankly.

'This is not my home, this is a party house we've come to. A lot of my co-workers live in this beautiful city, but me?' He waved his hand in the air as if to do away with the concept. 'I live just outside the city.'

The low thud of bass rumbled through the air. As they approached, the sound of dance music became clearer, coming from the end house in a row of six. The faded yellow kitchen light spilled out into the dark garden as Dimitru went in first. Muffled voices from the inhabitants grew louder with the music. Brendan stopped at the back door. His intuition was always something he could rely on. He was trying to read it, but it wasn't as if he could stop and think. Anything that would make Dimitru second-guess the reason why Brendan was there could be a big problem. He was walking into a house full of druggies, probably off their heads, and he could handle them. But given the housing estate he was in, it would be unwise to let the wrong people know he was there. Ever since his and Lorna's recent escapades, regardless of whether they were set up by the government or not, there would still be many people who would love to claim his life. The UDA controlled many loyalist estates in Belfast, and the fact Brendan had killed one of the commanders, his blood would be sought by many.

Brendan followed Dimitru inside, an overwhelming smell of beer and cigarette smoke attacking his senses. He shut the door and turned to follow Dimitru into the living room. A few steps behind, he could hear Dimitru telling the crowd that Brendan was coming in. The room fell quiet for a moment. Brendan looked around the kitchen, noticing one of the knives was missing from the rack. He went to grab his pistol, then decided not to. He was more than capable of taking a knife off a would-be attacker if he had to. Especially if they were under the influence. He just needed to keep himself cool. Calm.

He stepped into the living room. All eyes were on him. Three men sat at the dinner table – two of whom were the bouncers he'd floored in the Red Brick. The other looked at Brendan, his eyes glazed as if he didn't know what day it was.

'Here he is, the hard man of the night.' The gym head stood up from the sofa, stumbling towards Brendan, his hand outstretched. 'Where's the pretty lady?' He shook Brendan's hand, falling into him at the same time.

'She's not feeling very well.'

'That's a shame, we were going to get her to dance for us.' He looked back at the sofa where Dimitru now sat with a blond-haired lady around the same age as Brendan.

'Good luck trying to get her to do that.' Brendan spoke more seriously. 'She'd quicker chop your balls off and feed them to you.'

Dimitru laughed. 'He does have balls, this one, doesn't he?' He lit a cigarette. 'Grab a seat, Brendan. Relax. You're not in any danger.'

'Not at the moment,' Andrei shouted from the dining table.

Brendan took a seat, facing the rest of the room. He looked across the room at Andrei. 'You had your chance in the bar. Look how that worked out for you. If you want another shot, just say the word.'

Silence briefly fell over the room. Brendan knew this type. He'd dealt with them all his life. He knew if they thought he was an easy target they'd walk all over him and he'd get nowhere. The lady sitting bedside Dimitru cleared her throat, twirling her hair with her left index finger.

Brendan pulled his phone out and looked at the screen. 'Look, maybe we should chat tomorrow instead. I'm not into drugs or alcohol. I don't want to interrupt this party.'

'You're in the wrong business, then,' Andrei said. 'Maybe you should just fuck off then and let us get on with our party.'

Brendan put his phone in his pocket and stood up.

'Sit down, Brendan,' Dimitru complained. 'I'm going to make a call to the boss back home tomorrow, I'm pretty sure he'd like to sit down with you and talk about your little business proposal. Tonight is simply a chance for us to get better acquainted.' He slowly stood up, balancing himself on the lady next to him, and walked over to the fireplace. He grabbed a cigarette lighter off the mantel and lit a joint. 'But, we need to be sure you're not working for the authorities.'

Brendan sniggered. 'Me? Are you for real? Think you need to give the drugs up. They're fucking up your head.'

Dimitru laughed as he blew smoke from the joint. His phone rang. Answering it, he spoke in Romanian, looking at Brendan. 'Delivery,' he rushed across the room, through the door into the kitchen. Brendan's blood pressure went up. He stood up and followed Dimitru out to the kitchen. He almost walked right into the lady they'd met that morning.

The Romanian lady who was now their inside man. Diana. Dimitru's girlfriend. She looked at Brendan, her brows furrowed. Brendan's eyes shot open. He thought that was it. But she was a good actress, politely excusing herself, walking around him into the living room. She was so good that Brendan almost believed she was a complete stranger.

'Where do you think you're going, my friend? The party is just getting started.' Dimitru put his arm around Brendan playfully, dragging him back into the living room, in higher spirits now that his girlfriend had arrived. 'She's come bearing gifts.'

Diana pulled out a transparent plastic bag full of white powder. Cocaine. The hard stuff. Dimitru was right. The party was just about to get started. She looked at Brendan as she walked out into the kitchen. Her expression was one of those discreet "what the hell are you doing here" type of looks. Brendan looked at her again as if she were a complete stranger. It was a good thing she'd brought what she did. Everyone in the room was more concerned about getting a line of the white stuff than whether or not they knew each other.

Brendan walked over to the table, watching as Dimitru spread out six lines. Dimitru pulled a five pound note out of his wallet and rolled it up. He looked at Brendan, offering him the roll. Brendan refused. Dimitru wasn't going to force him. He was happy to take it himself.

'I appreciate you inviting me to your party; thanks for allowing me to come meet you all. But this is just boring the shit out of me. I'll call you tomorrow.'

Dimitru snorted two lines, one in each nostril, then dropped the rolled note down onto the table for whoever wanted to go next. 'I've something I'd like you to help me with tonight.'

Brendan knew what was coming next. He was going to have to incriminate himself for Dimitru to trust him.

'We've had a problem with someone. We need to go and teach them a lesson. Sort of send out a message to them and the rest of their group of nobodies that we are not fucking about. You happy to help?'

He had a split second to decide yes or no. Any reluctance would all but destroy any chance of meeting the big boss from Romania. What Brendan used to justify anything that he was about to get involved in was that whoever they were going to see was likely involved with them for the wrong reasons and wouldn't be completely innocent. 'You want to rough someone up?' He looked at Dimitru, then at the group at the table, all sniffing, snorting or wiping their noses. He shrugged his shoulders. 'I've got absolutely no problem with that. Let's go.'

Dimitru now looked like the one who was taken aback. He looked at the table of sniffers. 'Let's go; leave this shit until we come back.' He walked past Brendan, leading the way out into the hallway. He grabbed a rucksack that dangled over a coat stand in the corner next to the door. The clonk of metal inside the bag meant that there were not drugs inside, likely guns or blades. Dimitru pulled the front door open and stepped out into the front garden. He lit a cigarette and offered one to Brendan. Brendan quickly refused.

There was a slight drizzle. Brendan zipped his jacket up to the neck. He wanted to check his phone, knowing Lorna would be worried. If he didn't contact her, she'd end up acting. What Brendan was starting to realise about her was that she was as fearless and impulsive as he was. If the shoe were on the other foot, Brendan would have no problem bursting into the house to get her. So he thought she'd be inclined to do the same.

He pulled his phone out of his pocket. 'I'm calling Lorna. Tell her to go home.'

'Where is home?' Dimitru asked, as he pointed a key at a silver Mercedes, unlocking it.

'We're staying in a B&B at the minute. We're building a house in Italy.'

Dimitru turned and looked at Brendan. 'Italy? Why there?'

'With the intel Lorna has from her old job, she's become quite a valuable asset to the Italian underground.'

'You mean to tell me she's got dirt on the Italians?' Dimitru pulled the driver's door open, but didn't get in. He stood looking across the roof at Brendan, astonished.

'She was one of the top agents for British Intelligence, mate,' Brendan said, looking back at him. 'She's got contacts all over the world. If she wants to cause upset in America, she can. If she wants to wind up the people over in Russia, or North Korea...' He laughed, sounding impressed himself at what she knew. 'She can cause a lot of problems for people.'

'Shit!' Dimitru laughed, his cigarette dangling from his mouth, getting soaked. 'Better be nice to this lady, then.' He gestured for Brendan get in.

Brendan was about to get into the front passenger seat when Andrei and the other bouncer he roughed up in the Red Brick made their way towards the car. He decided he didn't know them well enough to spend a journey into the unknown with his back to people who'd probably stick a knife in him at the first opportunity.

He sent Lorna a text, telling her that he was just taking a drive with his 'new friends.' He told her not to worry; he had his gun ready to draw, and two out of the three he was travelling with were so doped up that they'd probably not pose much of a threat anyway. She replied; frustration could be sensed from her words. Brendan put the phone back in his pocket and ignored what would be a thread of messages from Lorna accusing him of being stupid.

Andrei took the front passenger seat. The other bouncer sat next to Brendan in the back. The radio just about broke the uncomfortable silence. The laughter and high spirits that were present in the house were now non-existent.

As they exited the estate, they drove past the car Lorna was waiting in. None of them took any notice of the vehicle, except Brendan. As the Mercedes pulled out onto the Shore Road, Brendan spotted Lorna's car creeping out. She was following them.

'Where are we going?' he asked, pulling his pistol out, checking that it was loaded. This was more of a signal to them that even though he was outnumbered three to one, it still wouldn't be wise if they decided to make a move on him. His nerves were on high alert, but even more so when Dimitru answered his question.

'You know the Shankill Road?'

Brendan looked at Dimitru in the rear-view mirror. His expression did everything but say 'are you serious?' 'I know it, yes.'

'Well, we've had a few issues with our merchandise over there. Our friends in the UDA have wanted the issue dealt with, and instead of getting their hands dirty, they've asked us to send a little message to anyone who wants to fuck about.'

'The UDA have sub-contracted their punishment beatings out to the Romanian mafia?' Brendan said.

The bouncer sitting beside Brendan in the back seat lit up a joint and said, 'we're taking over this little fucking city.' He put the window down in the back of the car and joined Andrei in laughing. 'Little Belfast is going to become little Romania.'

Brendan looked at the giant who was now laughing through a cough. Not wanting to antagonise the people he was trying to get on his side, Brendan humoured the guy and asked for a puff of the joint.

The car exited the city's west link motorway system and turned right onto Cliftonstreet, heading north towards the roundabout at Carlistle Circus—the roundabout where this had all started for Brendan. Where Agent Hughes had been sniped out and where Brendan and Lorna were also meant to be assassinated, had Damien Cleary not intervened and taken out the number one hitman at Her Majesty's disposal.

'Who're we dealing with here?' Brendan said. 'I'd be surprised if I don't know them.'

'Ian Murphy?'

Brendan smirked as he heard the name. Murphy was there the night Brendan had gotten into the fight with Johnty Burrows. From what Brendan recalled, Murphy had hit Brendan with a few bottles, trying to get Brendan off his mate, the late Burrows.

'I'd like a word with him,' Brendan said.

# Chapter Eight

THE SHANKILL ROAD WAS a heavily Protestant, loyalist estate that stretched from North Belfast over to the west of the city. The infamous peace wall had been erected in the late 1960s to separate the estate from the equally-as-heavy Catholic republican Falls Road. Almost fifty years after it's construction, it still stood, acting as both an eyesore and a reminder of the depth of division that still to this day kept people on their own side. Kerbs outlined the roads, decorated with red, white and blue paint. Lampposts held union jack flags high in the sky, many of them tattered and weathered. UDA, UVF and UFF murals were still commonplace. Images of masked gunmen dressed in guerrilla clothes were still seen as acceptable and normal.

Dimitru kept the car in third, not going any higher than twenty mph as the car progressed deeper into the estate. The houses were terrace rows of eight to sixteen, each possessing it's own tiny piece of concrete garden to the front. The eerie silence in the car was testament the horrific things that happened on these streets, many of the previous generation left with more psychological scars than physical.

Brendan shot to full alertness, only realising he'd gripped his pistol so tightly when he tried to release the grip and found his skin had glued itself to the cold metal.

The bouncer beside Brendan acknowledged the gun. 'Are you keen to get the job done? You sure you know how to use that thing? This is big boy stuff.' He tapped Dimitru on the shoulder, sniggering, apparently proud of his comment.

Brendan didn't respond. He was busy keeping his eyes peeled for anything that didn't look right, his finger on the trigger, ready to start shooting.

'Is he still in the same house?' Brendan finally spoke.

'Yes, the one on the end, just at the gate to the peace wall,' Dimitru said.

Brendan nodded his head, recognising it. 'So, what has he done?'

'He's been trying to close down our shops,' Dimitru said. 'He's a racist son of a bitch and doesn't want Romanians coming over here and taking over from the paramilitaries.'

'What do the leaders of the UDA say about this?'

Dimitru laughed dismissively. 'They don't give a shit as long as they get paid. Either way, they don't care. But this little son of a bitch has threatened to close us down and send us all back to Romania with nothing but our dicks in our hands.'

Brendan grunted. 'Sounds like Murphy, alright. Who's he working for now?'

Dimitru looked at Brendan in the rear-view mirror. 'You need to do your homework, my friend. You should be the one giving us the information about this place.' He pulled the car over along the side wall of Murphy's house, shutting the engine off. 'His wife and kids are staying with her parents this week. We're going in there to make an example of what will come to anyone who tries to fuck with us.'

Brendan heled Dimitru's gaze in the mirror, seeing in the eyes of the Romanian that he meant business. This did not bother Brendan, not in the slightest. What bothered him was the chain of events something like this was likely to spark off—a group of foreigners moving into an estate like the Shankill to rough up one of the Shankill's own. Word would quickly spread throughout the local community and there would be big problems for the Romanians.

Brendan kept the bigger picture in mind, the thought of bringing down the Romanian mafia was what propelled him out of the car.

As he stepped out of the car, he heard Dimitru whisper to one of the others to get behind the wheel and keep the engine running. He said they were going to be in and out and he wanted a clean getaway.

Brendan walked towards the back of the house. A six-foot-high panelled fence outlined the back garden. The bins had been left outside the gate to be emptied the next day. He reached his hand through the gate hole, discreetly trying to slide the bar across. It was padlocked. He looked at the car, Dimitru and Andrei stood over the car's open boot, looking in as if they were trying to make a decision. Brendan approached them. They both looked around at him; their faces weren't as confident as he'd have expected.

'You're not deciding whether or not to donate a lung. Just fucking choose something,' Brendan said.

After they'd both selected a weapon, Dimitru had chosen a pistol similar to Brendan's Dessert Eagle. Andrei had decided on something quieter and shoved a meat cleaver down inside his jacket.

'Let's go.' Dimitru led the way. He went towards the gate to the back garden, but Brendan informed that it was locked and that they'd need to climb over.

With the assistance of the bin, Brendan scaled the fence first. He jumped over, landing in the muddy grass. Dimitru was next, then Andrei. The garden was a twenty-foot square. A steel pole shot out of the grass, with a clothesline extending out from each side. The house was in complete darkness. One of the upstairs windows was wide open. They could hear someone snoring. Whoever it was had no idea what was about to happen. Brendan checked the kitchen window. It was locked. The window to the right, below the open bedroom window, was locked. The door was locked.

The three gathered around in a close circle.

Brendan whispered. 'We've got two choices. Either we kick in the back door and run up the stairs before he has any idea of what the fuck is happening...'

'Or?' Andrei hissed.

Brendan gestured to the thick plastic drainpipe that ran all the way along the wall from the ground to the roof, passing the open window.

'You're crazy,' Andrei whispered. 'We can come back tomorrow.'

'Fuck tomorrow,' Dimitru hissed. 'We are here now.'

Brendan knew if he was to impress them, he'd have to show a certain level of value to them. Value to people like them was having balls. Before they debated the situation anymore, Brendan shoved his pistol down into the back of his trousers and went for the drainpipe. He heard Andrei snigger and say something about 'fucking spiderman,' but

Dimitru was quick to suggest Andrei go up instead. No response came from Andrei.

Brendan grabbed onto the drainpipe and hunched himself over as he forced his feet into the gap between the pipe and the wall, beginning his climb. He managed to get up two steps when he arrived at two redundant screws, which made it easier for him to get a grip. He placed his feet on them and pulled himself up farther, the snoring getting louder. After one more step, he was three feet away from the window ledge. He looked down; both Dimitru and Andrei watching, smiles on their faces as if being entertained. With his left hand, he reached up and grabbed the window ledge. Pulling himself up, his hand slipped and his body weight fell back into the wall. He frantically grabbed hold of the drainpipe, his breathing and heart rate elevated, his sweaty hands beginning to lose grip. He heard Dimitru curse from below him. His pistol had slipped out from the back of his waist and was now flying back down to the ground. Dimitru managed to catch it, but now Brendan was heading into the house unarmed. He paused for a second, catching his breath, then he continued.

Making sure he hadn't woken the person inside, he made a second attempt at the ledge. This time he was aware of the slippery surface. Flinging him arm up, he caught the ledge and pulled himself up, this time slower, with all his focus on maintaining his grip. When his head reached level with the ledge, he peeked in through the open window. Complete darkness. He flung his other arm off the drainpipe, catching the edge of the window. Now with a firm grip, he pulled himself up onto the ledge and sat side-on to the window. His shoulders were too broad to go in face front, so he'd have to go in sideways. He looked down at the other two. Both still grinning. As another snore came from the room, he craned his head inside and looked around. Nothing could be seen. He could just about see the outline of the bed, the streetlight sending a tiny bit of light into the room, but not enough for him to recognise who was sleeping in the bed. Then he spotted a collection of rose gold knuckle duster rings sitting directly below him on top of the bedside cabinet. He grabbed one of the rings and dropped it down to Dimitru. Dimitru looked at it, then looked back up at Brendan, nodding his head. He signalled Brendan with a thumbs up. Brendan took that as his signal to go for it.

Using the side of the window frame, he pulled himself off the ledge and into the room, carefully placing his feet on the cabinet, now fully in the room. He slowly stepped down off the cabinet onto the carpet-lined floor. From the outline of the bed he saw the figure move, rolling over onto the other side of the bed. Brendan felt around for something he could use as a weapon. He had a choice between a cup and a glass bottle that were sitting on the side of the cabinet next to the rings. Neither of those would be worth more than one blow. He needed something that could be used more than once, if need be. He slowly reached under the bed, finding a baseball bat. This was better. From outside he knew Dimitru and Andrei wouldn't have been following him up the wall and in through the window, so he had to bring Murphy down to them. Brendan reached for the lamp on the cabinet and switched the light on.

'Haven't seen a fat mess like you in a long time.' He spoke casually, as if it was the most normal thing in the world.

Murphy grunted, still half asleep. A few seconds passed until he reached full consciousness and realised what was going on. He rolled around, terror written on his face. 'Who the fuck are...'

Before he could finish Brendan swung the bat down on top of his head, once. He pulled the duvet off the bed to reveal a fully naked body, now squirming up the bed against the headboard. 'Get your fat ass up and dressed before I move onto the next level of this. And trust me, you don't want that.'

Murphy froze. He didn't move, his hands covering his head, his body shivering with fright.

'Move!' Brendan swung the bat down on the headboard, sending splinters into the air. Murphy jumped off the bed. Brendan stood over him as he snatched up his clothes, which were strewn across the floor. He pulled his boxer shorts on but before he put on anything else, Brendan told him that was enough and ordered him to lead the way out of the room and down the stairs.

As they entered the kitchen, Brendan whacked him again on the back of the head, sending him face first into the ground. The key to the back door was in the lock. Brendan opened it and let the other two in. 'I've done my part. I'll be in the car.' He wiped his prints off the bat and handed it to Dimitru.

'Well done, James Bond!' Dimitru said. 'You sure you don't want to stay for this?'

Brendan shook his head and stepped out into the back garden.

# Chapter Eight

ARRIVING BACK AT THE Rathcoole estate, Brendan looked for Lorna's car. He knew she'd attempted to follow them, but hoped she'd turned back. She wasn't there. The other three passengers in the car were still joking about the Irish James Bond scaling the wall of a house in the middle of the night and climbing into the bedroom of the enemy. They were right in a sense; it was something that took both a lot of skill and balls. That's what made Brendan the person he was. Was he reckless, or courageous? It depended on individual opinion.

He didn't ask in what state they left Murphy; he didn't want to know. He didn't need to know. All he needed to know was that they wanted him around, at least long enough to get close to the boss and finish the job. His father's dying words rang through his head. Use his skills to do good. What he'd done in the Shankill was neither good nor bad, but it was simply for the greater good, a lesser of two evils perhaps.

As they got out of the car, Brendan's phone rang. It was Lorna.

'Brendan, where the hell are you?'

'Back in Rathcoole.' He spoke sharply as he watched the other three get out of the car.

'I'm coming back for you now. Don't move.'

He looked at Dimitru. 'I'm gonna to get going. I'll speak to you tomorrow?'

'You sure you won't come in for a drink?' Dimitru asked, sounding victorious. 'You're one ballsy son of a bitch.' He threw his arm around Brendan affectionately.

'Nah, go and enjoy your party. I'm just waiting for my lift.'

'Ah, the beautiful English lady. Have fun.' He winked his eye at Brendan as if he'd rather be going home with Lorna, too. 'Okay, my friend. I'll call you tomorrow.'

Brendan stood against the closed door of the fast food joint, leaning against the steel shutter, taking shelter from the drizzle. He listened as the guys in the party grew increasingly louder. The rest of the estate was tranquil. He stood and watched as if in a trance as the drizzle caused a constant stream under the orange glow of the streetlights.

After few minutes of meditative staring into the rain, Brendan was woken from his daze by Lorna's arrival. He jumped in, glad to be out of the rain and grateful to be in the company of someone he wanted to be around.

'You scared the shit out of me, Brendan.' Lorna put the car in neutral. 'I thought they'd served you up to the paramilitaries.'

'If they'd done that, then they'd have no chance of getting any business from us.' Brendan adjusted the dial of the heating. 'These guys don't want to be giving their dirty money to the UDA just so they can use their turf to run their business.'

'Where did you go? I followed you as far as the west link but dropped off in case I was spotted.'

'I paid a visit to an old friend.' He looked at her. 'Remember Johnty?'

'The guy you put in hospital? He's the reason you were locked up when we met, wasn't he?'

Brendan nodded. 'Well, Ian Murphy was Johnty's best mate. He's been shouting his fat mouth off about Dimitru and his gang. He's threatened to put them out of business. He wants the UDA to take more control of their turf and not let it be taken over by some Romanians.'

'So, he's a racist,' Lorna said.

'They're each as bad as the other.'

'So, you paid him a visit.' She laughed, sounding astonished. 'You like pushing your luck, don't you?'

'I like doing whatever is necessary to cause fucking havoc inside the worlds that caused havoc in my life.' He looked at her, feeling himself bubble up. 'My father left me a shitload of cash to fund my life. Not to live happily ever after in some fancy house.' He grinned. 'Crazy bastard, God rest him, must have been planning my life out, long before I even knew it.'

'So, what's next with Dimitru?'

'He's impressed with what I did tonight. I'm pretty sure I'll be receiving a call from him tomorrow.' He looked out through the window as the rain got heavier. 'Let's go.'

# Chapter Nine

ARRIVING BACK AT THE hotel, Brendan jumped on his laptop while Lorna went to the bar to order some late-night food. Brendan had accessed the files that Lorna, as an agent for MI5, gained access to. He was genuinely impressed by the level of clearance she had. The amount of information shared between governments was phenomenal. At his fingertips, he had information that could easily start a third world war. Information that brought into disrepute not only the British government, but the Americans, the Russians, the Chinese. All the superpowers around the world had been involved – in some fashion – in dirty dealings to line their own pockets. Brendan had always thought his father was joking, or perhaps it was just bitter words coming from an Irish Catholic growing up in Belfast during the troubles, but it turned out his father's opinion was not entirely inaccurate. And if the late Damien Cleary had gotten close and personal with these superpowers as the so-called global problem solver *The Ghost*, then his word would have been as true and accurate as anyone's.

He scrolled down the list of highly classified documents, selecting one titled *Romanian Underworld*. The file was a collection of the big players on the criminal scene in Romania. Past and present. Domestic, and those who'd expanded their business overseas.

'I'm going to organise those files better,' Lorna said as she entered the room with some food. 'Hughes was a messy bastard, and that was clearly how he treated those files. *So* unorganised.' She gave him a kiss on the cheek and set the tray down on the table, sliding the laptop away from him.

'You know, it's quite an insane amount of information you have there. This could start wars,' Brendan said as he reached over to the tray and grabbed a sandwich. The bread was presented in nice little triangles, as if a midnight snack in the bedroom required such diligent effort. He split open the two slices of bread. Thick pink cuts of ham were smeared with mustard.

'Jesus, Brendan, if I was going to poison you, I could have finished you a long time ago,' Lorna said, snatching up a triangle and biting a piece off in demonstration. She chewed it and swallowed. 'See, not dead!'

He laughed. 'I was just checking what was in it and was actually about to say you made a great choice.' He took a bite of it and chewed. He swallowed it and laughed. 'Looks like you're the one who's got the trust issues, not me.' He turned his gaze back to the laptop. 'But I'm serious about this stuff. If this falls into the wrong hands, it'd be catastrophic.'

'Well, we best not let it fall into the wrong hands, then.' Her face turned serious. 'But if we're to cut the head off this Romanian family, we have to be very smart about it. The boss of the organisation is one ruthless bastard. Trust me, he'd give new meaning to the murderers you'd find in this part of the world.'

Brendan shrugged it off. 'Ever heard of the Shankill Butchers?'

'Read a book about them in school....bastards.'

'We've had our fair share of them over here. Best leave those bastards in the past.'

She nodded her head. 'When it's political, it's always more difficult. Dimitru's boss has caused a lot of damage to innocent people in Romania, and it looks like he's branching out into other countries.'

'I want to get close to Dimitru,' Brendan said. 'We need him to believe that going into business with us would be good for the boss man back in the old country.' He lifted another sandwich. 'One of them let slip that they were going to try and take over the criminal network in Belfast. And what they did tonight leads me to believe that it's true. They don't just want to work alongside the paramilitaries. They want to take over.'

'They're trying to muscle in?'

He nodded as he chewed another mouthful of the sandwich. He picked up the bottle of Pepsi that accompanied the meal and washed down it down. 'Think so.'

'They're working with the UDA. The UDA is not likely to let that happen.'

'I don't know how strong the UDA is today. They may have to.'

Brendan looked at Lorna and pulled her off the edge of the desk where she stood. She straddled him on the office chair. 'Unless we cause the Romanians a lot of problems and have them retreat back over to their own country.'

'Diana will be our greatest asset. She needs a bit of encouragement, but she'll be fine.'

'She was at the party tonight. She scared the shit out of me when she walked in with a bag for Dimitru.' Brendan laughed. 'She's a good actor. Trust me, even I started to believe we'd never met.'

'Like I said, she'll be very useful.' She leaned in and kissed him on the cheek. 'She told me her son trains in one of the city centre gyms.' She paused. 'Think she said Club Twenty-Four Hours. Apparently he trains there really early in the morning on his own. Like about six, then goes to school. He's a bit of a loner but is handy with his fists.'

'What age is he?'

'Fourteen or fifteen, I think she said.'

Brendan thought for a moment. 'Might be a good idea to get him on our side, too. A problematic teenager is something we could do without.'

He pulled her in for a kiss, then carried her over to the bed.

# Chapter Ten

THE NEXT MORNING, BRENDAN woke at the usual time, five-thirty. His alarm had woken him for the first time in quite a while. Usually he'd be awake when his alarm sounded. He'd slept well and was feeling fresh. He rolled over to his right side to wake Lorna up, but she wasn't there. He sat up on the bed and called for her; perhaps she was in the bathroom. She wasn't usually up before him, so it too was a first. As he opened his phone, he had a message from her.

*Couldn't sleep. Just gone out for a walk. Sleep well, sleeping beauty, P.S. You snore like a pig! Xxx*

He laughed and got up from the bed, walking across the room to open the window. He looked down onto Great Victoria Street, one of Belfast's economic powerhouses. The city was starting to come alive. Cars, motorbikes and vans joined the queue of traffic waiting at the lights directly outside the Europa. The hotel promised to offer an exquisite view of the city once the sun rose.

Brendan went to get showered and dressed. After getting ready, he, too, wanted to take a walk. The morning air was fresh, and to him it was the best way of starting his day. Ever since having his duvet pulled off and being woken in shock by his father every morning during his training, he was someone who loved to be up and at them before the rest of the world.

He walked along Great Victoria Street, his hands in his pockets and his head sunk as far as into his jacket as possible, like a turtle drawing back into it's shell. The sky was now a mixture of pink and blue. A crisp chill was in the air, biting into whatever exposed skin it touched. He would have been happier jogging. A morning jog along the beach of Donegal was the best way to start the day. But being on the eastern Irish coast, Belfast didn't have the same sandy beach as the west coast, so he made do with the city centre.

He approached Club Twenty Four Hour, just a few streets away from the Europa. Impressed by the skills of the young lad hitting the dummy in the centre of the combat area, he walked closer. The kid looked like he could handle grown men as easily as he could lads his own age.

Brendan stood and watched for a few minutes. The kid was tall and thin, but his wiry limbs were toned and muscular. His body fat percentage was no higher than ten percent. If he wasn't competing, he should have been. Looking at him, Brendan thought about himself, when he was about that age. He'd seen that same expression, an expression of weathered hardness, a toughness, coupled with an unwillingness to accept defeat. If this was Diana's son, she'd raised a true fighter, both physically and psychologically. After a final ten seconds of the round, a blistering flurry of lefts and rights, Brendan watched the lad as he did everything but punch a hole in the dummy. When the bell sounded to end the round, the lad crouched down and lifted a bottle of water from the ground close to the wall. As he took a drink, he walked around in a circle, spotting Brendan watching him.

He didn't look at all impressed by the fact he had someone's eyes on him. Perhaps it would break his concentration.

Brendan opened the door and walked in just as the bell sounded for the next round. The lad got back to work. Brendan could feel the ground shake. Brendan stood at the security barrier. It was a members-only gym and he'd need a swipe card to get through the turnstile. He shoved his hands in his pockets and stood, watching the young boxer display a true show of pugilistic skill. It wasn't long before the lad's focus was distracted from it's target. He stopped.

'You alright, mate?' His accent proved he certainly wasn't of Irish origin.

'You're pretty good,' Brendan said.

'Thanks,' the lad said, turning his attention back to his target. He continued pounding the dummy, fast jabs and powerful crosses. His footwork was that of a professional. Through the side of his eye he could see that Brendan was still watching. He stopped. 'Listen, mate, do you mind? I'm trying to train here and having you stare at me is kind of off-putting.'

'You're Romanian.'

'So?'

'I know your mother. I told her I'd come down and see you.'

'Oh, yeah?' He became defensive and walked towards Brendan. 'What the fuck do you want, mate? You're not some fucking do-gooder, social worker or something are you?'

Brendan shook his head. 'I'm just a friend of your mum. She's worried about you.'

'I'm fine. And you shouldn't bother. Her and my old man are still together. As much as a fucking prick he is, she's still with him. So, don't bother going out of your way to help her.'

Brendan could see a lot of his younger self in the lad. For the first time, he was truly grateful for his late father keeping him in check. 'Are you competing?'

'No, I just do it because I like it. I get to pretend Dimitru's face is on the bag; it feels great.' He forced a smile as if his anger and uncanny hatred towards his father would somehow impress Brendan.

'Dimitru?'

'My father. If I had any respect for him, maybe I'd call him dad. But as it stands, I'll just call him Dimitru.'

Brendan laughed at the lad's loud mouth and apparent hostility towards the man Brendan and Lorna were now working to bring down. 'You remind me of myself many years ago.'

'Who are you?'

'Just a friend of your mother's.' He turned to make his way back out the door again. He turned and looked at the lad. 'Stick to the training, it'll do you more good than harm.'

The lad walked away from Brendan, his hostility still evident, but perhaps not personally directed towards Brendan, but towards life itself, or Dimitru.

After carrying on up through the city until he reached Queens University, Brendan turned and made his way back to the hotel.

He entered their room at just after seven thirty to find Lorna on the phone. From what it sounded like, she was trying to calm Diana down. After a moment, she hung up the phone. She dropped it down on the bed and sighed. She looked at Brendan.

'She's very unstable, Brendan. She thinks we're going to get her and her son killed. She said just knowing what she knows could get her killed.'

'He'll not kill his own family,' Brendan said. 'He's not that crazy.'

Lorna looked at him her eyes wide, hands on her hips. 'She thinks he is.'

'Well, let's continue what we're doing and close him down before he gets a chance to.' Brendan took his jacket off and sat on the edge of the bed. 'I've seen her son.'

'Teodoro?'

'That's his name?'

She nodded her head.

'He's a good boxer, and a lot of anger bottled up inside. He needs to get it out before he kills Dimitru.' He looked at her. 'Forget about Dimitru harming them, I think he's in more danger of the son hurting him.'

Lorna laughed. 'He's not a fan of his good old dad, then?'

'Think he imagines Dimitru's face when he's hitting the dummy.' Brendan laughed. 'And he hits hard, trust me.'

'You want to eat here or go into town and...' She paused as Brendan's expression kindly reminded her of the city they were in. 'Right, Belfast is a city where we can never be seen in public again.' She put the TV on and lay down on the bed. 'Once we've finished this organisation, we'll be out of here forever. I can't live all cooped up in a hotel room, hiding out.'

Brendan lay down beside her. 'Let's see what's on the news, see what bullshit they're talking today. Hopefully we get a call from Dimitru sometime this morning. We can...' He trailed off as he spotted the BBC news report. The camera was pointed at Murphy's house with the reporter talking about horrific scenes inside the house. 'Oh fuck.'

'What?' She looked at him, then at the TV. 'That was you?'

He nodded his head. 'Turn the volume up.'

The reporter went on to talk about the dead body that was found inside the house of Mr Murphy. Murphy was a well-known figure in the local criminal network, with long-standing ties to the UDA and the recently-murdered leading loyalist – John "Jonty" Burrows – who died in hospital following an altercation with the now on-the-run Brendan Cleary. The reporter went on to say how there was no reason to believe there was any link between the deaths of Murphy and Burrows.

Brendan looked at Lorna. Her narrowed eyes fixed on the screen. 'Fucking Dimitru!' He sat up on the bed. 'I swear if he was here right now, it'd be his body next on the news.'

'You knew you weren't going there to tickle someone, Brendan,' Lorna said, her voice calm in comparison to Brendan's. 'Look.' She turned the TV off and sat up, placing her hand on his shoulder. 'He was a scumbag. He's dead. Shit happens. Live by the sword and all that. We focus on the job at hand. What's best for you to do is use this as your way to get in with the Romanians. If they're thinking of going against the loyalists, then there'll be minimal chance of you coming into contact with anyone from your past.'

She made sense. Brendan stood up from the bed. He pulled open the bottom drawer of the bedside cabinet and pulled out his father's Desert Eagle. 'Wherever I go, this will go.'

'You're not superstitious, are you?'

He looked at her, his eyes narrowed.

'You think if that gave your father his nickname, it'll stop you from getting killed, too?'

'We'll soon see.'

'Let's go and get something to eat.'

# Chapter Eleven

AFTER THEY'D EATEN, they went for a drive. Lorna had never seen the beautiful view of the city from the cave hill before, so Brendan took her up to Belfast Castle, sat nestled centrally on the face of the mountain. Surrounded by a forest, a natural decoration from mother nature, the castle was something that not a lot of people knew existed. It was neatly tucked away a few miles north of the Antrim Road and few people other than the locals visited.

After an hour's walk around the trail, greeting dog walkers, cyclists, and joggers, they returned to the car feeling a sense of serenity provided only by nature. Brendan had left his phone in the car, not wanting any distractions. He wanted to use the nature walk to charge his battery, at least psychologically. As he got back into the car, the green light flashed at the top of his Galaxy, indicating a message had been received. He wasn't surprised when he called the number back to hear Dimitru's voice, sounding upbeat and victorious.

'My friend, Brendan. How are you today?'

'I'm good, thanks. Lorna and I were just talking about you.'

'All good, I hope.' He laughed.

'We wanted you to know, we think your organisation has the potential to grow. A small city like Belfast, if you can take control of the criminal underground over here, then you definitely have the potential to take over a few other cities in England, and who knows where else.'

'My friend, Brendan. With all due respect, how can I believe you and your pretty lady friend are telling me anything more than...how do you say it over here...porky pies?'

'I can assure you, we have information that discloses the whereabouts, places of residence, places of dealings and the influential people who run the criminal underworld, not just in England but all over the world. The reason the government wanted us to come in, I'd guess, would be to take that info back.'

'This sounds a little too good to be true. If it's true, why don't you just sell it to someone who wants it?'

'I've heard that the Romanian mafia is one of the strongest in Europe, and your family specifically is one that's had much success in taking over parts of Northern Italy, Spain and the UK. I know your family – The Rohozeanu – have had an important member murdered recently by rivals in London.' Brendan stopped, waiting for a reaction from Dimitru. There was a silence. At least this meant Dimitru had lost his humorous side. 'You want more? I know the person who ordered the horrific battering of Nikolai Albu.' Brendan spoke calmly and clearly. 'I can even tell you the fucking shop where they bought the baseball bats from.'

'Okay, you've got my attention.' Dimitru's voice deepened. 'But I must warn you, Brendan: you fuck with us, and we will come after not only you, but your entire family.' He paused for a second to see if Brendan would respond. He didn't. 'We must not be fucked with. You have proven yourself very useful last night. We could use someone with your balls. And with this information you have, the data on the whereabouts of the London attackers, I think it would be a beneficial goodwill gesture on your part if this information was disclosed.'

'Before we go any further.' Brendan matched Dimitru's tone. 'Don't ever threaten our families again. Or it'll be last thing you do. We have information on all criminal organisations, yours included. I want to go into business with you but keep mine and Lorna's family out of it.' Brendan looked at Lorna. She was looking at the phone, her expression as serious as Brendan's tone. 'As for giving you the attackers' location, we might be able to do that.'

'Might?' Dimitru's voice became sterner. 'This isn't a fucking game, Mr Cleary.'

'What happened to Brendan?' Brendan looked at Lorna. Her nostrils flared.

'Come to the pub tonight. If the information you give us is correct, then we'll talk more about what we can do together.'

Brendan cleared his throat. 'We'll be there after eight.' He hung up. 'He's very unstable.' Brendan put the key into the car and started the engine. 'We've got the rest of the day to do whatever we want. Fancy a bit more exploring?'

Lorna nodded her head. 'I've never seen the Antrim coast before.'

'Let's go look at the Antrim coast, then. I know a nice little fish and chips shop in Ballycastle.'

'That place rings a bell.'

# Chapter Twelve

AN HOUR LATER, BRENDAN parked in the almost empty carpark at the Ballycastle harbour, a small fishing village located on the cold, windy northeast coast of Ireland. It was a location not known to many. The greatest attraction the village offered was a ferry ride to Rathlin Island and the famous Bruce's Cave, named after the famous king of Scotland, Robert the Bruce. Despite the time of the year, quite a few people still lingered.

They walked along the beach and visited the golf course, letting the wind whip up around them. Passers-by would look at them, greeting them with the usual hellos. Lorna wanted to take photographs of the two of them. They'd not had a chance to spend quality time together in Ireland; instead they'd been on a constant run for their lives, under continuous pursuit by the corrupt government that had set them up.

'Let's have a seat for a moment.' Lorna shifted her direction, strolling towards the park benches fixed to the grass-filled walkway that circled the golf course's fifth hole. She closed her eyes and inhaled. 'The smell of that sea air is beautiful. Don't you think?'

Brendan sat down beside her and nodded. He put his arm around her, sitting back on the seat as if wanting to fall asleep right there. 'Those waves,' he said gesturing out to sea.

'You'd need some guts to go out there today.' Lorna curled up into him, wanting to contain their heat. He kissed her on the top of the head. 'Can you imagine what your life would be like, had we never met?'

She laughed. 'Does the seaside always make you reflective?' She poked him.

He laughed. 'I'm just thinking, that's all.'

'I'm only teasing. I've never really thought about it. You've never really given me much opportunity to breathe, let along stop and smell the roses.'

'How do you feel about Short?'

'What, the fact he killed your father or the fact that you killed him?'

'Or the fact that you both had a history?'

'I loved him once, Brendan. That's in the past. I love you.'

Brendan's eyes shot open. He sat up. 'You what?'

'I love you,' she said. 'I thought that's where we were at?'

Brendan paused for a second. 'Really? That's what this is? That's where we are? I thought we were just fucking about.'

Her jaw dropped and she sat up, moving away from him. 'What? You're joking, right?'

He smiled at her. He bit his lip to stop himself from laughing. Then he exploded into a fit of laughter. She punched him playfully on the shoulder. 'Of course, I love you. We can thank your ex, Short, for that. The thought of losing you in Italy made me realise how much I loved you.' He pulled her in close and gave her a kiss. 'I didn't want to lose you. I would have given my life for yours.' He looked deeply into her eyes. 'I thought I'd lost you.'

'Don't think about it,' she said. 'It's in the past. Didn't happen.' She looked out to sea into the distance. 'Maybe one day, we'll stop and think about how our lives could have ended up had we not met. But for now, let's become the biggest fucking menaces the criminal underworld has ever heard of.'

Brendan stood up and took her by the hand. 'Let's go and grab some proper food from the chippy. Before we do anything.'

# Chapter Thirteen

EIGHT THIRTY THAT EVENING, Brendan and Lorna parked their car directly outside the Red Brick. Both Romanian doormen stood on either side, drenched in long black overcoats, looking like undertakers.

Brendan shut the engine off and looked at Lorna. 'I've been thinking about what happened in Italy.'

'Brendan,' Lorna sighed. 'It's in the past. There's no point in thinking about it.'

'I know, but...' He paused, looking at the two doormen, who were joking with one another. 'Ever hear the saying "never put all your eggs in the same basket"?'

'So?'

'I think moving forward, we should split up. Not be together when we go into these places.'

'You want me to wait here, in the car?'

'Why not? You can keep an eye on the place. Keep me informed about what's going on out here.'

'You've got your weapon?'

He pulled his jacket open, displaying the Desert Eagle, resting nicely in it's holster. 'I'm not spending any more time with these scumbags than I have to. Trust me. I'll be out in thirty minutes.' He reached across the car, giving her a kiss on the cheek. 'Then we can go home and spend some alone time together.'

'You mean the hotel?' She forced a smile. 'We need to find a home together.' She pulled him back in towards her again. 'A proper home, where we can be together. In private.'

'After this is all done, we can look into that.' He got out of the car. Lowering his head down into the car again, he could see her glazed eyes not wanting him to leave. 'See you in half an hour.' He slammed the door shut and looked at Andrei and his larger companion, both of whom were warmer towards him than they had been the previous day. Clearly the stunt he pulled at Murphy's house had impressed them.

As he got closer, Andrei pulled the door open; dance music flooded out into the street accompanied by multi-coloured fluorescent lights.

'Here's Mr Bond,' Andrei joked. 'Or should we call you Spiderman? Scaling a building like that.' He reached his hand out to shake Brendan's. Brendan humoured him. 'Dimitru is in the office. Tell the barman to give him a shout.'

'Thanks,' Brendan said, stepping inside. The bass from the speakers sent vibrations through his body, tickling the inside of his ears. It was impossible for the patrons to have a proper conversation. The atmosphere suited the punters, however, who were more interested in feeling the effects of the alcohol than having a sensible conversation.

Brendan made his way straight for the office. The barman, remembering him from their previous encounter, smiled at Brendan. Brendan didn't respond. The barman pointed towards the office, beyond the bar and to the right.

Brendan entered the office, finding Dimitru on the phone, speaking in Romanian, perhaps on the phone to the old country. Brendan closed the door, pushing the noise back out into the bar. Muffled thuds of bass, causing the door to vibrate, was all that was left to accompany Dimitru's voice.

Dimitru, smoking a joint, offered some to Brendan. Brendan refused. Dimitru ended the call. 'Brendan. You had a nice day? Where is the beautiful lady?'

'Lovely day, thanks. She's not one for pubs or night-clubs.' Brendan grinned, trying to appear friendly. 'She needs to loosen up a bit.'

Dimitru exploded into a fit of laughter, false laughter that Brendan could sense a mile off. He didn't care about Brendan, but if Brendan could help at all, especially with something that could make him more money, then Brendan was perhaps the pot of gold at the end of the Romanian's rainbow.

'I thought about what you said on the phone,' Brendan said. 'If we are to be in business together, then I want you to trust me fully. And as a goodwill gesture, I'm happy to have Lorna email you across the details of the people you might want to pay a visit to in London.'

Dimitru turned his head at a slight angle, looking at Brendan, his eyes tiny slits. 'Why the sudden change of heart?'

'Let's just say a trip to the coast works wonders for clear-ing the head.'

Dimitru stood up and walked around the desk, reaching his hand out to Brendan. Brendan stood and shook his hand. 'I look forward to working with you, Brendan.' He swung his arm up and pat Brendan on the shoulder. 'You fancy a drink? Come join me at the bar; we'll have a drink to toast this new arrangement.' As much as Brendan wanted to get out of the bar, he needed to keep Dimitru sweet and prevent his unstable mood from dropping. The door opened and one of the waitresses came in with a tray full of cash. 'Come, we'll leave this lovely lady to count her hard-earned money.'

Dimitru pulled the door open and gestured for Brendan to leave first. Dimitru shouted to the barman to bring them over two coffees. Brendan led the way to a little room off the main bar area in a more private part, the farthest distance from the live band that was just setting up in the main bar area.

Brendan took a seat, not feeling comfortable enough to let his guard down. Belfast was his home, in the sense that it was his birthplace and where he grew up. He'd always feel a sense of attraction to the place, but the city, it's people and his past were things that could never let him settle there.

Dimitru joined him and pulled the sliding door across. He scratched his beard thoughtfully, looking at the ground, his face serious. He dropped himself down onto a two-foot-high stool that looked more suitable for a primary one class. He looked at Brendan, forcing a smile. 'Cheers,' he said as he lifted the coffee and took a sip. 'It's weird toasting with a coffee. You don't drink at all?'

Brendan shook his head. 'I like to keep my wits about me,' he said, mirroring Dimitru with the coffee. 'Slainte!'

'What's this slainte?'

Brendan laughed and set the cup back down, wiping the foam from his upper lip. 'It's cheers in Irish.'

Dimitru laughed. 'Slainte, then,' he spoke humorously. 'Okay, all the cards on the table time, Brendan Cleary.' He folded his arms. 'What's brought you back to Belfast?'

'I came back to breathe some Irish air,' Brendan said bluntly. He took another sip of the coffee while watching Dimitru over the rim of the mug.

'Can I tell you something, Brendan, off the books?'

Brendan felt as if Dimitru was about to open up to him, he sensed the Romanian's guard was down and that he was about to tell him something—until one of the doormen came in, causing Dimitru to jump in shock. Brendan looked at him, thinking how uncharacteristic it was for someone like Dimitru to act.

'Excuse me, is this a bad time?' the doorman said, a look of fear on his face as Dimitru's shocked expression turned to one of anger.

'No, it's fine,' Dimitru said. 'What is it?'

'You have a phone call at the bar.'

'Who is it?'

'London.'

'Why didn't they call my phone?' Dimitru pulled his phone from his pocket seeing the battery was dead. He looked up at the doorman. 'Put it through to the office.' He stood up.

Brendan stood up as well.

'Where are you going?'

'I've got to go,' Brendan said, looking at his phone. 'I've got a dinner date with a beautiful English lady, and she's growing impatient.' He reached out to shake Dimitru's hand. 'But thanks for the coffee.'

'I'll call you tomorrow morning. We can discuss our friends in London.' He shook Brendan's hand, then left with the doorman.

Brendan sat back down for a moment and finished his coffee. He had in fact received a call from Lorna.

As Brendan left the bar, Andrei had his head in the driver's side window of their car. He looked up at Brendan as he approached the passenger side. 'I was just telling her about your James Bond style stunt that took place last night,' he said through a cheesy grin.

'Stop it, you're embarrassing me,' Brendan said out of the side of his mouth. He pulled the door open and dropped himself down into the seat. He looked at Lorna. 'You okay?'

She smiled. 'I am now.' She stroked his face and looked out the window at Andrei. 'He was boring the fuck out of me.' She put the window up before the Romanian had a chance to air his response. She put the car in gear. 'Where are we for now?'

'You want to go looking for a place to live?'

Lorna looked at him. 'In Belfast?'

'Doesn't have to be Belfast, but I'm tired of staying in hotels.'

'Okay.' She giggled, sounding slightly astonished. 'Let's go back to the hotel, and we can look for places to rent.'

# Chapter Fourteen

*BRENDAN WAS STANDING in the back garden of his grandparents' house. He was playing toe-taps with his white O'Neill's Gaelic football while waiting for his Sunday morning fry. He was on tap number fifty-three when he was distracted by his uncle Ian, his mother's older brother. Ian was a former British solider who'd served in Derry and had eventually – along with his older brother Ivan – helped form the UDA in the early seventies, shortly after Bloody Sunday. Ian was always nice to Brendan, in spite of the fact that his father was so heavily involved in the Provisional movement.*

*Ian took the ball from Brendan and started doing taps of his own, reaching twenty-one before Brendan had returned the favour and distracted him, causing the ball to hit the grass. Brendan felt weird about the experience. His uncle was being too nice to him, paying him too much attention. Perhaps it was wrong that Brendan felt that way, simply because his mother's older brother was trying to do something nice by playing with him. But to Brendan it was weird that his uncle was even acknowledging he existed.*

*Brendan had started doing toe-taps again when the sound of his mother screaming at the top of her voice bellowed out of the kitchen window. She was in a fit of rage at her other brother Ivan. As Brendan entered the kitchen, his grandfather was shouting at Brendan's mother and Ivan, telling them both*

*to stop. They were at each other's throat over Damien Cleary
– Brendan's father. Ivan was accusing her of being a turncoat
and traitor to her own people. Brendan's mother screamed at
Ivan, calling him a narrow-minded bastard, and accused people like him being the cause of the conflict. People with his bitter
personality was the reason so many innocent people were dying on the streets. Ivan raised his hand and slapped Brendan's
mother across the face, sending her into the wall. She slid to the
ground, clasping her face. Before anyone knew what was happening, Brendan grabbed the poker from the coal bucket that
sat by the kitchen door and struck Ivan around the back of the
head with it. Ivan turned in a blind rage, grabbing Brendan by
the throat, screaming at him that he was going to kill him and
his fucking da'.*

Brendan's eyes shot open. Lorna was shouting at him,
telling him to calm down. He slowly came around into consciousness, realising where he was. In bed. In the hotel room.
Covered in sweat. His heart was racing. He looked to his left
and found Lorna sitting up, staring at him, an expression of
fear written across her face. It took him a few seconds to realise it had only been a dream. When he did so, he rotated his legs off the bed and placed his bare feet down on the
soft carpet. He crouched down, placing his head between
his bare legs while taking in a few deep breaths, calming his
nerves. He could feel Lorna place her hand on the middle of
his back. Then he felt her move in closer to him and kiss his
shoulder.

'Are you okay?' she said. 'Maybe you should see a doctor
about these dreams.'

'A doctor's not going to help me. They'll give me some medication that will do nothing but mask it.' He reached over and checked the time on his phone. It was ten minutes after five, twenty minutes before his alarm clock was due to go off. He turned around and gave her a kiss. 'I'm sorry if I scared you.'

'You don't have to be sorry, Brendan. I'm worried about you. I want to help you.'

He gave her another kiss and got up off the bed. 'I'm going for a run.' He walked across the room, snatching his gym slacks out of the wardrobe, pulling them on. 'Some fresh air and a bit of exercise will be enough to clear the head. I'm going to pass by that gym again and see if I can bump into Dimitru's son. For some reason I'd like learn more of his story.'

'Maybe you see a lot of yourself in him?' Lorna said as she got up and headed towards the bathroom. 'See you when you come back.'

He closed the door and put his hood up. He exited the hotel through the foyer, not acknowledging anyone. His mind was swamped with the thought of that dream. His uncles Ivan and Ian never spoke to him after that. That didn't bother him. What did bother him was how his late mother felt about it. She was who he cared about. Not the rest of them. He simply didn't give a shit about any of them. And the young Romanian lad he was hoping to bump into at the gym was as angry as Brendan once was. Brendan was grateful for his father taking him away those summer months. He needed it. Dimitru's misguided son needed it just as much.

After running a lap of the city centre, he sprinted from Millfield up the Falls Road, then jogged back down again.

As he approached the gym, he was glad to see Teodoro dancing around the bag as if he was Mohammad Ali. Brendan laughed, finding it funny because he used to do the same in their family garage. Opening the gym's front door amplified the sound of leather gloves slapping against the bag. He wiped the sweat off his face with his sleeve.

Teodoro looked at Brendan, not realising it was him until Brendan pulled his hood down, revealing his pink face and cropped hair. He turned away from Brendan, continuing to hit the bag. Brendan watched again, leaning on the stainless-steel railing that surrounded the turnstile.

The lad worked the bag for another thirty seconds—a mixture of jabs, crosses, and lower hooks as if to the body, finishing off with a flurry of punches that saw the bag almost jump off the chains it was hooked to. Sucking the air, like a fish that had jumped out of a bowl, his mouth and eyes couldn't have opened any wider. He walked around in a circle as if trying to suck every ounce of oxygen from the room.

'You're a good fighter,' Brendan said. 'If you learned to pace yourself a little bit more, you'd last a lot longer.'

'You sound like you've got some experience.'

'I know talent when I see it. I'm Brendan.' He held his hand out hoping Teodoro would accept the gesture. He did.

'Teodoro.'

'Nice to meet you,' Brendan said. 'How much is it to join this place?'

Teodoro pointed at the self-service booth behind the front door that Brendan had left open.

'You fancy a sparring partner?'

'It's your funeral.' Teodoro grinned, taking another drink from his bottle. The timer on his phone went off. 'Time to get back to work.' He turned and made his way back to the bag.

Brendan walked over to the self-service booth. The membership was only twenty pounds per month via direct debit with a thirty-pound joining fee. He would have paid it then, but he'd left his card back at the hotel. 'Will you be here tomorrow?' he shouted.

'I'm here every day,' Teodoro yelled back, not taking his eyes off the bag, continually battering it like he had a personal vendetta against it.

'See you tomorrow, then.' Brendan waved as he left the gym. Pulling his hood up again, he jogged the rest of the way back to the hotel.

As he entered the foyer, he reminded himself that he wasn't going to be in Belfast any longer than he had to be, and perhaps befriending Teodoro was a complication he could do without. But for some reason, he wanted to get to know the kid, perhaps help him, the same way he was helping his mother.

He entered the room. Lorna was on her laptop, the audio from BBC news resounding. He closed the door, pulling his hoodie and t-shirt off. Removing his trainers, he looked over at Lorna. 'What's new in the world?' he said light-heartedly, trying to counter the serious vibe he was picking up from the room.

'Just a continued story about your friend Murphy from the Shankill. They said they've gathered forensic evidence from the scene and are awaiting results before proceeding with their enquiries.' She sat back on the seat and swivelled around to look at him. 'How was your run? Feeling better?'

He sat down on the bed and pulled his socks off. 'Yeah, it was good. Feel much better, as always. I spoke with Teodoro at the gym. I'm going to go spar with him in the gym in the morning. Can you sign me up for the membership online? It's a direct debit. But you can also pay monthly. Just pay for one month. We'll not be here long enough to see into the second month.'

'Don't go making things complicated, Brendan.'

'I know, but I want to get to know more about the kid. He seems alright.'

'He seems a lot like you, you mean?'

He smiled at her and made his way towards the ensuite.

# Chapter Fifteen

BRENDAN STEPPED OUT of the shower, hearing Lorna's raised voice, but not second voice in response. He'd guessed the other person in the conversation was Diana, who'd proven her stability was not altogether intact—a loose cannon that he wasn't completely confident could hold it together and act as their eyes and ears when they wanted some information regarding Dimitru.

Brendan wiped the steam off the mirror and looked at himself, still listening to Lorna on the one-sided debate. He dried himself down then brushed his teeth. Wrapping a towel around his waist he stepped into the bedroom.

'Diana?' he said, sitting down on the edge of the bed. He reached towards the bedside cabinet. Pulling open the top drawer, he pulled out a pair of black socks.

Loran ended the call. 'I swear that woman's going to explode.'

'What's happened now?'

'Same old story. She said Dimitru came in drunk during the early hours of the morning, drunk and wanting to have sex with her. When she refused, he forced himself until she slapped him, then he beat her.'

Brendan sighed, pulling the socks on. 'I know what I'd like to do to the bastard.' He stood up and pulled on a pair of dark blue jeans. 'But we can't do anything. We can't get involved in their domestic life. If we do, then we'll have no chance of taking them down.'

'She also said, with a sigh of relief, that he's leaving for London on business.' She swivelled around on her chair. 'I'm guessing he's taking your little bit of advice and going to exact revenge on the rival group of Romanians.'

He pulled on a T-shirt then his overcoat. 'Good for him. It'll give him a bit of credibility.' He walked over to the service station and put the kettle on. 'It'll build the bastard up a bit before we bring him tumbling down.' His phone buzzed in his pocket. 'Bet this is him now.' He opened the message.

*How would you like to accompany me to London? It would be good to have someone quite handy with their fists. I have two flights booked for this evening. We'll be in London all day tomorrow, then we'll fly back the day after. What do you say?*

After reading the text, Brendan looked at Lorna. 'It looks like I'm going to London.'

She looked at him for a moment, as if trying to translate what he'd just said into something else. Something she'd prefer to hear. 'You go there with him, Brendan, you might not come back again.'

'I don't go there with him and we might lose whatever trust he currently has for us.' He prepared himself an instant coffee from one of the provided sachets. 'I think I should go, and you should stay here and try to keep Diana calm. Explain to her what we're doing. It'll be over soon.'

Lorna didn't look at all confident in the idea.

'Look, we're much better if we split up.' He made her a coffee too and handed it to her. 'Besides, it's only the two of us, and Dimitru I can handle.'

'Okay. I'll send you the info about where Dimitru's target is. From what I remember it was in Barking in the east of the city. Hold on a second.' She swivelled around on the chair and opened a new tab on her laptop. Dipping in to her emails, she clicked on a folder labelled 'Romanians in England.' She chose one of the tabs and opened a document, mugshots lining up page one. 'Yes, Dimitru's cousin was beaten to death by baseball bat wielding rivals from one of the other Romanian families.'

'I hope Dimitru has more sophisticated plans for his retaliation,' Brendan said as he responded to Dimitru's text.

'Don't be walking into a gunfight, Brendan.'

'Si, mama.' He teased.

'I'm serious.'

'I know.' His smile fell. 'It's simple. I'll jump on a flight, spend the day in London. Keep my distance while Dimitru does whatever he needs to do and be back in time for dinner the next day....' He paused, remembering his training session with Teodoro.

'What's with the expression?'

'I told the kid I'd train with him tomorrow.'

'Well you're just going to have to re-schedule.'

'He needs someone stable. Someone who will say something and follow through.'

'How about I go to London with Dimitru, and you can go have fun in the gym with your new buddy, then?'

'No, it'll be fine,' Brendan said.

# Chapter Sixteen

INSIDE BELFAST CITY Airport, Brendan and Dimitru sat on opposite sides of a small circular table outside Costa in the departures lounge. Brendan had an espresso. Dimitru would have preferred something with a bit more of a kick, but he settled for a cappuccino.

'You look nervous,' Brendan said as Dimitru dropped his phone back into his pocket.

'Do I?'

'You've pulled your phone out of your pocket at least five times in as many minutes, even though it hasn't sounded once.'

'I'm just waiting on a response from our brothers in London.'

'They're meeting us at the airport?'

Dimitru nodded, sipping his beverage.

The call came for their flight. Brendan lifted his black gym bag full of clothes. He wished he'd been able bring his late father's piece of trusty steel, but unless they were taking a private jet, that was simply not possible.

The queue for the flight was short: between twenty and thirty adults, a mixture of businessmen and women perhaps making their way home from a day at an Irish office.

The queue control girl quickly checked Brendan's passport and ticket and, without any conscious thought, nudged him on through with the rest. He followed a group of three middle-aged businessmen dressed in tailored suits as they slowly trudged across the runway and up the steps. The evening was windy, but dry, therefore there was no real rush to get into the aircraft.

The cabin was stuffy and smelled as if the flight that had just journeyed from London had been a little bit fuller.

The flight attendants, two women and one man, all looked tired. Their expressions – relaxed face muscles and heavy eyes – said they'd perhaps been on most, if not all, of the day's flights back and forward across the Irish Sea. After the usual safety procedures, the Bombardier Q400 slowly taxied along the runway, passed the terminal, and steered right onto the strip. After a few seconds, the metal bird was in the air. Brendan closed his eyes and put his headphones in. His choice of entertainment was Linken Park's greatest hits.

THE FLIGHT ARRIVED on time, without any delays—straight up and straight back down again. A little over one hour was all that was spent in the air, and the staff's more upbeat expressions lent an air of joy, perhaps indicating their final journey of the day.

Brendan reached up into the overhead compartment and pulled down his carry-on luggage. Dimitru flew with nothing but his overcoat and an umbrella. The Romanian led the way down the flight of steps at the rear of the aircraft seemed grateful to have brought his coat and umbrella. The weather was not as dry as it had been in Belfast.

As they entered the terminal, airport security checked Brendan's bag and politely let them go on without fuss. The second Dimitru deactivated flight mode on his iPhone, the device beeped.

'I hope this is our lift,' he complained. 'I want to get this done tonight and get back to Belfast again.'

'What's wrong, are you nervous?' Brendan joked, but Dimitru's expression didn't seem as if he were present in the airport. His thoughts were elsewhere.

'I don't like leaving my home for anything less than a sunny climate, a lounger by a pool and the sound of ice-cubes rattling off the side of my glass.' He spoke frankly and to the point. His good mood had been left in Belfast. But what Diana had said to them when they first met was that Dimitru did have an issue with his moods. He could be explosively happy one moment, then the next he'd be as low as a drizzly Monday morning.

As Brendan switched his Galaxy off airplane mode, it, too, went off as if it had been bursting at the seams with messages. It was Lorna. It didn't surprise him. She'd been less than enthusiastic about Brendan going to London. He opened the text.

*Don't be getting involved in their feud. You're there to simply prove the reliability of our information. Get back here in one piece, or I'll kick your ass XxX*

Brendan smiled to himself and dropped the device back into his jeans pocket.

As they passed through the arrivals terminal, Dimitru received a call. He spoke in Romanian. Brendan could speak the language, one of the many languages his father forced him to learn, but Dimitru spoke fast and with a local dialect, so Brendan had to rely more on his intuition to get the meaning of the conversation. Whoever it was, they helped raise Dimitru's spirits. His thin lips curled up at the sides and he walked taller with an extra spring in his step.

As they stepped outside the terminal, Dimitru pointed in the direction of the short stay carpark and led them that way. As they got within fifty yards of the carpark, a black Mercedes illuminated it's headlights and the engine ignited.

Brendan was aware that he was now in a dangerous situation. He knew these Romanians would gut him and leave him somewhere in London if they felt they could. But like most human beings, they were led by their greed. And if Brendan could prove to them that his data was legit, not only would Dimitru become the guy who'd exact revenge on the rival gang who'd taken his cousin's life, he'd also have a chance at a takeover from other underworld bosses. If Brendan could prove to the big boss back in Romania that he was in a position to help expand his empire, then Brendan's life was as safe as the rest of them.

Twenty feet from the car, Dimitru shouted something, again in Romanian. He raised his arms in the air as if he were about to greet their driver in a hug. The driver opened his door and got out. As he stood up, he closed his long grey overcoat as if trying to contain something on the inside. He stood a few inches shorter than Brendan's six-foot frame, and at least four inches wider. He looked like his favourite sport was the highly popular European sport of strongman.

He greeted both Dimitru and Brendan—first Dimitru with a hug, invited by Dimitru's body language, then Brendan with a handshake. The way he was constantly checking his jacket led Brendan to believe he had a nice surprise that would eventually be produced for the individuals Dimitru was in the city to see.

Dimitru made the introduction. 'Brendan, this crazy bastard is Neculai. Neculai, meet the infamous Brendan Cleary.'

'Pleasure to meet you,' Neculai said.

'You too,' Brendan said, tossing his bag onto the empty back seat. He followed the bag in. Dimitru circled the car, taking the front passenger seat.

As Niculai got behind the wheel, he spoke in good but not perfect English. 'I think you're going to become very popular within our Romanian family, my Irish friend.' He swivelled the rear-view mirror and looked at Brendan. 'You know where to find these sons of bitches?'

Brendan looked at his phone, opened his email box and selected the thread from Lorna. He nodded and looked back up at the mirror. 'I have the bastard's location. Not only do I know where he lives, but also where he conducts his business.' He looked at Dimitru, then back at Niculai. 'Just in case you'd like to take a little tax for what they've done.'

Dimitru laughed, slapping Niculai playfully on the shoulder. 'Bloody genius or what?'

'The time is just after nine,' Brendan said. 'Maybe we should wait until a little later before paying them a visit.'

Dimitru nodded in agreement. 'Let's go for a drink. It's been a long time, my friend.'

'Yes, we can have a toast to old friendships, and new ones.' Niculai looked at Brendan in the mirror, smiling at him. Brendan smiled back, zero authenticity behind the expression.

# Chapter Seventeen

ARRIVING IN EAST LONDON'S borough of Red-bridge, a short distance from the rival gang's heartland, they cruised through the town's high street and parked directly at the door of Your Lucky Day betting office. The shop sat nestled in the middle of a row of six shops – a hairdressers, a newsagents, a café, a laundrette and a used electronics shop. Each of the small businesses were shut. Aside from the signs above their premises, you'd never have known what they were. Each had metal shutters dropped to the ground, padlocked shut. The hairdressers, called Luscious Locks, had local slang and profanity spray painted across the silver protective front.

Getting out of the car, Brendan spotted a homeless man lying in a sleeping bag in the doorway of Luscious. The area was clearly in need of a facelift and some regeneration. He was sure that local crime rates were sky high, and that the Romanians were taking full advantage of that fact. He looked at the homeless man, curled up in a ball, a bottle of cider next to him, looking directly at Brendan. The expression on the man's face was one of hopelessness. The man had clearly given up on life and was now reduced to not much more than an animalistic state. Many dogs had a better quality of life.

'Don't take drugs, my friend,' Dimitru said as he followed Niculai into the bookies. 'If you can't handle drugs or booze, don't do it.' He stopped at the doorway and looked at the homeless man. 'Otherwise you end up like this guy over here.'

Brendan grunted, following them into the bookies. The shop was one person away from being empty. The customer stood staring up at the plasma mounted to one of the four pillars. A betting slip clutched in his hands, his expression was similar to the man sleeping outside. But unlike the homeless man, it wasn't an addiction to drugs or alcohol that was the cause of his sorrow, but it would eventually have the same results.

There was a cheer, a victorious eruption in the back office as the driver and Dimitru entered. Brendan followed them into the office to find a group of three men sitting around an office desk. One was sitting on the business side of the desk. He wore a black hoodie with the sleeves rolled up to his elbows, showing off some tribal style tattoos that marked the front of his forearms. He had a shaven head and another tattoo running up from under his hoodie, travelling up his neck and finishing at his chin. He looked at Brendan, his brown eyes narrowing into tiny slits. He was in the middle of sharing a pleasant exchange of words with Dimitru when Brendan entered the room.

Brendan closed the door. The atmosphere in the room was heavy, it was certainly too small a space for some many personalities. The other two who sat on the opposite side of the desk looked as if they were employees in a disciplinary with the tattooed boss man. The two looked like brothers, almost identical, only one was thin with a wiry moustache, the other was slightly more muscular without any facial hair. The thin one looked at Brendan, welcoming him in broken English. He spoke in a tone of mockery. His broader accomplice just turned his head back to the shaven-headed boss who was still staring at Brendan.

Brendan looked at Dimitru, then at Niculai, shrugging his shoulders. 'Are we going to stand here and look at each other, or are you lot going to pay these guys a visit?'

The shaven head stood up from his seat. He walked around the table, not once breaking eye contact with Brendan. He didn't smile, and the aggressive vibe he was giving off thickened as he approached Brendan. He reached his hand out to shake Brendan's. 'I hope for your sake you're right. It wouldn't be good for any of us if you send us into a bloody massacre.'

'The information I give you will be better for you than for them. After that, I don't give a shit what you all get up to when you go in there.' Brendan embraced the handshake, mirroring the Romanian, squeezing so tight he almost broke bones.

Dimitru cleared his throat and approached them. He placed his hand on Brendan's shoulder. 'Brendan, meet Alin. He's my younger cousin.' He stood in the centre of the two, like a referee in a bout. He turned and placed his hand on the shaved head's shoulder. 'Alin, meet Brendan. Now both of you stop trying to measure your dicks. We're on the same team.'

Alin released his grip, Brendan smiled at him.

'Pleasure to meet you, Brendan,' Alin said.

'Pleasure's all mine,' Brendan responded.

The wiry guy with the moustache jumped up from his seat. 'Brendan, welcome to London. I'm Marian.' He offered Brendan his hand. Brendan accepted. Marian turned, and pointed to the guy with similar features. 'That's my older brother, Marku.'

'Pleasure,' Brendan said.

Marku stood up, his face as serious as the job they were about to do. 'Welcome.'

'Let's go,' Dimitru said, leading the way back out of the office.

Brendan's phone vibrated as he followed Dimitru out the office. Lorna asking for an update. He ignored it, at least until he had something to update her with.

As they exited the shop, a second black Mercedes – identical to the one Niculai drove – had just shut off it's lights.

Dimitru looked back at Brendan as he made his way towards the car. His confidence had returned. That bounce in his step, the untouchable swagger that Brendan had first witnessed in Belfast was now alive.

Brendan looked back at the homeless guy still lying in the doorway, the bottle of cider clasped tightly in his hands. He started the think of how grateful he was to be in a position to walk away from everything he was doing. Why was he putting himself in danger? Putting his and Lorna's future at risk. Damien Cleary's dying wish was for his son to make good use of the set of skills that he'd passed on, but was it worth losing everything good he had in his life?

Brendan got back into Niculai's car. Alin taking the front passenger seat. Dimitru opened the rear passenger side door and got in. He looked at Brendan, handing him a weapon. A black Sig Sauer. 'Just in case you need it.'

'I'm not going into a gun fight with you.' Brendan handed the pistol back over to Dimitru. 'I've come here with you to prove our information is good. A goodwill gesture.'

Dimitru put his hand up to Brendan in refusal. 'Just take it. Just in case.'

'You sure he knows how to use that thing?' Alin sniggered.

Brendan looked at him and smiled, dropping the magazine out of the bottom of the gun, checking that it was full. It was. He pumped one round into the chamber, so it was ready to fire. 'I think I'll figure it out.'

The other Mercedes pulled away first. Niculai followed. Brendan watched through the window, out into the streets that were London. He tuned out the noise of the others in the car. Their topic was the people they were going after. They appeared excited, not at all nervous about what they were about to take part in. There was a disturbing reality about the fact they were on their way to take a life—or perhaps lives, plural—yet they sounded almost as if they were talking about who'd won the football. Brendan had witnessed the coldness of Dimitru in Belfast. He'd thought they were going to rough Murphy up a little, scare him perhaps, not leave him bludgeoned to death in his kitchen, only to be found by some stranger. But Brendan didn't lose focus on what he was doing. He reminded himself of the fact that so many people were suffering because of the way these organisations were operating. A justification if nothing else.

As they arrived at the location, the car fell silent.

Dimitru looked at Brendan. 'Are you sure you don't want to come and join us?'

Brendan shook his head, but he looked at Dimitru. 'You're not carrying out the attack here?'

'Of course.'

'With all due respect...are you fucking stupid?'

'You watch your fucking mouth, Cleary,' Niculai shouted.

'If you want to get yourselves into bigger trouble, go right ahead. Unless you're thinking of killing everyone in that pub, including innocent people, think again. You'll be caught and will all go down for it. You'll also start more chaos.'

'What do you suggest then, smart man?' Dimitru said.

'You wait for them to close up for the night and leave. You take as many of them as there are away from here and torture them before you execute them. But you leave one of them to tell the tale. You leave them so fucked up in the head that they never recover. The word will spread through your criminal world about what you did.' Brendan looked around at them all. None of them seemed opposed. 'You advertise yourselves as the most sophisticated group in the area. You send out a clear message that says, without question, that none of you are to be fucked with. Ever again.'

Dimitru slapped him affectionately with the back of his hand. 'You know, that might work.' He looked at the other two in the front. They both looked like they agreed, but that they didn't want to display how impressed they were.

Brendan's phone rang. It was Lorna. He stepped out of the car to answer it. He didn't want her to worry about him.

After what had happened in Italy, both realised how easy it would be to lose the other. And neither of them was willing to let that happen. 'Hey, are you okay?'

'Am I okay?' Lorna sounded both grateful and surprised. 'Are you okay?'

'I'm fine. I'm just giving these guys some recommendations on how to go about their business a little better.'

'Don't get too cocky, Brendan.'

'I know, I know,' Brendan said, feeling like he was being nagged. 'But I can't come across as a sniffling little weasel either. If I do, then I'm in trouble. These guys are animals. Nothing more, nothing less.'

'I met your little gym buddy this evening. He was with Diana.'

'How are they?'

'Like two people who've had to live with Dimitru for too long.'

'Did you give her a little pep talk, tell her that we're on the case?'

'That's what I'm getting to. We had another idea.'

Brendan looked at the car. The three others in the car were all having a discussion. 'What?' He put more distance between himself and two vehicles.

'One thing she gets from being with him is financial security.'

'I don't think they have piles of notes sitting around in grey bags with dollar signs on them,' Brendan said humorously.

'No, but Diana has access to Dimitru's accounts. He has lots of money in them. I'm thinking the least she deserves is to get her hands on some funds with which she'll be able to disappear.'

Dimitru got out of the car and made his way towards Brendan. 'I've got to go. If you guys can think of how you can clear out his funds, then, of course.' He hung up, looking at Dimitru. 'Lorna's jealous she's not over here, too.'

Dimitru grinned. 'The lovely English lady is missing her home?'

Brendan nodded, then gestured with his chin towards a group of five men making their way into the pub. 'I recognise the one with the suit. He's one of your targets.'

Dimitru turned his back to them, looking in the opposite direction. 'Yes, that is one of them. The son of a bitch is dead.'

'Well, I've told you what I would do. But that's just me. I frankly don't give a shit. As long as I'm on that flight back to Belfast tomorrow and not in a station or funeral parlour then you can do what you want.'

'Yes, I've talked it over with my associates.' He gestured for Brendan to accompany him back to the car. 'We're having reinforcements join us with a transit van. We'll be removing them all from here tonight. But I need to ask you a favour.' He made his way towards the rear passenger side. He gripped the handle of the door and looked across the roof at Brendan. Brendan mirrored him on the opposite side.

'I told you I'm not getting involved in whatever it is you're doing.' Brendan pulled his door open and got in. Dimitru followed him. 'I've proven myself and my word good to you. That's it.'

'You don't want us to go in there and start shooting the place up?' Alin said. 'Then, we need you to go into the pub and find out how many of them there are.'

'Brendan, you're right. I don't want to start shooting innocent people just going out for a pint,' Dimitru said in a persuasive tone of voice. 'If you go in there and eyeball the ones we're after, the job will be a lot cleaner. And when our friends arrive with the van, we'll know exactly who's going in the back of it.'

Brendan looked around the car. All three of them were looking at him. He felt pressured. He couldn't back out. Their plan made sense. Brendan didn't want his information to cause innocent people to get killed. He looked through the window, towards the entrance to the bustling establishment. He sighed. 'Fucking hate pubs.' He threw the door open and got out. As he slammed it shut, he could hear Dimitru say something, but his voice faded away as the door closed. He didn't bother to ask what he'd said. He shoved his hands in his pockets and made his way towards the bar.

As he approached the front door, he saw from the condition of the outside furniture that he was entering a pub that had seen better days. He'd seen pubs like this before, back in Belfast. Usually they were locals that had experienced the force of criminal muscle moving in and pushing the good punters out. The wooden tables and chairs were badly chipped and splintered. The rubbish, cigarette packets and butts were strewn everywhere. And if there was a manager of the place who cared more about serving regular paying customers, instead of local hoods using it as a hangout, then the area would have been a little more presentable.

'Evening,' Brendan said to one of the doormen, who held the door open for him.

'Evening, mate,' the doorman responded.

'Cheers.' Brendan nodded politely as he entered the pub. There was an atmospheric chatter. Multiple individual conversation from the various groups seemed to come together, almost in one tune. Without making eye contact with anyone, Brendan made his way straight for the bar. He could see a group of men and women, probably early twenties, becoming rowdy as they egged one another on to down another shot. The casual jeans and plain shirts that the men were wearing, along with the revealing skirts and skin-tight tops of the girls, led Brendan to believe that perhaps this was only going to be their first stop before heading on to another club. And it was this kind of people Brendan didn't want getting caught in the crossfire. Having their young lives stripped away from them needlessly was something he wasn't going to let happen, even if he had to put down the ones who posed the threat to them.

'What can I get you, mate?' The barman spoke loudly, leaning across the bar.

'Just a Pepsi, please,' Brendan said. He looked around. The group Dimitru had recognised entering was sitting in a booth in the far corner. Six of them. All looked older than Brendan, perhaps early-to-late forties. Three sat on one side of their table and three sat on the opposite.

Brendan turned his attention back to the barman. He pulled his bank card out of his phone wallet.

'Cheers.' The barman took it. 'Can I use the contactless?'

Brendan nodded his head. One of the lads from the young group came to the bar, asking for another six shots. He leaned on the bar, as if his body needed the support. His head bobbed around on the spot, as if unable to focus. He caught Brendan's gaze in the mirror that ran across the wall behind the bar. He smiled at Brendan. Brendan took a sip from his Pepsi and checked his phone.

'Alright mate?' the lad shouted, turning to look directly at Brendan.

Brendan thought this was the beginning of it, a drunken conversation with someone who'd had a little too much to drink. He looked at him. 'Having a good night?'

'Fucking lush, mate.' He slurred his words, and felt the need to fall into Brendan, shouting it in his ear. Brendan didn't allow it to bother him. The lad was a little over the limit. 'Here, where are you from?'

'Belfast.'

'You're Irish? I fucking love Ireland.'

'Thanks. Me, too.' Brendan laughed. 'Go easy on the booze, mate.'

The barman arrived with a tray of six shots. The lad handed the barman a crumpled-up note that he dropped twice before it finally reached the barman's grip.

He put his arm around Brendan and told him to have a good evening, spitting as he spoke, but it was unintentional, no harm was meant by it. No aggression. Brendan could understand and appreciate friends out having fun together. That's what life's all about he thought. At least for most people. Brendan watched as the lad staggered back to his friends; they all looked happy to see him return with more shots. Brendan allowed himself to see the humour in the interaction. The guy was harmless, unlike the group sitting in the corner, acting as if they owned the place.

Brendan took a seat in the opposite end of the pub from the group he was watching. He was in a position that would not attract too much attention, but it wouldn't look as if he was trying the stay out of the way. He sipped on the Pepsi, the gas causing the beverage to fizz around his lips. He checked his phone. Dimitru had sent him a text.

*Don't be having a party in there. Just find out what you need to know then get out of there.*

After people-watching for ten minutes, pretending he was more interested in the replay of the earlier game of football on the widescreen above his head, Brendan finished his drink. The time was eleven thirty, and the bar was beginning to clear out. The group of youngsters had left for the next leg of their binge tour. A middle-aged couple had finished off their drinks and left. Brendan followed them out, leaving only the group of six Romanians inside.

He wished the doormen goodnight and made his way back to the car, noticing that the two Mercedes had moved farther down the road, almost out of view of the pub's entrance. A black transit was now parked beside the Mercs. He got to the car and jumped into the back again, pulling the door shut. He looked at Dimitru. 'There are six of them in there.'

'Do they look armed?' Niculai shouted.

'I didn't go up and frisk them,' Brendan responded to the simple question.

Alin sniggered. 'He always has an answer, this guy,' he said dismissively.

'We wait. When the pub closes and they leave, we'll hit them,' Dimitru said, glaring at his phone, as if he was in receipt of bad news. His expression was distant. Not in the car.

'You get some bad news?' Brendan said.

Dimitru shook his head. 'No, the boss man is planning a trip from Romania. He's paying us a visit.' He locked his phone and looked at Brendan. 'I've told him about your little business proposition, and he wants to come and meet you personally.'

'I'm touched he's coming all the way,' Brendan said sarcastically. 'But let's just focus on getting back to Belfast.' He looked at his phone. Another text from Lorna. He decided not to open it.

A short while later, the doormen had retreated into the pub and closed the doors. The six would be leaving any moment. A silence had fallen over the car. Brendan realised he'd gripped his pistol so tight that he'd caused an imprint on his palm, perhaps subconsciously preparing himself for the worst-case scenario. He had lowered his window for a clearer view, removing the tints.

'There they are. Now we go,' Dimitru called to the guys in the van. 'Let's get these bastards.'

The moment Dimitru said this, Niculai started the engine and led the convoy towards the targets.

The Mercedes came to a skidding halt on the footpath right at their feet. The six froze. Before anything registered with them, the van's sliding door flew open and four men wearing ski masks jumped out, armed with pistols.

The six raised their hands and dropped their jaws. Brendan watched with the other occupants of the car as the targets were bundled into the van through the sliding side door.

Dimitru's phone rang. He spoke in Romanian.

Brendan could loosely comprehend the exchange. Niculai was to lead the convoy to the location. As Brendan recommended, they would make an example of the group and send out a clear message to the rest of the criminal underworld that there would be consequences if someone crossed them, striking a new level of fear amongst others in their world.

Brendan expected there to be an upbeat enthusiasm from the group with which he'd shared the car. But there wasn't. Instead, a silence. It made him feel uneasy. He wondered if his choice to join Dimitru on his trip to London had been the right one to make. But there was nothing he could do about it now. His choice was made, and he continued to advertise his quiet confidence that would ultimately convince the bosses of the Romanian crime family that he'd be a worthy asset.

The streets in East London were damp and deserted. The driver led them towards Barking Industrial Estate, and turned off the main road, entering what was at that time of night a dark, derelict area, making for an optimal location to carry out their plans.

The car was guided in through the gates of a warehouse. Above the building's reception area was a dirty white sign reading Smith's Meats. The reception side of the building was in darkness, but faded light shone through the tiny windows that ran along the top of the brown-bricked walls of the warehouse's main production area. Nightshift staff were perhaps working late.

Brendan pointed to the sign. 'You're really going to make an example out of them, then.' He shook his head. 'You'll certainly send out a message.'

'How do you know this place isn't for you, too?' Alin said.

'Because you wouldn't be that fucking stupid,' Brendan said. 'I can help your business grow bigger than your boss could make it in two lifetimes. If your boss got wind of you screwing up his business plans, I'm pretty sure you'd be next under the meat cleaver. So less attempted intimidation; that's carrying zero weight.'

The van pulled up beside them. Brendan watched as everyone got out. He got out, too.

'I thought you weren't getting involved?' Dimitru said. He walked around the car towards Brendan. 'You've proven your worth, Brendan.' He lit up a cigarette and put his hand on Brendan's shoulder as they walked towards the van. 'Let us deal with this vermin. Take the keys to the Mercedes and we'll meet you back in the city tomorrow.' He pulled out a roll of notes and stuffed them into Brendan's pocket. 'Enjoy London. Take in the scenery and forget about what will happen here tonight.' He held his hand out to shake Brendan's. 'I look forward to a flourishing business between us. I can see a bright future.'

Niculai joined them and handed the car keys to Brendan. 'Don't scratch it.' He grinned, his teeth biting down on the butt of a cigarette.

Brendan took the key and made his way towards the driver's door. The sound of the six men and their terrified screams sent a chill down his spine. He shut his mind off to the noise and to the idea of what was going to become their fate. He got into the driver's seat and pulled the seat forward, closer to the wheel. He started the engine, but before he put the car into gear, he called Lorna.

She answered almost instantly. 'Brendan, are you okay?'

'I'm fine.' Brendan put the window down. He could just about catch the remains of the captive's screams. He put the window back up again. There were times when he had to close himself off to things. Things like what was about to happen inside that warehouse. 'I'm looking forward to seeing you tomorrow.' He felt himself longing for Lorna. 'I think we're in with the Romanian mafia now. So, let's see how long it takes us to bring these bastards down.'

'Brendan, what's wrong?'

'Nothing.'

'Then what's with the voice?'

'I'm just tired. How's it back in Belfast?'

'Fine. I'm going to spend the day with Diana tomorrow. She's a nervous wreck.'

'You need to make sure she doesn't break. Dimitru instils fear in people and I'm pretty sure she's no different.' He put the car into reverse and backed out through the steel-panelled gates. 'I'm going to grab a snack. I'll speak to you in the morning.'

'You take care and get home safely.' Lorna ended the call.

Brendan put the radio on. BBC Radio One was playing the graveyard shift, a playlist of slow-beat trance music. He switched the station to one more upbeat. Not in any rush, he cruised the streets of East End London. Even in the middle of the night, there was life to the city, a buzz. The air was damp and humid. The streets were deserted, but still, the atmosphere was heavy. It was as if the air carried with it the energy of the daytime when the city was truly alive.

Spotting a McDonalds's, he pulled into the drive through and joined a queue of five idling vehicles. The car directly in front of him was a silver M3 with BOSS on the registration plate. Brendan looked through the rear window of the BMW and wondered who the BOSS was. The BOSS, or at least the person behind the wheel, could barely be seen from the other side of the seat. Brendan could just about see the peak of a baseball cap pointing towards the roof of the car. The passenger seat was occupied by a female who looked no older than early twenties, and that was stretching the imagination as far as possible.

After ordering two Big Macs and fries with coke, he followed the queue to the service window and patiently waited for the food. He finally got a glimpse of the BOSS as he had to step out of the car to collect his order. Brendan could hear the BOSS explain to the member of staff that his window was broken and he couldn't put it down, which was why he had to open the door and get out.

After getting his order, Brendan pulled into one of the shopping outlet's parking bays. Alongside seven other cars, at that time of the night he felt as if he was at one of those American outdoor movie theatres, where the customers would pull up and watch the flick from the comfort of their own vehicle. But instead of a widescreen blockbuster movie,

Brendan was provided with entertainment by a group of petrol heads at the far, more secluded part of the carpark outside a Halfords.

After finishing his meal, he made his way towards the city centre. Given the size of London, he knew it wouldn't be like travelling around Belfast. Belfast was perhaps the size of one of England's smaller cities, but with a London population double that of the entire thirty-two-county island of Ireland, he was at the mercy of his phone's sat nav.

After cruising the streets for an hour, he decided to find a place to put his head down. He found a Premier Inn six miles from the airport. Fortunately for him, there was a room. He checked in at three a.m. and texted Dimitru to tell him he'd meet him at the airport the next day. Dimitru didn't respond, but Brendan was focussed on nothing else but getting to the airport the next day.

He had a shower, then prepared his clothes for the next day, a daily habit of razor-sharp precision. He set his alarm for eight-thirty. Considering the time, he decided to give himself a lie in. His normal waking time was in two hours, and sleep deprivation was perhaps more dangerous for someone with Brendan's life than a gun that jams.

# Chapter Eighteen

THE NEXT MORNING, BRENDAN'S alarm went off. His eyes shot open, momentarily unsure about where he was. He reached over and grabbed his phone, shutting it off. After a few seconds, his eyes came into focus. He sat up, resting against the headboard. He'd begun practising meditation when he was training with his father in Donegal. The late Damien Cleary always preached to his son about how the practise was good at clearing the mind. A clear mind was the best way of maintaining control of the body. Brendan hadn't meditated for a long time, but for some reason, he felt it would be good to take it up again. After remaining in bed with his eyes closed for ten minutes, practicing deep breathing, he got off the bed and finished his morning ritual by blasting though a five-exercise upper and lower body circuit. Usually he went for a run, but the rain was pelting off the window like marbles, therefore he opted for the warm water of the shower.

After this, he felt more alive. Fresher and alert, he jumped out of the shower, shaved, and, after asking the receptionist for an iron, took the creases out of his shirt and trousers. He put the kettle on and made himself a cup of coffee. He de-activated airplane mode on his phone and before he could even check his emails, his phone went into a fit of messages, vibrating and beeping. When the device settled back down, he recognised he had three missed calls and two voicemails. All from Dimitru.

As he played the first voicemail on loudspeaker, he could hear the celebrations of Dimitru and the others. Dimitru was only just coherent. Between laughing and slurring his words, he told Brendan how they'd sent out a clear message to the other gangsters that they were not just there to take part but were about to take over the entire criminal underworld. Brendan continued to listen as Dimitru began singing along with the others in the background. Whatever they were singing was in Romanian, but Brendan didn't need to translate to understand their meaning. Had it been the festive season, they would have been described as merry.

As the singing continued, the call ended. Brendan looked at the phone, waiting for another call. It didn't come. He decided to forget about the night before and go for his breakfast.

The hotel's reception was alive, even at that time of the day. A queue of eight people waited to be served, bags slung over their shoulders. Brendan didn't know whether they were checking in or out, but they were anxiously waiting to be processed. As he cut through the middle of the group to get to the restaurants, he picked up a foreign accent. Perhaps Eastern European.

As he entered the restaurant, he acknowledged a young couple, perhaps around his age; both looked like the blood had been drained out of their faces. The only redness visible was the rings around their eyes. Brendan smiled at them and took his seat. The couple made him cast his mind back to the night before, and the group of youngsters, they were pretty much pissed before leaving the pub. He was sure that group was feeling worse for their actions, but at least they hadn't been caught up in the deadly turf war between the two Romanian families.

After ordering a full English breakfast, he switched his phone back onto pilot mode, choosing to clear his mind from any artificial distraction. He wanted to spend the morning at a slower pace than his life had recently been going. And other than Lorna, he didn't care to hear from anyone.

However, he quickly came to realise that he couldn't escape the life he was living simply by removing his phone's connectivity and shutting off his mind. He watched as the waitress pointed the remote control at the TV and switched it on to it's default channel ~ Sky News. The top story came to life. A meat factory in the East End of London, where Dimitru and his crew had well and truly sent out a message. A message in the bloodiest form possible. A massacre was how the reporter was describing it. It was clear Dimitru was ready to do some extreme things in order to grow his business and satisfy the boss back at home.

After his breakfast, Brendan took his bag and checked out, thanking the hotel staff for putting him up at such short notice. He still had Niculai's Mercedes. The car was parked in the corner of the hotel's facilities. Mist had coated the entire car. The air must have been cool and fresh the night before, leaving the residue visible.

He opened the door and got in, dropping his bag and overcoat on the front passenger seat. Switching the engine on, he fired the heating up to twenty degrees and the fan power up to full. He took off and, for once, felt he was able to just go wherever he'd like. As long as they got to the airport on time for their flight that evening, he had the freedom of a car full of fuel and the open road. He didn't know where he was going to go, but for some reason he was happy with that.

After spending two hours behind the wheel, Brendan felt like he did whenever he practised his morning meditation. His mind felt calm, collected, certainly much better than it had for a while. He pulled over at a Tesco supermarket and re-fuelled the car for the return journey. After filling the tank, he went into the petrol station and got himself a double espresso and a sandwich. He de-activated flight mode and called Lorna.

'Brendan, are you okay?'

His facial expression lifted as soon as he heard her voice. 'I'll feel better when I get my hands on you. I'm on my way to meet with them now. We'll be leaving for the airport soon.'

'Get home safely. I've seen on the news what's happened over there.'

'He's really sent out a message to the other gangs. Nobody will be fucking about with that organisation again.'

Lorna grunted. 'We've given Dimitru and his crew false hope. Because when they've been taken down, they'll wish they'd have chosen to go to work and earn a living.'

Brendan laughed as he started the car. 'Maybe it's not too late for them.'

'They've got a lot of making up to do for a lifetime of crime,' Lorna said, a sting in her voice, venom towards the Romanians. 'Last night, I went through the documents our

British agents have gathered on the mafia family over the years. They've created a lot of broken families. A lot of people have suffered at their hands.'

Brendan pulled out of the Tesco carpark and followed the road markings for East London. 'Speaking of families, have you spoken to your sister?'

'I can't, Brendan. If the government knows I've contacted her, it'll be bad for us, and for her.'

There was an awkward silence. Brendan cleared his throat. Lorna sniggered.

'But thanks for asking,' she said. 'I'm looking forward to seeing you, too. Perhaps we can pay a little visit to Chelmsford and pay Lisa and Josh a visit. Have a look at them without attracting any attention to them, or us.'

'Josh is your sister's husband?'

'No, her teenage son, who I hear is becoming an adolescent pain in the ass.'

Brendan laughed. 'We all were at that age.'

'I'm on my way to meet with Diana. She's fucking depressed, Brendan. She needs looking after.'

'It's not surprising, living with that piece of shit.' Brendan joined a queue of slow-moving traffic. 'Listen, I'll chat with you later. Have a nice day.'

'Take care.'

# Chapter Nineteen

BRENDAN ARRIVED AT the bookies where he'd met the rest of the family's London branch. He parked the car behind the black Mercedes's twin. As he got out, he spotted a foot-thick scratch running the entire length of the driver's side. If that was his car, he'd be pissed. But he kind of guessed it was done while driving home in a drunken state sometime in the early hours.

Brendan entered the shop. A group of three young lads in school uniforms pushed past him, looking at him as if he were a high school attendance inspector. He approached the office door, hearing laughter coming from the inside. He knocked the door, not to be polite, he simply didn't want to walk into something he didn't want to see.

Alin shouted to come in. Brendan entered. An overpowering stench of smoke and cider lingered, and a clear sign none of them had showered in at least twenty-four hours. Dimitru sat on the sofa, his left leg casually slung over his right, his hands joined behind his head. He looked at Brendan through glazed eyes. A smile spread across his face.

'Brendan.' Alin looked at Dimitru. 'Our man with the plan.' He slurred, standing up, perhaps a little too fast, as he had to balance himself off the desk to stop from toppling over. He trudged around it with his hand outstretched towards Brendan.

Brendan shook his hand, but it was more like catching the big man before he fell.

'I look forward to working with you again,' Alin said, his voice no steadier than his walk.

'Maybe some sleep might be a good idea?' Brendan said, honestly, not sarcastically. He'd made some friends within the Romanian mafia. He needed to make sure they continued to feel that way. At least for now.

He smiled at Brendan, making Brendan unsure about what was going on in his mind. 'And I'll sleep when I'm dead.'

'Like those poor bastards who thought they could fuck with us,' Dimitru chimed in. He stood up and patted Brendan on the shoulder. 'Let's get back to Belfast; I miss that depressing place.'

Sitting at the airport, Brendan watched as Dimitru paced up and down the departures lounge, his face downcast, his phone glued to his ear. Brendan didn't know who it was, but the moment the call came through, Dimitru put some distance between them before he picked up. Brendan didn't care. He was tired, both physically and mentally. Tired of listening to all the bullshit that came out of Dimitru's mouth.

He watched the news on his phone, still talking about the terrible events that had taken place in East London, described as being the most barbaric display of brutality that London had seen for a long time. There had been a message written on the walls of the warehouse in blood: *lesson learned we hope!* The slogan was written in Romanian, but undoubtedly it was a message from those who were about to take over the criminal scene.

As Brendan continued to kill time, scrolling through his phone, he received a text message from Lorna.

*Just met Diana's son. Teodoro. He's a piece of work. No wonder Diana's nerves are shattered, trying to contain him. Maybe he should hit that bag in the gym a bit harder. Have a safe flight home, and text me when you arrive. I'll come and pick you up. Lorna xXx*

Brendan responded with a smiley face.

They had another forty-five minutes until they were due to board the flight, so Brendan offered to buy them dinner in the lounge pub.

Dimitru looked like his hangover had just begun to kick in. His eyes tiny slits, his olive-coloured southern European complexion had become drained. His liver had clearly received some assault, and he was suffering the consequences of it.

Brendan had a steak and chips, with fried onions. Dimitru had a chicken burger and a foot-long hotdog. It was amusing for Brendan to watch him try and eat it without covering himself in chilli sauce. Brendan washed his meal down with a Pepsi Max, Dimitru savoured a Rum and Coke.

Nine-fifteen finally rolled around and they joined the queue of passengers to board. Like their flight from Belfast, it was the last flight of the day and there were not many passengers. Dimitru was grateful when the air hostess allowed him to take a complete empty row of seats A, B, and C on row twenty-eight. Brendan was happy with his seat and pleased he didn't have to smell the remnants of Dimitru's late

night celebrations. After giving the flight attendants their respect and humouring them while they demonstrated for the
passengers the emergency procedures, he put his earphones
in and selected Guns and Roses Greatest Hits, a playlist that
would last perhaps the entire length of the flight.

# Chapter Twenty

SHORTLY AFTER TEN, Brendan's eyes opened as the air hostess alerted him that they were preparing to land and he needed to remove his headphones. Brendan turned and looked back at Dimitru. The Romanian was out cold, and snoring. Sophistication was the furthest thing from Brendan's mind when he watched Dimitru straighten himself up once prompted by the hostess. He laughed to himself and turned back around to face front. He put his seatbelt on and waited for the aircraft to touch down.

The night was windy and damp and they were welcomed back to Belfast by the famous Irish drizzle. Brendan led the way down the rear flight of steps, gripping the cold steel handrail for balance.

Once in the terminal, Brendan de-activated flight mode and called Lorna.

'You've arrived?' She said, sounding relieved.

'We're just exiting the terminal now.' Brendan looked at Dimitru, who'd began to walk with more swagger in his step. His ego had taken a tremendous boost after what they'd just done. 'Where are you?'

'Are you on loudspeaker, or can I speak freely?'

'Go for it.'

'I'm with Diana. She's less than excited to see him come home. Pity you couldn't have left him there with the rest of them.'

Brendan smiled and looked at Dimitru as the Romanian fumbled with his phone. 'Yes, it's a pity. How long will you be?'

'I'll see you in twenty minutes.'

'Great.' Brendan hung up the phone. 'You need a lift?'

Dimitru shook his head. 'No... Thank you. Andrei is coming to get me.' He shoved his phone in his pocket and pulled out a box of cigarettes. As they exited the terminal, he put it between his lips and bit on the butt. Pulling a lighter out of his back pocket, he tilted his head as he puffed off the end, almost dragging the flame down into it through the opposite end. 'My bitch woman should have picked me up, but she's not answering her phone. Useless bitch.' He rubbed his head.

'You need to get some rest,' Brendan said as they made use of the zebra crossing, entering the airport's short stay carpark.

'I need my bed, you're right.' Dimitru took one last draw of the cigarette and flicked it into a puddle that had formed beside the taxi rank's pickup shelter. He looked at Brendan, his eyes straining to remain on their target. 'Our boss in Romania has heard about our little escapade in London. He's very impressed. He says he wants to meet you.'

'Great. Tell him to come to Belfast,' Brendan said.

'He's paying a London a visit in two days, then he'll be in Belfast the day after.'

'Great, then we can get down to business.'

Dimitru grunted in agreement. 'Business, yes. We can do lots of business together.'

Ten minutes later, Lorna pulled up at the shelter. Brendan shook Dimitru's hand and told him they'd be in touch. Dimitru asked for Brendan's address, but Brendan refused. He made it clear to Dimitru that no matter how much business they were to do together, both he and Lorna would be going home at night with the ability to sleep easy knowing that their anonymity remained intact.

'Fancy a takeaway before we go back to the hotel?' Lorna said as she guided the car through the airport's security barrier.

'What do you suggest?'

She shrugged her shoulders. 'Fish and chips?'

'Why not.' Brendan sounded gassed. 'I think I'll go for a run tonight before bed.'

'You're stressed?'

He looked at her as she focussed on the road, pulling the car onto the Sydenham By-pass, city bound. He touched the top of her hand that rested on the gear stick. 'I'm better now. I've missed you.'

She smiled, keeping her eyes on the road. 'You're becoming soft, Brendan Cleary.'

He laughed and nodded his head. 'Maybe.'

'So, you're glad you went to London?'

'I think it's secured our entry into this organisation. The boss is coming over from Romania in three days. He's going to London first, then he's paying us a visit here.'

'Promise me something.'

'What?'

'That you'll let me cut the dirty bastard's cock off when we're finished bringing down his dirty little empire.'

'You promise me something?'

She sniggered, 'what?'

'If we ever fall out, promise me you'll leave my cock out of it?'

She exploded into a fit of laughter. 'What about the house in Donegal?'

'What about it?'

'How about we stay there for a while, at least while we're over here?'

Brendan didn't look at all enthusiastic.

'Come on, you can't ignore the house forever.'

He didn't respond. To Brendan, that house would always be the place where his father died, but to Lorna it would always be the place where his father broke Brendan down as a child and re-built him into someone not many people in the world would be able to mess with. He was a walking, breathing example of a one-man army, who'd come from the most sought-after contract killer—his father, a man known only as The Ghost on account of the fact he never seemed to die, no matter how many sticky situations he found himself in.

'I don't know, Lorna.' His voice was low, deep. Emotionless.

If Lorna wanted to find a way to touch a nerve, she'd found it. There was an awkward silence in the car as they cruised through the town towards the Lisburn Road. Lorna put the radio on to break the silence.

Brendan put the window down to let some fresh air in. 'I'm starving.' He was grateful to see the Monty Carlo fish and chip shop. 'We need to start eating proper food,' he said.

Lorna pulled the car over outside the shop and switched off the engine. There was another silence. She turned and looked at him. 'I'm sorry for mentioning the house.'

Brendan turned to her. He looked at her for a moment, then stroked her face with the back of his hand. 'I'm the one that's sorry. And maybe you're right. I should be going back to it. I can't run away from it forever.'

She leaned over to his side and gave him a kiss on the cheek. 'I bought you a month gym membership, too, in case you still want to go and train with young Teodoro.'

'Thanks.' He kissed her back.

'But, if you decide you want to spar with him, let him win.'

Brendan grinned. 'I don't think I'll need to let him. He's pretty skilled. And full of energy.'

'Okay, well how about we just stay in the hotel tonight? Then we can go to Donegal tomorrow, after you're done playing in the gym.'

'You're the boss!' He got out of the car. 'I'm not going to argue with you.'

# Chapter Twenty-One

BRENDAN'S ALARM WOKE him up at the usual time – five-thirty. He rolled over and checked his phone. Nothing from Dimitru. He was happy with that. He'd done what he needed to do. Now his sights were on the big boss. Getting in close to him, perhaps winning an invitation to work a little closer to him, would make it much easier to cut the head off the organisation.

He quickly pulled on a pair of tracksuit bottoms, a vest, and a hoodie. Pulling up his hood, he leaned over the top of Lorna, kissing her on the cheek. She rolled over and smiled at him.

As he made his way towards the door, she mumbled. 'Have fun at the gym.'

Brendan pulled the door open, looking back at her. 'See you soon.'

As he descended the stairs, he passed the cleaner, who was a little shocked by his approach. A hooded man would be enough to put anyone on edge, especially one approaching from behind.

'Jesus, you scared the life out of me, love,' the elderly lady said, shock written on her face.

'Sorry,' Brendan said, politely. He put his hand on her shoulder affectionately. For some reason he thought of his grandmother, his mother's side. Then he thought about his mother. After the disappearance of his father, Brendan and his mother Vanessa had suffered daily torment, worried of where Damien Cleary had ended up. He'd give anything to go back in time and tell his mother that everything was going to work out for the best. But, until he discovered the existence of time travel, there was no point in wasting time or energy on the thought.

He kept his head down and his hood up as he crossed the foyer, stepping out into the rain. The famous Irish drizzle didn't feel like much; it was very light. But if you stood in it for very long, you'd quickly add a few extra kilos in water weight.

He decided to go for a short jog first to warm up before entering the gym.

He arrived at the gym soaked inside and out. As he approached the gym's front door, he saw Teodoro at his usual place in front of the punch bag, going hell for leather with a barrage of lefts hooks, right crosses and snappy jabs.

As Brendan stepped inside, the smell of stale sweat mixed with leather brought him back to those days in the gym in Donegal. It used to be a bad reminder of all those summers of torture and torment that his father put him through. Now, it acted as a reminder that he wasn't made of glass; he was built of extraordinary resilience, a mental toughness that only the elite in the world of war and combat could maintain.

He closed his eyes and inhaled, imagining himself back in that gym on the western Irish coast, going up against his father, never able to get the better of him. It wasn't until their little scrap in the dark, inside The Gents House just out-

side London that Brendan had fought an opponent so gifted with their hands. It was strange how that stranger whom
he'd fought in total darkness ended up being the man who'd
taught him to fight in the first place.

'Morning.' Brendan took his trainers off and stepped onto the blue matting of the gym's dojo. 'Fancy trying it on
with something that will throw back at you?'

Teodoro stopped and smiled. He took his gloves off,
dropping them to the ground he picked up his bottle of water. 'I don't want to embarrass you.'

Brendan grinned. The lad was very confident. That was
good. Confidence would make him feel good. If boxing
made him feel good, then that was what was going to stop
him from going down the wrong path, joining his father and
the rest of the soon-to-be dead or rotting in a prison gangsters. Brendan didn't want to shatter the lad's confidence; he
was too young, and at his age it was too fragile. He opted to
not spar with Teodoro until he knew what he could do.

'How about we do some pad work, then?' Brendan
grabbed a set of striking pads at the bodyweight circuit area.
'You up for displaying your power to me?'

Teodoro took a swig from his bottle, then set it back
down on the ground. Lifting his gloves up, he forced his
hands back into them. 'Let's go then.'

The look he had was a look that Brendan hoped he could
help maintain: that innocent fearlessness of youth. Teodoro
was at the stage of his adolescence where he could easily go
down the wrong path. Brendan felt, in a sense, that giving
him some guidance was kind of like going back in time and

giving himself some guidance—perhaps like the guidance his father gave him before he vanished.

AFTER TWENTY MINUTES, Teodoro was exhausted. The sweat was pouring off him. Brendan had worn him out, but the young lad was warming to Brendan. His defensive wall had come crumbling down. The attitude that he'd displayed previously was simply a that of a misguided young boy, desperately searching for the male attention that Dimitru wasn't giving him.

'You hit hard,' Brendan said as he pulled his pad off. 'How long have you been training?'

'As long as I can remember,' Teodoro said. He pulled his gloves off, throwing them down on the mats. He dropped himself onto the ground and grabbed his bottle of water. 'I used to watch my father beat my mother. I always told my mum when I was older, I'd return the favour to him.'

Brendan's eyebrows lifted. 'You've been training to beat up your father?'

Teodoro took another swig of the water. He looked at Brendan with a childish grin on his face, blowing out his cheeks with his lips closed as if water was about to burst out of his mouth. He nodded his head. He swallowed the water and set the bottle down. 'That's bad, isn't it?'

Brendan didn't answer either way. He tapped Teodoro on the cheek. 'It is what is it, but I think you're a very gifted young fighter and should focus on getting better, rather than getting even.'

'I don't think I'd ever hit him anyway. My mum was distraught the last time I said I was going to.' He smirked. 'She said he's too dangerous. She literally begged me to put the thought out of my head.'

'Maybe she's right?'

He didn't reply. 'Will you be here tomorrow?'

'I'll be here tomorrow, yes,' Brendan said.

'I've gotta go get ready for school.' Teodoro threw a playful punch at Brendan. Brendan ducked it. 'See you tomorrow, Brendan.' He pushed his way through the turnstile and lifted his gym bag out of the first locker that ran along the wall towards the door.

Brendan grabbed his gloves and went towards the dummy to finish his workout. He was hitting it with a high roundhouse kick when he heard Teodoro shout his name. He turned and looked towards the door. The lad was watching him.

'Thanks, Brendan.' He smiled, then left.

Brendan waved to him, then turned and caught the dummy with a thunderous right hook. He worked out for another half an hour. He was always of the mind that a half-hour blast in the gym was ten times better than a low-intensity workout that took half the morning to complete.

After he was finished, he decided to take a long route run back to the hotel and cool down after his session. Belfast was just beginning to wake up for the day, and he was grateful he wasn't one of the early-morning rush hour commuters making their way to work.

As he entered the hotel, the staff were also a tad livelier-looking than when he'd left. He quickly said good morning

to the receptionist and the manager, who looked to be setting the tills up for the morning shift.

The same cleaner whom he'd frightened half to death
was now cleaning the first floor close to their room. But she
was ready for him this time.

'You're keen, being up at this time of the day.'

Brendan laughed. 'Best way to start the day.' He swiped
his room card across the locking console. The red light
changed to green and the lock clicked. He opened the door
and stepped in. Hearing the shower run, he decided to surprise Lorna by joining her.

He could hear her humming a melody to herself, clearly
in a good mood. He pulled off his clothes and slowly opened
the door to the bathroom. He could just about see the shower at the other end of the room. He swam through the steam,
seeing the small of her back. He slowly opened the door and
stepped in, gently touching her shoulders with his hands.
She flinched. Her head shot around. Her initial shock dissolved into the air with the steam when she saw it was him.

'How was your workout?' She turned and moved in closer to him. He just smiled. She pressed her firm breasts against
his chest as she slowly moved in to kiss him. He ran his finger
through her soaking wet hair. She softly stroked his face as
the kiss grew more intimate. He pushed her against the tiled
wall and lifted her. She wrapped her legs around him and
continued as the hot water washed over them as if washing
the rest of the world away, leaving nothing but them.

# Chapter Twenty-Two

AFTER BREAKFAST, THEY checked out of the hotel and thanked the staff for their hospitality. Brendan smiled again as the cleaner was vacuuming the black and gold carpet.

'You're everywhere I turn,' the cleaner joked.

'I'm not stalking you; don't worry.' Brendan stepped past her and out into the cool air. The rain had stopped, and the blue sky was swimming across their line of sight, pushing the grey clouds west. He took Lorna by the hand and they made their way to the underground carpark.

'You want to drive, or will I?' Lorna said.

'I fancy a drive.' He took the keys off her and opened the car. He tossed his bag onto the back seat then got behind the wheel. He started the engine. The fuel gauge jumped to the opposite side, just one mark away from being a full tank.

Lorna got in beside him and set the heating to twenty degrees. She rubbed her hands, as if hoping the motion would cause the air to heat up quicker. Brendan quickly put the car in reverse and manoeuvred out of the bay. As they emerged onto level ground, he guided the vehicle onto Great Victoria Street and followed the one-way system towards the motorway.

Brendan felt an uneasy sensation in his gut. He was re-turning to a place where he'd been impacted heavily, not only during his teenage years, but also recently, when he and Lorna had taken Brendan's father as he bled to death after being sniped out by Short.

'Are you okay?' Lorna broke the silence as the car merged onto the M1, leaving the city.

'Yeah,' he said bluntly. 'You're right. I can't avoid going back.' He felt her placing her hand on top of his, which was resting on the gearstick. 'We can face anything together,' he said, quickly glancing at her through his side eye while keeping his focus on the increasingly dense traffic.

'You're right.' She squeezed his hand. 'You know we should write a story about this one day.' She giggled.

'Yeah, the real-life Bonnie and Clyde.'

'The good Bonnie and Clyde,' Lorna said. 'Just one thing you need to be careful of, Brendan.' Her tone grew serious 'When you're working closely with these guys, these scumbags, they may at times become friendly towards you. You might even start to like them as people. Just remember who they really are.'

'I'm not going to let any of them drag me into their world.'

'It's happened to agents before,' Lorna said. 'Good, actually brilliant, agents with bright futures within the intelligence world, falling victim to getting in too deep. They ended up turning on us and going with their new *friends*. But it's a sure way to die or end up in jail.'

'Every night when I close my eyes, I see my father taking his last few breaths, dying in my arms. The last few words he spoke to me will live with me forever. I can either let them haunt me, or I can become the real son of The Ghost and haunt every crooked bastard I can get my hands on.'

'What about the rest of your family?'

'Fuck them,' Brendan spat. 'After he left, they left my mum and me to sort ourselves out. The only people that was there for us were my grandad and my aunt Mary.' He paused for a second. 'Fuck the rest of them. They can all burn in hell.'

'Do you still think of your mum?'

'Every day.'

'That's why you don't drink.'

He nodded his head. 'She was a beautiful lady. All she ever wanted was us to be a family. Us three. Until that fucking government tore us apart.'

Lorna cleared her throat and turned to look out through the passenger door window. 'I'm sorry, Brendan.'

He looked at her. 'What are you sorry for? You didn't do it.'

'Yes, but I worked for them.'

'You're not them, Lorna. If I'd had your upbringing, in England as an English person, I could have joined them.' He looked at her briefly. 'You're the best thing to come into my life for a long time. Don't ever forget that.'

She reached over and gave him a kiss on the cheek. 'Don't you ever forget that the feeling is mutual.' She dropped herself back down onto her seat. 'Now, are we going to make a home out of this place we're headed to, or what?'

Brendan laughed. 'You've really got your sights on finding us a place to live, haven't you?'

'Well, we need somewhere to stop for a while. We can't keep running around, living out of hotel rooms. Unless you want your father's money to quickly dissolve.'

'You're just a little wannabe home-maker,' he teased. 'But you're right. I just think we'll be better off in another country. This house is lovely. It's a private location, but I don't know if I'd be able to sleep at night without wondering if someone will come through the door.'

'We'll figure it out.' She pulled out her phone and checked for any messages. There was a text and a missed call from Diana.

*I don't know how much longer I can handle this good-for-nothing piece of shit. He's out of control. I feel like just sticking one of the kitchen knives right through his heart.*

'Oh, no!' Lorna dropped her head into her left hand as she continued to read her phone from her other hand.

'What's he done now?'

'She's threatening to take matters into her own hands.'

'What do you mean?'

Lorna scrolled back up the text. 'She's considering taking a kitchen knife and... well, you can imagine.'

'Tell her to give us a few days.'

'You think that's all we need? To take down their family, including the boss?'

Brendan nodded his head as he negotiated the traffic, weaving around the slower vehicles. 'The boss will be here in a couple of days. Dimitru said he's coming to the UK to meet with the leader of the largest criminal network in the UK. They're a bunch of nasty bastards, and I want to make it look like a set-up. We assassinate the boss man and create an internal feud. Let them all kill each other while I befriend Dimitru, get him to disclose the location of the boss's greatest financial resources, then rip them all to shreds from the inside out.'

'What about Diana, and Teodoro?'

'I don't think they'll really miss him that much.' Brendan spoke humorously, knowing both the son and partner of Dimitru would probably pull the trigger if they had the chance.

'Wait a second.' Lorna's voice livened up. 'I think this guy is the paranoid boss man.'

'What do you mean?'

'He lives in fear that one of his own men will eventually take him out and take over the organisation. This is not like the old Sicilian mafia, where loyalty and blood ruled all. These are just a bunch of animals who'd not give a second thought to wiping someone out for a bit of cash.'

'Dimitru is exactly that kind of man.'

# Chapter Twenty-Three

AS THEY ARRIVED IN Donegall, there was an eerie silence. Brendan had been quiet for the last thirty or so minutes. Lorna had kept herself entertained by taking in the beautiful landscape that passed by. The house was a beautiful modern construction, set on the coast of Ireland, with nothing but the Atlantic Ocean for as far as the eye could see.

As they approached the gate, Brendan jumped out and punched in the passcode to release the security lock, setting the gate in motion, sliding across electronically. The rusted runners on which the gate travelled creaked as more and more of the grounds came into view. He put the car in gear and proceeded up the driveway and around the circular pond that acted as a mini roundabout to what little traffic the ground ever saw. The car idled for a moment as Brendan looked at the black wooden door that led into the place that had once given him nightmares. His teen years flashed across his eyes. His facial muscles tightened; his eyebrows joined in the middle. He clenched his fists and his jaws.

'Hey.' Lorna gently placed her hand on top of his thigh. He flinched. 'It's okay.' She stroked his face gently. 'Come on, we'll face this together.' She lowered her head, while maintaining eye contact with him. 'Remember? Together.'

He kissed her hand as it caressed his cheek. 'Come on.' He shut the engine off. As he got out, he closed his eyes and inhaled the salty sea air. He could imagine being thirteen again and being beaten and battered, going through what that could be described as both physical and mental torture. He approached the door and opened it. He entered. Lorna followed. They'd left the house open with the keys on the mantelpiece. The house was open for the world to enter, but that's how it always was. The secret Cleary household was simply a place to sleep. It was not a home, although it had all the potential to be.

Brendan stood and looked at the photo of him and his father on his seventh birthday. In the photo, Brendan was wearing a pair of black trousers and shoes, topped off with a blinding white shirt. He looked happy in that photo. It was before he'd been introduced to the very house in which they stood.

Brendan looked at Lorna; she had a look of fear on her face—perhaps not fear in the sense that he would do something to her, but fear about how upset he was going to become about coming back again. But she was wrong. He reached in close to her, kissing her on the cheek. 'I'm glad you're here with me.' He gave her a hug. She clung to him. He looked at the ceiling, smiling, as if he were at peace with what had happened at the house. 'How about we go and have a workout, then I'll race you in the pool afterwards.'

'I don't want to keep embarrassing you, Brendan. But if you insist, then that's fine.'

'We'll see.'

'And screw the pool. We're on the west coast of Ireland. Let's go for a dip in the ocean.'

They took their bags up to the bedroom. All the belongings they'd left behind remained there. They changed into their casual clothes and made their way towards the ground-floor gym.

Later that afternoon, they'd returned from the beach feeling fresh and rejuvenated, perhaps lighter than either of them had felt since walking into the other's life. Brendan prepared lunch – a smoked salmon salad. Lorna sat by the open fire, conserving as much heat as possible while resting her exhausted limbs on the fur rug the ran along the mantle.

As Brendan prepared the meal, she gave him a bullet point update of the local news on the BBC. The Romanians were beginning to cause more worry in the city of Belfast. Their growing confidence, especially Dimitru's, was going to get a lot of people into trouble, not least himself.

'Any more trouble on the Shankill Road?'

'It's funny you should say that.'

'Why?' Brendan's ears perked up. He wasn't in the mood to hear bad news, but he knew more would come before they left Belfast.

'Your little mate, the one that Dimitru and co beat to a pulp... well, his family and friends have reason to believe your family's to blame.'

'Why?' Brendan laughed. 'Actually, you know what, screw it. After what happened before, can you really be surprised they're trying to pin it on someone with the Cleary name?'

'Yes, but that means your family could be open to attack.'

'I'll pay Mary a visit, but she can handle herself anyway. I'm not bothered about any of the rest.' Brendan slid the fish onto the plates. 'If we can bring down the Romanian mafia's shop in the city, save a few lives, and stop this city from getting worse, then I'll be happy to say "cheerio" to it.' He grabbed the plates and brought them into the living area, handing them to Lorna as he got down on his knees on the rug beside her.

'Anyone in particular you want to help? Like a gifted young pugilist?'

Brendan smiled, gazing into the flames of the fire as he crossed his legs.

'Admit it, you want to help him more than anything else.'

'What's the problem with that?'

Lorna moved in a little closer to him. She leaned into him and rested her head on his shoulder, following his gaze into the flames. 'There's absolutely nothing wrong with it. It think it's lovely. It's sweet.' She paused for a moment. He didn't respond. 'Just be careful you don't get too attached to him. His father is someone we're about to destroy. His mother is an emotional wreck, and I'm guessing he is, too.'

Brendan lowered himself back-first onto the rug and looked at the white ceiling above. He was deep in thought, and still didn't respond to Lorna's words.

She turned to face him, hovering over the top of him. She smiled softly and lowered her lips onto his. They kissed slowly. She lowered her body, resting on top of his. He could feel her firm breasts press against his toned chest. They kissed continuously for a few minutes, until Brendan sat up. He looked into her glazed eyes, stroking her face.

'Let's go upstairs,' he said. 'It'll...'

Before he could say another word, she pressed her index finger onto his lip. 'Let's just stay here. It's nice.' She kissed him again, then guided him back down onto the rug. The level of passion between the two of them grew with an intensity that mirrored the flames of the now roaring fire.

# Chapter Twenty-Four

SHORTLY AFTER SEVEN that evening, Brendan woke on the rug. The fire had extinguished itself, but Lorna's naked body heat below the blanket had kept them from them suffering a chill. He went to move, but she groaned. She said something, but the words that came out of her mouth were incoherent—something about washing the dogs and cleaning out the kennels. He grinned, then laughed as she let out a loud, bellyaching laugh. She laughed for a few seconds, then settled herself down again and snuggled up into him.

He reached over and grabbed his phone, which was resting just about within arm's reach. He had a missed call and a text message. When he opened the massage, he was surprised it was from an old friend. Stefano Botticelli.

*Ciao, Brendan. I hope that you're well, my friend. I have some information that you may or may not like. Either way, I thought you'd like to know that some people your father had an issue with in England, when he went to Leicester in search of Indino, have re-surfaced after going into hiding from The Ghost. The cowardly bastards went into hiding for fear your father would come after them again. I just thought you should know, in case you wanted to even the score. Or at least finish the job your old man started. Take care, my friend. If you ever need anything, let me know. Stefano.*

Brendan closed the phone and left it on the ground. He lay himself back down and looked up at the ceiling again. 'Even the score' He spoke under his breath, not wanting to wake Lorna up. She mumbled something else under her breath that let him know she hadn't woken up yet. He set his alarm for nine, to wake them up for some dinner, then drifted back to sleep again.

Two hours later, at nine, they both woke, groggy, their eyes tiny slits trying to adjust to the light.

'What do you want for dinner?' Brendan said as he sat up and reached for his shirt which he'd left strewn across the floor along with the rest of their clothes.

'Whatever's easiest,' she said as she reached for her bra and panties. Brendan watched her as she stepped into the matching black delicates. She turned and looked at him. 'Or you can have me.' She crouched down and stroked his face. 'Actually, I feel like some vegetables. But you can have me for dessert.' She straightened herself up and made her way towards the kitchen.

Brendan grabbed his phone and re-read the text from Stefano, almost walking into the wall as he followed Lorna into the kitchen. He responded to Stefano, simply saying he hoped everything was okay and that he and his father were safe and trying to live their lives in relative peace in comparison to what had been their lives to date. He also suggested that they should meet sometime when he and Lorna had found themselves a slightly more permanent residence.

'We've got mince and spaghetti strings,' Lorna shouted, her head inside the cupboard next to the fridge. 'If we've got...' she paused for a second. 'Great, we've got Spaghetti

Bolognese for dinner tonight.' She pulled himself out of the cupboard. 'Hope you fancy something Italian.' She looked at Brendan, who was leaning against the work top, his eyes fixed on his phone. She cleared her throat. He looked up at her.

'It's funny you should mention something Italian. I've just received a text from Stefano Botticelli.'

'And?'

'He's said a few guys that were out to get my father have re-surfaced from hiding after he went to England looking for Paolo Indino.'

'Where are they?'

'Leicester.' Brendan laughed. 'Since when has Leicester been a hotbed for Italian criminals?' His tone sounded as if he didn't expect Lorna to respond.

'Since the Italian influx when the Italian boss of Leicester City Football Club brought the eyes of the world to Leicester.'

'Well, looks like we're going to Leicester then.' Brendan dropped his phone into his pocket and jumped up, sitting down on the work top beside the sink. 'Spaghetti Bolognese is a great shout for dinner.'

Brendan offered to help with dinner, but she refused, telling him to go and relax. He didn't argue and took himself off into the garden. As he stepped outside, he shivered, zipping his coat right up to the neck. Being on the coast was always relaxing, but the winning view came with it a price: the wind chill.

Brendan walked towards the summer house, which was like a second house that sat on the other end of the back garden. This, however, was more fit to be a one-man leisure centre. It had its own pool, gym, dojo, and study room, including a bedroom. As a teenager, Brendan had often lived there without ever needing to use the main house.

As he opened the single glass-pane door, he caught the smell of sweat and leather that came from the gym; this was the dominating scent of the entire space. He shut the door behind him; the sound sent echoes throughout. He stepped into the living area: a small kitchen and living room, including a TV directly facing a black leather sofa. The entire room was kitted out and decorated with a black and white theme. But Brendan was more interested in the gym. He continued on past the room and through a set of white wooden doors. Now he stood in the gym area, a vast expanse of space that could have served as a decent sized boxing club. He strolled around, his hands in his pockets, glancing absentmindedly at all the kit. The free weights area had been left with the same circuit that he'd last done. He laughed at the thought of himself slaving away, sweating bullets with a face as red as a tomato, his father standing over him telling him to push himself. He looked towards the dojo, or, as the late Damien Cleary called it, the unarmed combat room. He moved closer to it, feeling as if he were zapped back in time. He could see himself getting tossed around the room by his father. He felt a surge of anger. His fists and jaws clenched as he just stood and looked at the matted area. Spots of sweat and saliva could still be seen below the layers of dust.

Stepping up to the freestanding human-shaped dummy, he tapped the head. Smiling, he took a step back and threw his left shin into it, sending it backwards but not toppling it.

The base was filled with water, and an attempt to defeat gravity would almost always result in failure. This hadn't stopped him and his father competing to prove physics wrong. They never failed—Damien Cleary removed the word failure from the Cleary dictionary—they simply learned that physics was right. But what their attempts did do was develop their kicking power, and Brendan's kicking power was second to none. Had he been given a shot at a normal life, his physical capabilities would have become well-known in the sporting arena. But then, his father didn't want his existence to be wasted by having a highly-decorated trophy cabinet with Olympic gold. He wanted Brendan to suffer hard times, so that one day, he'd be able to give a helping hand to others who were also suffering hard or perhaps harder times at the hands of others.

He began to tidy the area, wanting to clean the place up and at least treat it with respect. After he'd re-stacked the weights and moved the dummy closer into the wall, he tossed the sparring gloves and contact pads into their storage compartment. He went back to the kitchen for the hoover. He quickly vacuumed the area, then searched for a mop and bucket. He dropped a cap full of disinfectant into the bucket and filled it with warm water from the kitchen sink. He put the surround sound on and went to work to bring his old home back to some kind of order.

'You expecting somebody?' Lorna shouted from the door that separated the lounge and the gym.

He laughed as he continued to mop around the weights area. 'I'm just trying to take a bit of pride in what was once home for me.'

'Dinner's ready,' she said as she approached him. 'I love this place.' She sat on the free weight bench, mockingly flexing her biceps in a pose in front of the floor-to-ceiling mirror that ran all the way along the wall. 'Your father must have invested millions into this place.' She stood up and ran towards the dummy. She jumped and spun in mid-air, clocking the chin of the rubber figure in a spinning hook kick. 'Come, on let's have some dinner.'

'I'm just finishing off, then I'll be in.'

Brendan spent the next five minutes in the gym. Then, having worked up an appetite, he switched off the music and left the mop and bucket in the kitchen. As he stepped outside, he felt the sea spray being carried inland from the beach. He shut his eyes and smiled, embracing the feeling of freshness. He looked in the direction of the house. Lorna was waving for him to get a move on. She was holding a plate up to her nose enticingly.

He entered the kitchen, welcomed by the smell of the freshly-cooked meal.

As they sat at the table, Lorna put the radio on to create some background noise. Brendan watched as she served the food. Steam shot up from the spaghetti as she pulled a plateful out of the pot with two wooden spoons. She then lifted the pan and scraped the Bolognese sauce on top. 'Buon appetito,' she said in a mock Italian accent, then sat down and served herself. Brendan reached for the jug and poured them both a glass of water. He looked at her as he took a sip. She looked happy. Happier than he'd ever seen her.

'You're even more beautiful when you're happy and content.'

She smiled at him, showing her bright white teeth.

# Chapter Twenty-Five

BRENDAN'S ALARM WENT off much earlier than usual. Lorna was less than impressed when, at three twenty-five in the morning—or, as far as she was concerned, the middle of the night—Brendan sat up and jumped out of bed as if the house were being raided. He quickly shut the alarm off and told Lorna to go back to sleep. She didn't need persuasion. She blew him a kiss and groaned with her eyes closed as she rolled over to the other side and burrowed under the duvet, sheltering away from the cool air.

Brendan quickly jumped into the shower to heat himself up then dressed in his gym gear. It was a two-hour drive to Belfast from Donegal, but the traffic would be quiet so it would be a relatively painless journey. After filling his travel mug with strong coffee, he grabbed the keys from the bedside cabinet and told Lorna he'd back in a few hours. She was only semi-conscious, so he sent her a text that she could read when she woke up.

He jumped into the car and blasted the heating. Pulling his hood up, he clasped his cup in between his hands while waiting for the revs to drop. Then he was off. The country roads of Ireland were treacherous at times, so he decided to take the journey through more frequently used and treated roads, taking himself through Derry City and down the

Glenshane Pass and on down through County Antrim, reaching Belfast safely and without any issue.

He parked the car on Adelaide Street, which was where he and Lorna had first met Diana. One of the hookers on the street asked him if he wanted some fun. He laughed and simply said no thanks. He snatched his phone from the car's central console unit and his gym bag.

Reaching the gym shortly after five-thirty, he found Teodoro was already pounding on the bag.

'Morning,' Brendan said as he passed through the turn-stile. Reaching into his gym bag, he grabbed his wraps and began wrapping his fists, starting with the left. He thought about the last time he'd had his hand bandaged up in the Crumlin Road's Mater Hospital. It was for giving one of the lads from the Shankill Road an emergency trip to the dentist. Brendan had broken the lad's jaw, shattered a couple of teeth, and bust the lower lip with what witnesses had called the sharpest right/left cross/hook they'd ever seen. The lad learned Brendan was not someone to be aggressive towards, and Brendan had learned not to lose his temper, as even though the other guy ended up worse off, he'd still needed to get butterfly stiches in his left knuckles.

'You ready for a bit of sparring? You haven't tired yourself out yet, have you?' Brendan shouted over to Teodoro, who'd just gone the final fast ten seconds of a round on the dummy and was now red in the face and arms.

'I've enough left in the tank for an old man like you,' he spat as he held his two-litre bottle of water.

Brendan smiled. 'If you call mid-twenties old, then...' He forced his left hand into his glove and lifted the right. 'Then get ready to be taught a lesson by this old man.' He dressed his right fist with the glove, then punched his two fists together, approaching the mat area.

As he got closer to Teodoro, he noticed the lad had a nasty laceration above his left eye, almost making an X symbol crossing through his dark, thin eyebrow. 'What happened there?'

'It's nothing, just a scratch.' Teodoro forced a smile, but the awkward expression was an indicator of how he was truly feeling on the inside. He clearly felt uncomfortable and didn't want to talk about it. Brendan didn't press him.

'You'll have to develop your defensive skills,' Brendan joked, playfully punching Teodoro. 'Your offensive is great, so at least now we've discovered the chink in your armour. But we can work on that.'

'Let's iron out your chinks, too then, old man. Teodoro threw a snappy jab, catching Brendan softly on the cheek, not enough to hurt but enough to make Brendan want to get to work and school the kid.

Brendan backed away into the centre of the mats, beckoning Teodoro to come at him. They both met in the middle, their gloves up guarding their heads, their elbows in tight to their sides. Brendan was a south paw, which initially made it awkward for Teodoro. The young lad was like many right-handed boxers; they hated having to go against a lefty. South paws, however, were more used to fighting against the greater majority of right orthodox fighters, so for them it was an immediate advantage. Brendan wasn't about to go easy on Teodoro, nor was he about to embarrass him. There was a fine line between being encouraging and being overpowering and dominating, and this to Brendan would perhaps be his greatest test.

The round alarm sounded for their first three minutes and Teodoro, as Brendan had anticipated, came at him fast. Quick to prove his skill, and even quicker to get the upper hand, Teodoro positioned himself in his boxer's stance, on his toes and bouncing around, trying not to become flat-footed. He threw a lightening-fast jab, and immediately followed up with a cross. Brendan blocked both and circled to his right. As he manoeuvred, Brendan only slightly tapped Teodoro on the cheek. Teodoro was clearly a different style of boxer than Brendan—offensive. Brendan was more of a counter-puncher and would use his opponent's momentum against them. Teodoro came in again for another shot, but again, Brendan dodged the flurry of blows, and each time, he was able to catch Teodoro while he made his sidestep. Brendan was playing a mind game with him. He knew that his constant sidesteps to the right would eventually be picked up by the trained boxer and he would be punished for it. He'd hoped Teodoro was paying attention to Brendan's habits and trying to outthink him as well as outbox him. That was undoubtedly what would make all the difference for him in the long run. And as Brendan went to sidestep, he was in fact about to step into a hook from Teodoro. Teodoro caught Brendan but had the decency to pull the punch and not lay the full force of leather into the side of Brendan's head. Brendan stepped back and covered up as Teodoro, growing in confidence, got in with a flurry of punches, first to the midsection and then moving to the upper body. The round bell sounded, and they broke away, both panting.

Teodoro looked at Brendan. 'You've got good defence. Were you a competitor?'

Brendan shook his head as he reached for his water. 'I only ever trained with my father. But he was quite good.'

That name, father, must have touched a nerve with Teodoro, as his smile dropped into an angry frown. 'You're lucky to have had a good relationship with him. Mine is a piece of shit.'

Brendan sat down on the rug and crossed his legs. 'There is a lot about my father that you don't know. Maybe I'll tell you one day.' He took a gulp from the bottle. 'Was it him that gave you that?' Brendan pointed at the cut on Teodoro's face.

He nodded his head. 'He was beating my mum. I heard her screaming from their room and when I burst in, I saw something that I shouldn't have seen.' He gritted his teeth. 'If I had a weapon, I would have killed him, I swear.'

'What was he doing?'

'They were in the bedroom,' Teodoro snapped. 'Use your imagination.'

Brendan shook his head. 'You guys should get out of there.'

'Where do we go?'

'I think I can help you and your mum. We met her on the streets a few days ago. We want to help. I know this is probably hard for you to believe because I'm simply a stranger, but I came home to Belfast to bury my past. I was very much like you when I was your age, but when my father disappeared, I had to find my own way. Learn how to do things myself. I want to give you the help that I didn't have, if you want it. You seem like a bright kid, and could have a good future, but if you and your mum stay with him, you're slashing your chances of a good life.'

Teodoro laughed off the offer. 'There's nothing you can do. He's too powerful. He's got a lot of nasty friends.' Teodoro looked at Brendan, smiling softly. 'But I appreciate the offer.'

'Would you miss Belfast?'

He laughed sarcastically. 'I have nothing here. My mother and I are stuck here. And all we have is each other.'

'Right, okay. Well, you go home and clear your stuff. Gather up everything you need. I'll speak to your mother. The moment Dimitru leaves the house today, I'm coming for you both.' Teodoro looked uncertain. Frightened. 'Don't worry. Where we're going, he will not find you. Nobody knows of this location. Trust me.'

Teodoro's expression lifted. 'Okay, if you're sure you don't mind...'

'Just you go and get ready. You got a number I can get you on?'

They exchanged numbers then left. Teodoro left the gym first. Brendan stayed behind five minutes to call Lorna.

'Brendan, I've received a call from Diana this morning...'

'I know about what happened. Teodoro told me all about it. I've sent him home to get his stuff. I'm taking them with me. They can stay with us at the house until we sort this bastard out.'

'He fucking raped her, Brendan.'

Brendan clenched his jaws. 'And Teodoro walked in on it. I'm surprised he hasn't stuck a knife in him yet,' Brendan said as he lifted his bag and dropped his drink into it. 'I'm going to hang around Belfast until they're ready to leave, then I'll go and get them.'

'You be careful.'

'I'll see you in a few hours.'

She didn't respond.

'Are you okay?'

'I'll be fine when someone cuts the bastard's balls off.'

Brendan laughed. 'You can do it if you want to.'

'Don't tempt me.'

# Chapter Twenty-Six

WITH A FEW HOURS TO spend, Brendan took a tour of the Antrim Road, towards O'Neill's. The café had just switched it's cookers on to get the food started for the first customers of the day.

Brendan looked at his watch. The time was just after seven-thirty. The shop was not due to open until eight, but he wasn't only impatient and hungry, he was also sure he'd need to dine in the place before any of the locals realised who he was. As much as Brendan loved his home town, Belfast did not feel the same.

He knocked the glass pane of the front door, directly above the sign that said "closed". He laughed as the lady in the shop appeared from the kitchen behind the counter. She didn't look at all impressed until she came closer to the door. Brendan pulled his hood down and smiled at her. Her eyes widened. Her jaw dropped, then she cupped her hand over the mouth, as if she'd seen a ghost.

She unlocked the door. 'Jesus Christ, Brendan. Where the hell have you been, love?' Her blue eyes glazed over, darting from his left eye to the right. He just looked at her, smiling mischievously, like a naughty teenager. 'Well, are you not going to give your Aunty Mary a hug?' She pulled him in close, wrapping both arms around him.

'How are you doing, Mary?'

She pulled him inside and shut the door again. She flicked the lock over and peered through the window, inspecting both up and down the street. 'Where the hell have you been? We thought you were dead.'

'Well, I guess I am kind of dead. I'm an acting ghost. A bit like daddy was.'

'What a mess you've been dragged into, love. It's not safe for you around here.'

'I'm only here for a few days. Then we're disappearing.'

'Who's we?'

'Agent Lorna Woodward.'

'That lady who was framed alongside you?' She laughed. 'God, it's like a real love story,' she teased. 'Us against the world.' She walked past him towards the kitchen. 'You're here for a fry? You hungry, love?'

'I'm starving, but I'm here to see you, too. Not just because you make the best fries in Belfast.'

She laughed. 'You always were a wee charmer, just like my little brother, God rest him.'

'It's hard to believe he was alive all those years.'

'Our Damien was a very secretive man.' She walked around to the serving side of the counter and switched on the coffee machine. 'Now you know why.'

Brendan followed her closer to the counter. 'How's the rest of the family?'

'We're worried about you, love.' She set a black ceramic cup under the coffee dispenser. She looked up at him. 'You sure you're okay?'

'I'm fine; don't worry about me.'

'Do you need any money?'

He smiled. 'I'm okay, thanks, Mary. But I'd like to send you guys some money if you need it. Daddy left me quite a bit.' He jumped up and sat on the edge of the counter. 'It appears he was off working for some very influential people around the world and had racked up a nice little savings for himself. Too bad he didn't get a chance to spend it.'

He looked down at the ground absentmindedly. He felt Mary stroke his arm. 'At least he didn't die in one of those countries around a bunch of strangers...'

'No,' Brendan said sharply. 'He died in my arms.'

She gripped his arm a little tighter. 'You know when we saw you on the news running around Stormont, it was like something out of a movie.' She smirked as she filled the machine with some fresh-ground Lavazza. 'You never were just a normal young boy. Ever since your daddy left, you were always the one the family thought about the most. You had it hard, love. Especially what happened with your mummy.'

Brendan's muscles tightened.

'Have you been down to see her recently?' Mary said.

He shook his head. 'I don't want anyone to spot me. Like I said, I'm only going to be in Belfast a few days, then I'll be gone and maybe won't be back again.'

She made two espressos. 'The fryers are still heating up. Let's go into the office for a minute. Don't want some nosy bastard seeing you in here.' She led the way past the kitchen and into the manager's office.

Brendan stepped into the office to find a desk with paper strewn everywhere.

Mary stacked the paper in a neater pile, clearing enough room to set the cups down. She sat down on the desk chair, and Brendan was gifted with the sofa that ran along the office window. Brown curtains were drawn. Apart from the messy desk, the rest of the room was in a decent state. The wall to Brendan's left had a bookshelf, a mixture of both fiction and non-fiction. He stood up and walked towards it.

'You're teaching yourself to speak Irish?' He pulled a book titled *Irish – for Beginners*.

'You're not the only smartass in the family,' she said in Gaelic.

He smiled at her as she sipped from her espresso. He then spotted the cluster of white photo frames hanging on the wall behind her. He took a sip from his espresso and stepped around the desk, taking a closer look at them. Mary swivelled around in her chair and stood up. She gestured towards one that sat high up and towards the outside of the group. It was one of Brendan and his father with Mary and two young lads who looked around Brendan's age.

'You were all so innocent back then. My little boys.'

Brendan sat on the edge of the desk, folding his arms. 'How are Sean and Tony?'

'They're alright. Nothing ever changes with that pair,' Mary said as she sat beside him on the edge of the desk.

'What did they say when they saw me all over the news?'

She giggled. 'I think they thought the same thing we all did: it had to be Brendan.' They both burst out laughing. 'But they were more worried about what would happen when Johnty Burrows died in the Royal. That scared a lot of us, Brendan. We don't want the loyalists targeting any of the Cleary family.'

'They'll not. I'll be putting them bastards out of business very soon.'

'It's not even the paramilitaries you have to worry about these days. The fucking Romanians are becoming the biggest problem around here.'

'Yeah, I know. They'll be going out of business very soon, too.'

'What do you mean?'

He just reached over closer and gave her a kiss on the cheek. 'Let's just have some breakfast; my stomach's rumbling here.'

'Don't you be starting anything and getting yourself killed, love. If you've got a chance to walk away from this place and start a new life, don't blow it. Just get the hell out of here and forget all about them scumbags. They'll eventually get theirs; don't worry about that.'

He looked at her. 'I wish I could just walk away, Mary. But I can't.'

'What do you mean you can't?'

'Daddy's last words, as he died in my arms, were to put everything he taught me to good use. And that's what I intend to do.'

'Brendan, you can't take on these groups. Jesus Christ, son.' Mary's voice lowered as if she were afraid of someone hearing. 'Get the hell outta here. This is not for you to take on.'

He broke her gaze and looked down at the ground. 'I can't do that, Aunty Mary. I appreciate your concern, but let's not argue while I'm here.' He looked up at her and grinned. 'Remember the Christmas I came to stay at your house?'

She burst into a fit of laughter. 'Do I remember? Jesus, you and Sean disappeared on your bikes and didn't come back for hours.'

Brendan laughed. 'Give young lads that type of freedom and you'll live to regret it.'

'You both scared the life out of us that day. God, we didn't know what had happened to you.'

Brendan smiled. His grin slowly dropped; his laughter faded away. He looked at her. 'I'll always have those memories. No matter where I end up. I'll cherish them.'

She kissed him on the cheek. 'Come on and we'll get you fed.' She stood up and made her way towards the door. He was about to follow her, but she turned to him. Actually, it's better if you stay in here, love. People don't need to know you're here. I'll bring your breakfast in. I'll be about ten minutes.'

Brendan turned, continuing to study the photos on the wall. Looking at them almost took him back in time, before he'd ever known anything about who his father was, or who he was about to become. Momentarily, he wondered what his life would have been like had none of that ever happened. Would he ever have been able to live a normal life? He caught a glimpse of a photo of him and his cousin Sean with their bikes. He smiled.

'Fuck it. It is what it is. I am what I am.' He said, as if talking to his cousin in the photo with him.

He sat back down again. Feeling his phone vibrate in his pocket, he pulled it out. It was Teodoro.

*Hi Brendan. It's Teodoro. Dimitru will be leaving our house at nine-thirty. He goes to the gym at ten, so we'll have a couple of hours where he'll not be here.*

Brendan replied. *Good. I'll come for you both just after ten. Be ready to go. See you soon.*

Just as Brendan sent the text, his phone rang. It was Dimitru.

'Dimitru, I didn't think you were an early riser.'

Dimitru laughed. 'You win the morning, you win the day, my friend.'

'True. What can I do for you?'

'I'm off to the gym this morning, then I'll be doing a bit of business this evening if you fancy tagging along.'

'What kind of business?'

'I want to show you our business in full. You've earned it.'

'What time this evening? I can't do the gym today; I'm in Newry with Lorna. But I can tag along with you this evening.'

'Great. I'll meet you up at the city hall at seven-thirty. Bring your pretty English lady friend, too, if you want to.'

'See you then.'

Just as Brendan ended the call, Mary walked in. 'A full fry, love?'

'Double of everything, please.' He said as he called Lorna. She answered almost instantly. 'Lorna, I've received a call from Dimitru. He's showing me more of their operations this evening.'

'That's generous of him,' Lorna said mockingly. 'What time can I expect you here?'

'I'm at my Aunt Mary's for a fry while I wait for Dimitru to leave the house. I've told Teodoro to make sure he and Diana are ready to leave as soon as I arrive. So, we'll see you about midday or shortly after.'

'Your Aunt Mary is your father's sister?'

He hummed to agree.

'What was her reaction to seeing your ugly mug?'

He grinned. 'Like she'd seen a ghost. But we've had a nice chat, talking about the old days.'

'That's good. I'm going to take a walk around this bloody homely estate you call a house. It's got a bit of character to it. Just needs a woman's touch to make it feel a bit more homey.'

'I recommend you try the gym.'

'You saying I'm fat, Brendan Cleary?'

He laughed, as Mary wheeled the breakfast in on a trolley. 'I've gotta go. I've got a date with the best food in Belfast.'

'Let me know when you get them two and are on your way back.'

He blew her a kiss and hung up.

'Was that the British agent?' Mary didn't sound as accepting of Lorna as Brendan would have liked.

'Ex-British agent.'

'You sure you can trust her?'

He looked at her as she set the plates down on the desk. 'I trust her with my life.'

Mary poured them both a cup of tea and sat down. 'Well, if you can trust her, then I'm happy.' She handed him a knife and fork, then lifted the ketchup. 'What's her story?'

'Briefly,' Brendan said, 'her father was killed in an IRA bomb in London. She grew up wanting to avenge his death...'

'Can't blame her,' Mary said, dousing her food in red sauce. She handed the bottle to Brendan, but he refused and went for the brown.

'Then, the government she'd devoted her whole life to serves her up alongside me.'

Mary looked at him. 'Just be careful, love.'

He smiled at her, his mouth full of soda bread.

'Now eat your breakfast. There's more out there if you need it.'

# Chapter Twenty-Seven

BRENDAN SAVOURED HIS breakfast, regarding it as the best tasting meal he'd eaten in a long time. He wasn't sure whether it was simply psychological appreciation for something that he'd perhaps never taste again, or whether it actually was, as he'd said, the best-tasting fry in Belfast. Either way, he'd finished with an appreciation equal to that of a death row inmate enjoying his last meal.

'You sure you've been eating okay?' Mary joked. 'You pretty much inhaled that.' She lifted the plates and stacked them on the tray.

'I'm okay, Aunty Mary. Don't worry.' Brendan looked at his phone, the time was shortly after eight-thirty. 'I should get going. I don't want to bring trouble to the shop by risking people seeing me.' He stepped around the table, his arms out to embrace his loving aunt. 'I don't want to have to come back here again because the shit's hit the fan for you guys as well.'

She pulled him in and hugged him, almost squeezing the air out of him. 'Never forget we're here if you need us.' She cupped his face in her hands and looked into his eyes. 'We're a family, love. If you need us, we're here for you. Fuck what the consequences may be. We stick together.' She pulled him in for another embrace, planting two lipstick stamps on his cheek.

He pulled his hood up and exited the office, weaving in and out of the tables, not looking at any of the customers. Opening the door, he turned around and waved at her as she stood by the office door, a hopeful smile displayed across her face.

'See you later, Mary!' He smiled from under his hood. She waved but remained silent.

As he stepped out into the street, the blue sky advertised it was going to be a good day. He didn't, however, lower his cover until he was safely behind the car's window tints.

He got behind the wheel and started the engine. Cool FM was playing an early morning playlist of old ballads. He sat and looked across the road at the shop, absentmindedly cast back in time to the days when he and his cousin would take to the slush-covered streets of Christmas morning on their bikes. The music being played by the radio DJ was from that time period, and he managed to grin, flashing his bright white smile as those memories washed over him like a comforting blanket that told him no matter what happened in the future, those memories would never die. It hadn't been his intention, but visiting his aunt Mary had given him a kind of closure about his youth. Perhaps a simple change in perspective was what he'd experienced. Whatever it was, he was grateful for it.

Not wanting to push his luck and remain in the area for too long, he put the car into gear and pulled away, making his way south, back down the increasingly busy Antrim Road towards Carlisle Circus towards the city centre.

His phone rang, automatically cutting out the music and patched the call through to the car's sound system. 'Hello.'

'Brendan, It's Teodoro. We're almost ready to go. If you'd like to make your way here at around half nine or just after, then we'll be ready. He's leaving soon.'

'Great, text me the postcode and address.'

'See you soon.'

The call ended. The radio came back on and the music continued. He drove along North Queen Street and turned right into the cityside shopping complex. Pulling into the petrol station, he parked at pump number six. It was the only available spot, and an imposing warzone type Land Rover used by the local police service occupied pump five, directly in front of him.

'Fuck!' For a split second, he didn't know where to look, his eyes darting everywhere but in the direction of the officer who'd just gotten out. He reached into the back, grabbing a New York Yankees baseball cap that lay on the floor. He pulled it on and grabbed his phone. He stepped out into the cold air and shut the car door. He inserted the credit card into the pump's payment console and thumbed in the code. Just as the officer left the shop with his lunch, Brendan, almost as if in synch, turned his back to remove the filler cap and lifted the nozzle. The car was already almost full, but with a little bit of time to spare while he waited for Diana and Teodoro, he made sure the car had as much juice as possible. Anything could happen; he had to be prepared for that, and a full tank in the engine was always better than an *almost* full tank.

Watching the PSNI vehicle pull away, his muscles loosened, and his heart rate slowly dropped to normal. He got back into the car. Teodoro had sent him the address. It was on the far north side of the city. The estate was on the heavily loyalist Ballysillan Road that sat nestled in the mountainous hills of the city.

He thumbed the address in and took off. Arrival time was ten minutes.

# Chapter Twenty-Eight

THE CAR NEGOTIATED the almost vertical hill with ease. However, Brendan considered the problems that would certainly be there for the locals trying to move on or off such a steep gradient in snow or ice.

He pulled into the street, and, seeing Dimitru's vehicle gone, pulled up outside number Thirty-four. He let the car idle as he called Teodoro, but before the call went through, both Diana and Teodoro exited the house, hands full with suitcases.

Brendan released the boot and got out to assist. 'Is that everything or is there more in there?'

'That's us,' Diana said. 'We travel light.' She looked at Brendan, forcing a smile on her battered face.

He just shook his head. Now wasn't the time to bring it up. He grabbed her suitcase and lifted it into the boot. 'Jump in,' he said as he grabbed the second suitcase, placing it neatly in the boot alongside the other. He grabbed Teodoro's and tried to slide it in, but the cases were too big. 'We're going to have to put these in the back of the car. You can take the passenger seat.' Brendan spoke with authority, but without trying to sound bossy. He knew Teodoro had seen enough overpowering males in his life, and therefore recognised that it was not the tone to use to get off on the best foot.

'Where are we going?' Teodoro said, setting the suitcase on the floor behind the passenger seat.

'You'll love it, don't worry,' Brendan said. He slammed the boot closed and got back into the driver's seat. He looked at Diana in the rear-view mirror. 'You sure you haven't left anything behind? We're not likely to be coming back here again.'

Her eyes were glazed, red rings highlighting the outer perimeter. She was staring absentmindedly out of the window, not even paying attention to what was happening in the car.

'Diana,' Brendan said.

She jumped, her eyes shot around, meeting his gaze in the reflection.

'You okay? You sure you've got everything?'

She nodded, wiping a tear from her face.

'She'll be alright when that bastard is six feet under,' Teodoro shouted, fastening his belt.

Brendan put the car in gear and circled the miniature roundabout that directed traffic around the street. As he approached the junction, he indicated right, taking them further up the Ballysillan Road, towards Antrim Town.

'Where are you taking us?' Diana finally spoke as the car pulled onto the tree-lined country road. The Crumlin Road was long and windy, meandering through North Belfast through all the troubled hotspots and reaching the tiny village of Crumlin near the International Airport.

'We're going to Donegal,' Brendan said.

The car quickly picked up speed, climbing the mountain with ease. He put the window down to let some fresh air in.

'It's a safe place, don't worry.' He looked at Diana in the mirror. 'You're safe now.'

'Where's Lorna?' she said.

'She's there.' Brendan smiled. 'She couldn't be arsed coming all the way to Belfast for a gym session this morning, so I'm here by myself.'

Diana forced a smile.

Teodoro hooked his playlist of music up to the car's sound system. This made the lad happy, cheering Diana up a little.

As he negotiated the country roads, Brendan regarded Diana in the rear view mirror. She was looking across the car, towards her son. Young Teodoro had managed to close the door on whatever else was going on in his head, bobbing and humming in synch with the beats coming from the ballad.

'Thank you, Brendan,' Diana said. She reached forward, placing her trembling hand on his left shoulder. Still looking at him in the mirror's reflection, her eyes looked heavy, like dark clouds, ready to burst with rain water. 'Whatever happens, I'm grateful for you and Lorna.' She squeezed his shoulder, then sat back in her chair. 'You're both good people.'

'We haven't done anything yet,' Brendan said. 'But one thing I can promise you both...' he paused and looked at Teodoro, then turned back to the road, briefly shooting his gaze into the rear view. 'Neither of you will have to go near him again, if you don't want to.'

'We don't want to,' Teodoro said. 'If I see him again, I'll fucking kill him.'

'You don't want someone's blood on your hands,' Brendan said, briefly looking down at the car's logo on the centre of the steering wheel. 'It's not something you want on your conscience.'

'So, why did you come back to Belfast?' Diana said.

'Yes,' Teodoro said, sounding impressed. 'We saw you on the news at Stormont. There are a lot of people over here who would like to get their hands on you.' He looked back at his mother and laughed. 'You've got some balls coming back here.'

'I needed closure from this place.' Brendan's voice didn't match Teodoro's. It was more of a dull, matter-of-fact tone, simply delivering information regardless of the stories the Romanians or even the local Irish had heard about him. He didn't see himself as a hero, and certainly not as someone who should go down in folklore. He was simply a product of his environment. He looked at Diana, then Teodoro. 'My father once joked about how the government that forced him to become the man he became would one day regret ever making that decision.'

'What did he mean by that?' Teodoro said, as he shifted the beats to something a little heavier. 'I love Metallica.' He increased the volume. 'What did he mean by that, Brendan?'

Brendan glanced down at the radio and laughed. 'He made me. I'll show you once we get to Donegal.' He raised the window on his side. 'It all started there.' He turned his gaze back to the country road and zoned in on negotiating the infamous local roads that brought new meaning to the word treacherous.

# Chapter Twenty-Nine

SHORTLY AFTER MIDDAY, Brendan pulled the vehicle up to the estate's black gate. It activated, slowly revealing the inside. He guided the car along the drive towards the front door. He stopped at the steps that led up to the front door, which was now opening. Lorna leaned against the door frame, her arms folded inside a woollen jumper as if trying to conserve heat.

'Who owns this place?' Teodoro gasped, looking around the gardens.

'It belonged to my father.' Brendan shut off the engine. 'Let's go.' He opened the door and stepped out, pulling the rear door open for Diana. Once she stepped out, he dragged one of the suitcases off the back seat.

'Hey, are you okay?' Lorna approached them, pulling Diana in for a hug who broke into a fit of hysterical sobs as Lorna pulled her in close. 'Don't worry, the bastard won't get near you here.' She looked at Brendan over the top of Diana's shoulder.

Brendan turned and indicated for Teodoro to give him a hand with the bags. He released the boot and took and bag out, handed one to Teodoro, then lifted the second one out for himself.

Diana turned to Brendan, wiping her nose on the sleeve of her jumper. 'Here, give me one, I can still be of some use.'

She forced herself to smile and took one of the suitcases off him. Lorna took the fourth from the back seat and led the way into the house.

The TV was on in the living room: a news report about the increase in foreign nationals who'd been found dead in and around the London area. The moment he heard that the murdered were part of the Romanian community, he knew it was a retaliation for what had happened in London, when Dimitru and his guys took the information supplied to them by Brendan and Lorna.

As she set her suitcase down on the floor, Diana's eyes locked on the flat screen at the first mention of Romanians in London. She said something in Romanian, speaking fast and under her breath.

'What was that?' Brendan said.

'That bastard is part of the boss in Romania's crew,' she spat, clenching her fists.

'How do you know?' Brendan said.

'Because that is where I was before they brought me here.' She turned and looked at Teodoro, who stood beside her, also fixed on the screen. 'Teodoro was born in London.' She stroked his face. 'He was only a baby when we were moved to Belfast. When Dimitru struck a deal with the local UDA to open a brothel, he moved to Belfast to run things for the boss at home and brought me to run the whore-house for him.' She sniffed, wiping her nose on her sleeve. 'He wanted me to himself. Nobody else was allowed to fuck me, only him.'

'Mum...' Teodoro shouted. 'I don't want to listen to this.'

Brendan grabbed Diana's suitcase. 'Come on and I'll show you the gym, Teodoro.' The lad ignored him, but Brendan grabbed him by the forearm. 'Come on, mate. You can do some training. I'll teach you a few things.'

'I'm sorry, love,' Diana said in Romanian. She switched to English. 'Go with Brendan, let him help you.'

'Or maybe you can show me where Dimitru keeps all the stash and let me shoot the bastard.'

Brendan stopped and looked back at Diana, his eyes wide, his eyebrows raised. 'You know where he keeps all his stash?'

She nodded her head.

'She knows everything about his little empire, where he keeps all his guns, drugs, cash,' Teodoro shouted. 'You should have just let us take it all. Let him try and get out of that one.'

'I think we need to discuss this,' Lorna said. 'But not now. Go and get yourself washed up. There are clean towels in the bathroom on the first floor to your right, just as you go up the stairs. I'll go and make some lunch, while Brendan and Teodoro go and play in the gym.'

'What do you mean "play"?' Teodoro said defensively.

'She's just kidding,' Brendan laughed. 'Come on.' He led them down the hallway, through the kitchen and out into the garden.

'Where's this gym?' Teodoro said as he followed Brendan through the patio door out into the garden.

'Down here,' Brendan said, pulling his hoodie up. The coastal wind was blowing in all directions. A stabbing chill came in off the Atlantic, and Brendan's cropped hair did nothing to shield him from it.

He opened the pool house's door and stepped in, holding the door open for Teodoro.

'This is all yours?' Teodoro stepped inside, shutting the door behind him, sending the wind back outside.

Brendan just nodded his head as he looked around.

'You're so lucky to have all this.' Teodoro walked in past Brendan, looking like a child who'd just been given free access to his favourite toy store.

'I wouldn't say I'm lucky.' Brendan's phone rang. It was Dimitru. 'Have a look around, make yourself at home. I've to take this call.' He stepped outside. He answered it, putting the phone to his left ear while pressing his right index finger into his right ear. 'Dimitru, it's very windy where I am so you're going to have to shout.'

'It's okay. I'm just checking if you still want to come with us tonight? I have a little surprise for you.'

'Don't really like surprises, mate.'

Dimitru laughed, like he always did. It appeared everything that came out Brendan's mouth was amusing. 'Don't worry, this surprise is simply a thank you for the help you gave us in London.'

'What kind of surprise.'

'She has two of the sweetest breasts you could ever have in your mouth, and a hot piece of ass. If you want her, she's all yours to break in. Fresh meat from the old country.'

Brendan clenched his jaw and made a fist. He looked through the window into the gym where Teodoro was loosening up. 'You know Lorna and I are an item?'

'Fuck that, my friend; you are not married yet.'

Brendan didn't respond.

'Anyway, it's just something for you to think about. She's all yours if you want her. If you don't, I'll take her.' He grunted. 'See you tonight.' He hung up. Brendan stood on the spot, continuing to watch Teodoro. A few seconds later, he received a message. A photo from Dimitru. He opened it. Dimitru was right about one thing: the girl he'd given to him as a present was very attractive.

# Chapter Thirty

AFTER LORNA HAD GOT Diana settled into the house, and Teodoro had worked up a sweat in the gym, the four of them ordered takeout from the local village. After a democratic debate, they all opted for something Chinese. Wanting to maintain the property's anonymity, Brendan and Teodoro went to collect, instead of having it delivered.

Instead of taking the car in which they'd left Belfast, they went to collect in the black Range Rover. Like all the cars they drove, it had fully tinted windows, addressing Brendan's paranoia more than anything.

'Are all your cars dressed like a gansta rapper's?' Teodoro joked as he pulled open the passenger door. 'Not that I'm complaining.' He jumped in; the smile on his face was the first Brendan had seen.

'You'll soon get used to it,' Brendan said. He jumped in behind the wheel and started the engine.

'You think I can drive it?'

'What age are you?'

'Coming fifteen in a couple of months.'

Brendan grinned as he put the car in gear. 'We'll see what your mum says.'

'She's not thinking straight. Her head is up her arse, man.'

'It's not surprising, is it?' Brendan guided the car down the driveway and hit the button on the gate's remote control.

'No, but she doesn't help herself either. She gets stoned or drunk, thinking it's all going to help her. It just makes her mind into mush. Then she walks around the house feeling sorry for herself. I've told her before that I'd kill him, and we'd be free of him forever, but she demands that I put the idea out of my head. Then she goes back to numbing herself with the booze and drugs.'

'You've got to understand the situation she's in, mate.' Brendan guided the car through the gate and indicated to turn right, slowly edging the car forward to get a clear view. 'If you were to kill him, you'd have that hanging over you for the rest of your life. And trust me, it's not something you want.' He quickly glanced at Teodoro, who was watching him as if hanging off every word. 'She's in a very difficult situation, and you've got to be the man of the house and stop acting like a boy.' He laughed. 'You know, you're so much like me it's unreal.' He accelerated, sending the revs through the roof. 'And believe me when I tell you your mum's going to need you to be strong for her. And that doesn't necessarily mean acting out in violence.'

'What makes you think we're the same?'

Brendan sighed. 'My mother drank herself to death, torn apart from the belief that my father was murdered and left in a ditch somewhere. The thought of him coming to an end like that – she couldn't face, and just like Diana, she gave herself what she believed would help numb the pain.'

'She's dead?'

Brendan nodded, as he slowed down on an approach to a roundabout. 'And the worst part of it was, he wasn't even fucking dead.'

For Brendan, this was all new, too. Usually he had a father figure, and he was the one with the childlike attitude, carelessly joking around, knowing that someone else would be the responsible adult. After all, he'd still not reached the age of thirty. But over the last few months, since meeting Lorna in the cell of the PSNI station in Belfast, he'd had to grow up very fast. He'd had no other choice.

'Thank you for your help,' Teodoro said. 'I don't know why you're doing it. But thank you.'

Brendan pulled up into the carpark of the restaurant. He shut the engine off. 'I haven't done anything.' He looked at Teodoro. 'But you're welcome.' He opened the door and got out, pulling his hoodie up to shelter from the rain that had begun to fall.

As they arrived back at the house, Teodoro had gone quiet in the car. Brendan was straining to keep the conversation flowing, getting nothing but one-word answers. Perhaps reality was slowly seeping into the mind of the young lad, just as it had felt when Brendan had realised he wasn't normal or had only the slimmest chance of ever living a normal life. Teodoro would have to do some growing up, quickly. But with some guidance from someone who'd been through it before, Brendan had faith that he'd be alright and would bounce back, stronger than before.

They made their way towards the front door, but Lorna called them from the side of the house close to the garages. She'd set a table for them under a heated canopy that sat on the black-and-white heated patio to the right of the out-door pool. The wind would have been a nuisance to their outdoor dinner, had it not been for the see-through canopy that dropped over the table like an over-sized umbrella that reached all the way to the ground.

'Who's idea was it to dine outside?' Brendan said as he set the takeaway down on the table.'

'My guess is her.' Teodoro gestured towards his mother. 'She hates being inside.' He put his tongue out at Diana. 'It's almost as if she's allergic to four walls.'

'I know the feeling,' Brendan said. He looked at Diana. She looked at the table, not holding eye contact with any of them. 'Hope you all like Chinese noodles. We've enough here to feed half of the country.'

'I'd eat anything.' Teodoro reached over and grabbed the bag of containers off Brendan.

'Teodoro,' Diana shouted. 'Where are your manners?'

Brendan looked at Lorna. She looked back at him, not sure where to look.

'It's not how I raised you,' she spat. 'You're not your fa-ther.' She spoke her last two words with emphasis.

Teodoro handed the bag back to Brendan, but Brendan put his hand up in refusal. 'Help yourself.' He cleared his throat. The tension beneath the canopy was heavy. 'Diana, I'm going back to Belfast this evening to meet with Dimitru. He's bringing me with him to his local arms and drugs dumps. If there's anything you can tell me that will give me an idea what to expect tonight, it will be much appreciated.'

'It's simple.' She spoke sharply. 'All of his dumps are in one of two places, and they're protected.'

'Where?' Lorna said as she took the food from Teodoro and began scooping noodles from the container. 'And who's it protected by?'

'The whorehouse, just off Cliftonpark Avenue, or in a warehouse down at the city docks.' She took the container off Lorna and helped herself to a minuscule portion of the food. 'PSNI officers have been taking money and free bribes off them in return for assurance that their operation will be safe.'

'Can you find out a name and get it to me?' Brendan said. He piled his plate with the remains of the food. 'If Dimitru breathes a word about my being back in the city, it could be a problem.'

'It's the big boss; that's the bastard you want to get your hands on. You give me a chance, and I'll kill him with my bare hands.' Diana spat.

'Just get me the info on the bent cops, and I'll worry about serving up justice to the rest of them.'

'I want to come with you,' Teodoro said, blowing the steam from his noodles.

'No chance,' Lorna said.

'What do you mean, no chance? I deserve to be there.'

'You deserve to be there, but you'll just make things more difficult.' Lorna argued. 'And you could put yourself and Brendan in greater danger if there are too many people around.'

'I can help,' Teodoro complained. 'I'm not useless.'

'You're definitely not useless,' Brendan said. 'But you have a chance of walking away from this life, and that's what you're going to do. That's the only condition. And it's not up for debate.' Brendan scooped up a fork-full of noodles, twirling them around the fork. 'I'm going by myself.'

# Chapter Thirty-One

AFTER THEIR MEAL, THEY all returned to the house. Diana hadn't opened up from her traumatised, closed position. Her body language was defensive. Teodoro, on the other hand, had a little extra bounce in his walk. Whether or not he was blocking out what he'd seen, he'd eventually need some serious counselling. A young boy wanting to take the life of his father was an individual with an abundance of trust issues. That type of person would be dangerous, not only to themselves but to the people around them, and to the greater population.

'Before you go to Belfast, Brendan, there's something you should know about what you're getting involved in,' Diana said. She sat down at the kitchen table, inviting Brendan and the others to join her. 'Dimitru's an idiot. A piece of shit who deserves to have his cock chopped off. And given the chance, I'll certainly be the one to do it.' She looked around the table at them all. 'But he isn't completely brainless. He plans on taking over the entire criminal racket here in Belfast. He's coked off his head, and his confidence is as high as the jet the Romanian boss will be flying in on.'

Brendan looked at Lorna, nodding his head. 'We had a feeling this is what he was up to. And he's undoubtedly grown in confidence since his little trip to London.'

'Thanks to you,' Diana said, folding her arms, her eyes fixed on the stainless steel cutlery set in the middle of the table. 'He told me all about *Brendan*, the Belfast man who would help him turn his little empire into a more dominant one by helping crush the local scumbags.' She looked at Brendan, then Lorna. Then back to Brendan. 'He's planning something very big, and I'm afraid many people will get hurt, or even killed.'

'That's not going to happen,' Brendan said.

'How do you know?' She spoke with mock humour. 'I mean, like you can bring down the entire Romanian mafia.'

'I don't have to,' Brendan said, his tone calm. 'We cut the head off the organisation, shut down a few of the biggest money makers, and we'll cripple their business. We just need someone who can help tell everyone what exactly is going on.'

'I might have someone,' Lorna said, her arms folded, imitating Diana's body language. Her face was frozen in a serious expression, as if deep in thought. 'I think I have just the person who'd love to get their hands on a story like this.'

'Who?' Brendan said.

'She's a friend from London. A reporter for the BBC. But she's also a women's rights activist. And if she gets wind of this kind of story, if she's still in the news business, she'll make some publicity for the Romanians, and any piece-of-shit corrupt cops you find are tied into them.' She laughed. 'They'll go down with them.'

'Okay, well, you get on the phone to her, see what she can do,' Brendan said. 'What can you tell me about Dimitru?' He looked at Diana. 'Anything that I don't already know that will bury him.'

'Where do I start?' Diana laughed without humour as she looked across at her son. 'His father came into Belfast after a deal was made between the local UDA and the head of the Romanian mafia. The UDA didn't want to be seen involved in such business, so they simply gave out their streets, with guaranteed protection, for a slice of the action. Therefore, the Romanians bring in the sluts, the drugs, and the guns, and in return, the UDA gets a big fat piece of their pie for simply letting them run the streets.' She looked at Lorna. 'But Dimitru is just like any man with a growing empire; his confidence is growing to dangerously high levels, along with his greed. It's only a matter of time before he sets his expectations too high, and he ends up in a box.'

'He's been taking more and more drugs,' Teodoro added. 'And his head is turning to mush.' He looked at his mother, then Brendan. 'I'm glad the man that I once called my father is now dead. It'll make it easier for me to put a bullet in his head if I'm given the chance.'

'You're not fucking getting involved in this,' Diana shouted across the table. 'I don't want that lousy son of a bitch tainting your soul.' Her lower lip quivered. 'You're the one thing in my life that's pure. You're the one thing I've got to be proud of. I will not have that dirty bastard take that away from me, too.'

Teodoro didn't respond.

'Your mother's right, Teodoro,' Lorna said. 'It's not worth it.'

'You don't want that hanging over your shoulders for the rest of your life.' Brendan stood up and grabbed his phone. 'When this is all done, we'll try and help you get started with a new life.' He looked across the table at Lorna. 'Maybe we can find some capital to help.'

'I've got an idea of where we can find some for ourselves,' Diana said.

'Where?'

She smiled at her son. 'Dimitru does not trust anyone with his funds, except the mother of his son. He's never wanted to have large amounts of money in his own bank account, so he's spread it out among three different accounts, under three different names. I have access to all of them.' She looked across the table at Lorna. 'I can wipe the bastard out and put him back on the street where he belongs.'

'What do you know about the boss, who's coming over next week?' Lorna said.

'Apart from the fact that he's my cousin?' Diana spat, her arms folded defensively. 'He's given our family—a good, honest, hard-working family—a bad name, and he's brought too much misery to people not only in Romania, but in England, and now Ireland. He treats me like his beautiful cousin, and the only lady Dimitru is not allowed to put on the market for sale.'

'How close can you get to him?' Lorna said.

'As close as a family member can get. As close, if not closer, than Dimitru can.' She forced a laugh. 'No matter how much money my loving partner puts in his pocket, he's still very old-fashioned and believes in blood being thicker than water.'

Brendan looked at his phone. 'That may come in handy. But we may not need you to get close to him. I may have already secured that ticket.' He pushed his chair out and stood up. 'That's Dimitru. I'll see you all later tonight.'

'Be careful,' Diana said.

'Don't kill him without me being there to see it,' Teodoro shouted after Brendan as he headed for the door.

Lorna followed him out. 'Hold it there, Lone Ranger.' She marched after him.

He held the door open for her. They passed through the dining room into the living area and towards the front entrance. 'You heard what Diana said.' She grabbed his hand. 'You be careful.'

'I'll be alright. I know these streets better than he does.' He pulled her in for a kiss. 'I'll be fine.'

'You got some protection?'

'I'm not really going to shag one of the hookers.' He grinned.

'Very funny. I mean do you have a...'

'I know,' Brendan said. 'I've got my father's weapon in the car. Loaded and with some backup ammo.' He kissed her again. 'Don't worry. I'll be back shortly. Before midnight, anyway.'

He decided to take the Range Rover. As he got in the car, he checked to make sure the gun was where he'd left it. It was. He started the engine and sent Dimitru at text to tell him he'd be in Belfast in the next two hours. He put the car in gear and was about to take off when Lorna appeared at the window. She pulled the door open and gave him another kiss. She told him she'd get on the phone to her mate in London about bringing some bad publicity to the organisation, kissed him again, then shut the door.

He took off just as the rain started. The gate opened and he was off. Belfast bound. A place where he thought he'd left behind.

# Chapter Thirty-Two

BY THE TIME BRENDAN arrived in Belfast, the rain had stopped. During the journey, he'd fallen into an almost hypnotic trance with the constant back-and-forth motion of the windscreen wipers. The time was shortly after seven. It was dark and damp. Although the downpour had ended, there was a constant swoosh of rainwater as cars went by in the opposite direction. Belfast's most common feature. Still, the city would always be Brendan's home.

Always making a point of topping up his vehicle, he made a return to the petrol station he'd used earlier in the morning before he'd gone to pick up Diana and Teodoro. As he stood at the pump, his phone went off in his pocket. He ignored it until he'd filled the tank. He paid the fee at the pump and got back into the car as the wind picked up, bringing with it a chill that could almost cut through the skin.

He started the engine and quickly pulled out of the bay to allow the next customer in the growing queue. He pulled over into one of the service station's parking bays. Checking his phone, he saw the call was from Dimitru. He returned the call.

Dimitru answered almost immediately. 'Brendan, just to let you know, we've stopped off in the Europa Hotel. The boss man wanted us to check it out.' He laughed, as he always did. 'He likes to be put up in nothing but the finest of establishments. He's a businessman and sees this as a business trip.'

Brendan sniggered. 'Very professional. Does he claim back expenses?'

Dimitru erupted into a fit of laugher, almost choking. He appeared to be very happy and considering what Brendan had done earlier, that was good. At least he was none the wiser with regards to what Brendan was really up to.

'Do you want me to come and pick you guys up?' Brendan said.

'Where are you now, my friend?'

'I'm close to the city centre. I can be there in the next thirty minutes.'

'Great. I will see you soon. I'll be on my own; these other lazy bastards have work to go to. But this is good – I'm glad we can spend a bit of time together. We can get to know each other a bit more.'

'Sounds good, mate.' Brendan almost believed himself; he sounded that convincing. 'I'll see you soon.' He hung up. Before he took off, he ran into the petrol station to grab a cappuccino from the self-service Costa machine.

As he left the station, his heart almost skipped a beat. Standing at pump eight was none other than his uncle. His mother's older brother. A bastard of a man, whom Brendan had grown to hate. He'd witnessed him hitting his younger sister when he was a child, punishing her for going with Brendan's father and giving birth to Brendan, or what he'd seen as a 'dirty taig.'

Everything in Brendan's body, every cell of his being, wanted to strangle his uncle with the hose he was using to fill the Range Rover. Judging from the car his uncle was driving, and the fancy suit he was wearing, business was good. Whether his lavish lifestyle was still being funded by the UDA, or he'd seen the light and gone legit, he looked well.

Brendan clenched his jaws and put his head down. It wasn't worth it, not at that moment anyway. He wanted to focus on the job at hand. If his uncle were to run into him again, he'd settle the score for his mother. Now, his mind was on Dimitru and the others. He got back into the car and took off.

The streets of Belfast were quiet. This time of night, there was nothing but the odd taxi racing through the streetlights. Knowing the streets well, Brendan was able to time it so the lights were green as he approached. This was a skill he'd taught himself over his years of cruising Belfast with his teenage mates.

He pulled up outside the establishment, directly behind a black taxi. It flashed his mind back to the days when his uncles on his father's side of the family drove black taxis, down the Falls Road and into the city centre. That was known as the safest way to travel. It was known within the city that most taxi cabs were operated by the paramilitaries. Safe, however? Brendan wasn't so sure. One of his father's older brothers had been shot dead while making his journey home one night.

Brendan snapped out of his daze when he heard Dimitru's loud, accented voice. As usual, the Romanian could be heard before he was seen, on the phone while his eyes scanned the road, eventually meeting Brendan in the SUV.

Dimitru hung up the phone and patted the door security on the shoulder.

'That was quick,' Dimitru said, flicking his cigarette into the gutter below him. He jumped in. 'You ready to have a good night?'

Brendan nodded and indicated to move away from the kerb. He pulled out behind a bus and joined the queue of three taxis waiting at a temporary roadworks. 'I'm interested to learn more about what you guys are doing. From what I hear, you're becoming more notorious within the city. Which is surprising, because the paramilitaries, I thought, would have preferred to maintain control of these streets.'

'You're surprised a little group of Romanians could come over and take over?'

'Not Romanians, per se, but the paramilitaries on both sides were always keen to maintain their power. A bunch of control freaks.'

'That is something you're right about, my friend. That you're right about.' Dimitru put his window down. 'Mind if I smoke in here?'

Brendan looked at him. 'You just had one.'

'I like smoking. It calms my nerves.'

He shook his head. 'I don't mind.'

'You know where the Ballysillan Road is?'

'Of course I do.'

'Good, I need to get a shower and freshen myself up.' He pulled a cigarette out of a twenty box and put it in his mouth. Pulling a lighter from his jeans pocket, he lit it up and took a long drag. He exhaled, blowing the smoke out the window. 'You can meet my lovely family.'

'Great,' Brendan said. He cleared his throat, then put his window down. 'Those things smell like shit.'

# Chapter Thirty-Three

ARRIVING AT DIMITRU'S house, Brendan found himself grateful that he'd chosen to take a different car. He wasn't sure whether or not Dimitru had other friends in the street, and if he did, their eyes could have landed him in something a little too premature.

He shut the engine off and got out. Scanning the street, he was glad his appearance was not the same as it had been when he'd run around these streets. He grabbed his jacket from the back seat and shut the door, following Dimitru along the slabbed path that cut an almost straight line through the front garden, leading up to the door.

'Doesn't look like Diana's here,' Dimitru said. There wasn't a light on in the entire house. A ginger cat sat at the door, looking up at them, crying to be let in. 'Aw, Ginger, has mummy gone and left you out here on your own?'

'You called a ginger cat Ginger?' Brendan laughed. 'Very creative.'

'It's Diana's cat.' Dimitru lifted it, cradling him in his left arm, while his right hand searched for his keys. 'I got the bloody thing for that little shit I call a son. The ungrateful little bastard complained because he wanted a dog instead.' He opened the door, and dropped Ginger onto the floor, letting him run in first. He turned and looked at Brendan. 'He wanted a bloody pitbull.' He laughed. 'Thinks it would make him look like a fucking tough guy if he had one.'

Brendan smiled, stepping into the house. He turned and looked down the garden before closing the door behind him. The hallway was narrow, with white walls along the top half and yellow paint along the bottom half. A shiny black bannister lined the stairway along the right side. Dimitru hit the light switch in the hallway. He looked confused. 'I wonder where the fuck she is. She doesn't normally disappear without saying.'

'Did you guys have a fight or something?' Brendan pressed him, giving Dimitru the idea that Brendan was none the wiser about what had taken place.

Dimitru shook his head. 'She was being a bitch last night, but nothing more than usual.' He stood at the bottom of the stairs. 'Go and make yourself at home. I won't be long. Help yourself to the kitchen if you're hungry or want a drink of tea.' He pulled his phone out of his pocket. 'I'll try and find out where this crazy bitch is.'

Brendan continued down the hallway. Glancing at the family photos as he passed, he noticed the three looked much younger and happier. He stepped into the kitchen to find Ginger sitting by his bowl, looking up at Brendan as if to ask for some food. Brendan reached down to stroke the animal, but before his hands could make contact, the cat ran and jumped onto the worktop towards a bag of cat biscuits, which he was *really* after. Brendan, obliged, gripped the bag and lifted the cat back down onto the floor, filling his dish.

After the cat was fed, Brendan looked for what he could make for himself, settling for a cup of tea. As he waited for the kettle to boil, he pulled out his phone and sent Lorna a text.

*I'm in Diana's house with Dimitru. Tell her she forgot her cat, Ginger.*

He smirked, dropping the phone back into his pocket. He made the tea, then dropped the soaked teabag into the sink. He looked out the window that sat directly above the sink, casting his eyes across the back garden. It looked as if it hadn't been treated in some time. He wouldn't be surprised if there were a dead Romanian rival lying somewhere in the grass. One could certainly be hidden in the length of it.

Casting his eyes farther down the garden, he saw a corner flattened down by concrete slabs. A free-standing dummy that was undoubtedly Teodoro's most prized possession stood looking up at Brendan, as if he were the catalyst to all the abuse that the piece of equipment had taken over the years.

His phone vibrated. He pulled it out of his pocket. It was Lorna.

*She said if you could bring Ginger back with you, she'd be very grateful. He wasn't there today when they left. Congratulations, you've now been promoted to saving cats' lives!!*

He was about to respond when she called him.

'Well, you've taken on your biggest assignment to date, Mr Cleary.'

Brendan laughed, blowing on his tea. 'I know. I think I can retire after this one.' He cleared his throat. Making his way through the kitchen door, he went back down the hallway, turning right, through another door into the living room. 'How are they?'

'It's weird, because Teodoro seems unfazed by the whole thing. Diana, on the other hand, well...what can you expect?' Her voice lowered with the sound of a door closing. 'But her eyes glazed over and she almost broke down the moment I mentioned the cat.' She laughed. 'I love the name, by the way.'

'I'm just waiting on Dimitru getting out of the shower, then we're off to the whorehouse. Have you managed to contact your friend, the activist?'

'I've called her, but she hasn't replied. I've left her a voicemail.'

'Will she call back?'

'I'm certain of it.'

'Can she be trusted?' Usually Lorna was the one who operated with extreme caution, but this time, Brendan was the one with the concerns.

'Brendan...come on.' She sounded offended. 'You think I'd contact her if it had a chance of causing us problems?'

'You've been in this game long enough, I guess, to know what not to do.' He sipped on his tea, looking at the fish tank in the corner of the room, a tropical tank almost as large as the seventy-inch plasma that occupied the adjacent corner. 'It's a nice house they have here. It has a homely feel to it.'

'Well, they seem like a normal, nice family. If only the man of the house wasn't such a bastard.'

Brendan stepped closer to the fish tank, crouching down, following one of the fish that looked like someone had blown air into it, causing it to swell. 'Sleeps with the fishes.'

'What?'

Brendan straightened himself up and walked over to the fireplace, looking at himself in the mirror. 'Nothing. "Sleeps with the fishes" is just a saying from one of the biggest gangster movies of all time.'

'Yes, I know: *The Godfather*. But this isn't a gangster movie,' she said. 'I've got to go. Be careful.'

'Yes, Mum,' Brendan joked.

She blew him a kiss then hung up.

He dropped his phone into his pocket and sat down, his attention still on the fish tank. He sat clasping the hot mug in his hand, almost hypnotised by the tank. The low hum from the tank's motor gave him an almost therapeutic feeling, until the ceiling began to shake—thumps from Dimitru upstairs, trudging around. Brendan looked up at the ceiling, following the sound of the footsteps across the room. He could hear muffled shouting but couldn't understand what was being said. Perhaps Dimitru was used to Diana ironing his clothes for him and had found a nasty surprise when she'd left him with his shirts in balls of wrinkles. Brendan found some levity in the thought.

He finished his tea and brought the cup back out into the kitchen. He stood leaning against the worktop, checking the news to see if there were any more developments in London. Nothing on London, but there was a story closer to home—a shooting in the Rathcoole Estate, where they'd been invited to the party. He clicked on the story.

*A man has been found badly beaten close to a fast food takeaway shop during the early hours of this morning. The establishment, which is run by a local Turkish family, is said to be a place where local youths congregate. Drinking and drug*

*use around this area, as the locals have complained, has been a*
*growing problem and one that needs more attention from com-*
*munity leaders. It is not known whether or not this man was*
*involved in any kind of altercation, but the individual, who is*
*from the area, is said to be in stable condition in hospital. An*
*early-morning dog walker found the young man, and immedi-*
*ately called an ambulance.*

'This is the beginning of it,' Brendan sighed. The sound
of Dimitru thumping his way down the stairs snatched Brendan's attention from his phone. He struggled not to laugh at
the expression on the local crime boss's face, sporting a baggy
pair of jeans that looked like they'd been ironed with a brick,
and clasping a shirt in his hands that looked even worse.

'Stupid bitch can't even do the laundry anymore,' Dimitru complained, strutting over to the corner of the room
where a white fridge-freezer sat. Reaching down the side of
it, where the appliance met the wall, he pulled out an ironing board. Flipping the legs out, he slammed it down on the
ground. He pointed towards the cupboard below the sink,
next to where Brendan was standing. 'Grab the iron for me
please, Brendan.'

Brendan did so.

'Have you heard about some guy getting a beating in
Rathcoole?' he said as he handed Dimitru the iron. 'From
what the news said, he's been given quite a tanking.'

Dimitru took the iron and plugged it in. 'Yes, he's one
of our guys. But this isn't the time for us to have a beef with
someone,' he mumbled to himself, spraying his shirt with water and then covering it with steam.

'Well then, why the fuck did you go around to the Shankill?' Brendan leaned back against the worktop, folding him arms. 'I mean, come on; that was clearly going to spark a reaction from someone.'

'That was for us to see if you were legit, and not a shit-talker.' Dimitru ran the iron across the shirt, a grin appearing on his face. He looked up at Brendan. 'We didn't expect you to be that ballsy. You've done well.' His grin dropped again into a frown. 'We'll sort this out after the boss leaves again.' He looked up at Brendan, shifting the shirt's position on the board. 'You should be honoured the boss man's coming here. He generally doesn't get off his ass and leave Romania.' He cleared his throat, looking as if he regretted what he'd just said. 'But when he heard about the info you gave us for our little adventure in London, he booked a flight straight away.'

'Stop, you're making me blush,' Brendan said humorously, folding his arm and crossing his left leg over his right. 'Looks like you've got bigger problems, by the way you're ironing that shirt.'

'Fuck you!' Dimitru laughed. 'She's a useless bitch, and when she gets home, she'll hear all about it. She's another problem I could do without. We work in a stressful job. I should be able to come home and not worry about this shit.'

Brendan felt like telling him Diana and Teodoro were gone and he was likely to never see them again, but he bit his tongue, knowing it was more important to keep him sweet, at least until the time was right.

A moment later, Dimitru reached over to the socket and unplugged the iron. He threw his right arm into the shirt's sleeve, flung the shirt around his back, and inserted his left arm. 'You ready to go and get laid?' He smiled at Brendan as he flicked down his collar and buttoned the shirt. 'Let's go, Casanova.' He grabbed his phone from the kitchen top and passed Brendan towards the fridge. He pulled out a bottle of beer and offered one to Brendan. Brendan refused.

Dimitru set the alarm and they left the house as the security device activated. Dimitru popped open the beer with the bottom of his lighter and led the way towards the car.

Brendan considered him. He seemed in a rush, as if running against someone else's clock. 'Why are you running?' Brendan said as he pointed the key at the car, unlocking it. 'Who are you running from, or to?'

Dimitru pulled open the passenger door and held Brendan's gaze as Brendan walked around to the driver's side. 'I'm eager to get away from this place before she,' he gestured with his chin back at the house, 'gets back and breaks my balls.' He sucked the foam from the end of the bottle and dropped himself into the passenger seat.

Brendan got behind the wheel and pulled to door closed. More out of habit than anything else, he scanned the area with his eyes, making sure there were no surprises waiting on him. He started the car, and the radio came on. The news of the hour talked about the attack at the Rathcoole Estate. Local residents were talking about how they'd heard someone scream during the night.

'Turn this shit off.' Dimitru changed the station, stopping on one that had some indie music playing.

Brendan adjusted the heating, setting it at twenty, and put the car in gear, taking off. He indicated to go left, down the steep, almost vertical hill and onto the Antrim Road.

'You know Cliftonpark Avenue?' Dimitru said, a ciga-rette resting between his lips.

Brendan nodded, his eyes focussed on the road.

Dimitru lit the cigarette, taking a long draw, as if he were inhaling it for his life. 'We're right on the end,' he said while exhaling the smoke. 'So, how serious are you and that lovely English lady, then?' He spoke with a hint of sarcastic humour rolling off his tongue.

'Pretty serious,' Brendan said. 'It's a long story.' He briefly looked at Dimitru, who was anxiously adjusting a plaster on his hand. 'What happened? Cut yourself shaving?' he joked.

Dimitru smiled, cigarette in mouth, eyes closed to keep from getting smoke in them. 'Long story.' He turned and looked at Brendan, smiling. 'But anyway, I'll get one of these sweet little ladies to kiss it better for me.' He slapped Brendan with the back of his hand.

Brendan smiled, simply humouring him.

# Chapter Thirty-Four

NUMBER TWELVE, CLIFTONPARK Avenue was a Victorian-style three-story building at the end of the line of terraced houses, standing on the corner of Cliftonpark, where it merged onto the Cliftonville Road.

Brendan parked the car directly outside the house, half on the path and half on the road. A rusted black gate, hanging off its hinges dragged along the ground as he pushed it open. The three-foot-wide pathway was uneven and split. More weeds lined the slabs than concrete.

The door stood around seven feet in height, painted in a sickly brown. A small mountain of cigarette butts lay next to the curled welcome rug.

Dimitru thumped on the door then beat the black rapper against the wood. Within twenty seconds, a female's voice shouted from inside. Her accent similar to Diana's as Brendan thought.

The sound of metal being slid off a hook caused the door to vibrate. Another two chains could be heard sliding across their housing, and finally the door opened. There stood a lady who looked to be in her early to mid-twenties. But it was difficult for Brendan to accurately judge, as she was plastered in makeup. She was an attractive goth. Her jet-black hair hung down the side of her face like dark curtains, lining her white face. Her dark lips and eyes made her look as if she were holding a Halloween party, but she wore the look well. Brendan found her extremely attractive, and had he not had eyes for Lorna, he certainly would have wanted to spend time getting to know this lady.

Dimitru turned and looked at Brendan, winking his eye as if he'd just produced a diamond in the rough. 'Brendan, meet the beautiful Elena.' He looked at her. 'Elena, meet Brendan.' He looked back at Brendan. 'Come with me, my good man.'

Elena opened the door and invited them in.

'Do we have many in the house tonight?' Dimitru said.

She looked at the ground, shaking her head. 'Not yet. But we have a party of three coming around in one hour.' She looked at Brendan as he stepped inside. She smiled at him, but her smile was not that of a happy person. It was more like someone looking at Brendan as if seeing him as a glimmer of hope, or a discreet cry for help, as if she, like Diana and Teodoro, had reached a breaking point and had had enough of the torment.

Brendan smiled at her softly, greeting her in Romanian. She responded in kind, and softly stroked his forearm as he passed, following Dimitru down the corridor and into the second left.

The room looked bigger than the house could have allowed from the outside. The ceilings were easily three feet higher than the front door, and there was enough room for the sectional sofa to run along three of the four walls, with plenty of room for a snooker table in the middle.

'Who is the party of three coming in?' Dimitru said, dropping himself down on the sofa, casually swinging his left leg up over his right.

'The usual trio who come together.' She sat down beside him. Brendan stood against the table, taking centre spot in the room. 'The two constables and their superior, from the local crime unit.'

Dimitru sniggered. 'That dirty bastard.' He pulled out a sandwich bag filled with white power. It looked like a bag of washing detergent, but the contents would not be going into the washing machine, instead up his nostrils. He looked at Brendan. 'Let's get this party started.' He unrolled the bag, then dipped the tip of his little finger in, pulling it back out covered in the white stuff. He dabbed it on his tongue, then grimaced. Closing his eyes, he pulled an expression as if to say the taste was sour, like taking something overly fizzy. He shook his head, then smiled.

Standing up, he joined Brendan at the table, laying the bag down. 'Elena, go and get a mirror. And put some music on while you're at it; it's fucking depressing in here.' He nudged Brendan with his elbow. 'This is going to be a good night.'

'Shouldn't you wait until after your business is tended to before you start to take all that shit?' Brendan sighed. 'I don't want to be pulling your drunk ass away from any problems you land us in tonight.' He sat up on the edge of the table, turning slightly towards Dimitru, at least growing a little amused by his actions.

'Don't worry about me; I'll be fine. A good shag and a few lines of coke will not cause you any problems, my friend.' He took another fingertip full of the stuff and licked it. There was some left on his finger after dabbing it on his tongue. He offered it to Brendan.

'Get that fucking thing away from me before I snap it off.' Brendan spoke firmly, and Dimitru's reaction said he knew Brendan was being serious. He didn't question him; he just took his finger back and gave himself the rest.

Dance music reverberated throughout the room, coming from the surround sound speakers. Elena entered the room again, a mirror under her arm. She set it down on the table, then pulled a razor blade out and handed it to Dimitru.

Dimitru poured out a small pile and began dividing it into lines. He pulled out his wallet, removing a ten-pound note. Rolling the note up tightly, he handed it to Elena. 'Ladies first.'

She took all of a split second to respond, snatching the note off him and crouching down, the roll inserted into her left nostril. One of the lines quickly disappeared up her nose, and she snorted. Then she inserted it into her right and did the same, coughing.

Brendan stood with his arms folded, defensively watching what was taking place. In spite of everything he'd gotten up to during his late teen years, he'd never been one for taking drugs. His father, in addition to carving his physical and psychological shape, had made sure Brendan was fully aware of the effect taking drugs would have on him, and subsequently had taught him how to just say no. Those two words, although so small, were sometimes the most difficult for many people in Ireland and throughout the world to say.

Giving in to peer pressure was something Brendan had never done.

Before him in that house stood two people who had given in a long time ago, and that was what had led them down the road they were currently on—a road that had brought Brendan into their lives. For one of them, meeting Brendan was going to be a blessing; for the other, not so much.

'You sure you don't want a hit of this stuff?' Dimitru said as he took the rolled note off Elena.

'I'm sure.' Brendan said.

Dimitru looked at him, his eyes tiny slits. 'I'm not sure about people who don't take drugs; it's very peculiar.'

'Get used to it,' Brendan affirmed.

Dimitru looked at Elena, nudging her with his elbow. 'He's a confident bastard, isn't he?' He crouched down and inserted the note into his nostril.

She looked at Brendan, her eyes more glazed than before, her nostrils red. She smiled at him. 'Yes, he is. But I like a man with confidence.' She stroked his forearm. 'I find it very attractive.'

'He's all yours,' Dimitru shouted, as he snorted and straightened up, wiping his nose. He looked at her and slapped her on the backside. 'And I want you to do whatever he asks, okay?'

She nodded, not taking her eyes off Brendan. 'I have no problem with that.'

Brendan wasn't looking anything off her. Lorna had quickly become the love of his life, and that was not about to change anytime soon, regardless of how beautiful Elena was. And beautiful she was.

Dimitru finished off the last two lines, then poured himself a drink. 'Take Brendan up to one of the rooms and show him a good time. I want to have a word with our friend from the local police service when he arrives.' He handed Brendan a glass of whiskey, which he quickly refused. 'You're a boring bastard, aren't you?' Dimitru said. He emptied the entire contents down his throat. 'But you're still a fucking legend, as you guys would say over here, after what you've done.' He looked at Elena, gesturing towards the door. 'I'll be down here, and remember: anything he wants, you give it to him.'

# Chapter Thirty-Five

REACHING THE TOP OF the flight of stairs, Brendan stood at the end of the corridor, which had three pale blue doors on each side. A constant banging noise was a clear indication that the staff were busy, earning their wages.

'We're in the first room, handsome.' She stoked his neck from behind as she passed him, slowly linking her fingers with his, gently pulling him enticingly towards to the door.

He played along. From the expression on her face, she had no problem delivering to him what she assumed he wanted. He smiled at her. 'You're very beautiful.'

'Thank you, Brendan.' She cast him a cheeky grin, biting her lower lip, as she pulled a key from her pocket, inserting it into the lock. Opening the door, she entered. He followed her in. The room was simple. Plain. White wallpaper was plastered across all four walls. The bed was a king-size, dressed in white and pale blue coloured sheets.

She closed the door after him. 'Have a seat; don't look so nervous.' She ran her hand slowly down his arm as he stepped further into the room.

He sat on the edge of the bed, looking at her. Playing the game. He watched her stroll slowly across the room, towards the wooden-framed window that ran all the way up to the room's high ceiling. Pulling the thick white curtains closed, she cast the room into darkness. His eyesight was reduced momentarily, until his vision could re-adjust. He followed her footsteps across the room towards the door. She hit the light switch and his sight was restored. She looked sexier under this light. Her eyes were smaller, her expression more relaxed. She strode towards him, holding his gaze. If he didn't have Lorna, he'd certainly be tempted to let her do whatever she pleased. But after almost losing Lorna in Italy, he'd learned to appreciate the lady she was, and wasn't ready to let someone else come between them. It was simply the two of them against the world. And that was something he was grateful for, thanks to the British establishment.

'I'm actually going to have some fun for a change.' She straddled him, slowly kissing his neck. Her perfume was strong enough to almost choke him. 'Lie down.' Her tone became more dominating, controlling.

He smiled and was about to do as she said. But his expression quickly fell into one more serious. 'I'm not here for this.' He looked at her. 'I'm not here for a free shag.' He spoke low, ensuring his voice wasn't carried.

She looked at him, her head tilted, unsure what he meant. 'I don't understand.'

'Do you like working here?' He looked at her. She didn't respond. 'You like sucking strangers' dicks for a living?'

'What is this?' She stumbled over her words, standing up straight, her hands on her hips. 'Is this a joke?'

'It's no joke,' Brendan assured her. 'I'm about to bring down the organisation you work for.' He stood up and stepped closer to her. 'I want to help you and anyone else who's been living like this.' He placed his hand on her forearm, an intimate gesture to bring her defences down.

She stepped back and shook his hand off her.

'Look, you know Diana?'

'Dimitru's wife? Yes, they have a son together.'

'Teodoro, yes. That's right. They've run away from him, this morning. He does not know about it.'

'He will be very angry when he finds out.' She folded her arms. 'And you helped them? That was very stupid. He will kill you for this, and you won't mean a thing to...'

'Fuck him,' Brendan hissed. 'You know he beats her, and rapes her? Their own son told me today he wants to kill him... His own father, he wants to kill.'

'Teodoro is such a sweet boy. I can't imagine him ever saying such a thing.'

'When a boy gets beaten up by his father, and walks in on him raping his mother, his feelings can quickly change, father or not.' Brendan paused for a moment. 'Come on, you must know he's a bastard and deserves to be brought down.'

'And how do you plan on doing this?'

'Let me worry about that, but you can help make the process a bit faster by telling me everything you know about his business. Diana told me he keeps some of his guns and drugs in this house. And She said he doesn't like to store all his money in banks.'

She walked past him and sat down on the edge of the bed. 'I don't know. He's a very dangerous man.'

Brendan sat down beside her, gently placing his hand on top of hers. 'Look, I know you're afraid. He's a very mean person, but if you don't help me, then you're going to be here, doing this, for a long time.' She looked at him, then back down at the ground again. 'You don't want to be here doing what you're doing, do you?'

She shook her head. 'This is crazy.'

'Sitting here, letting this all continue, is crazier when you can help me help you.' He sighed. 'Look, if I get Diana to talk to you, will you believe me then?'

She didn't respond for a second. Then a glimmer of a smile began to creep up her face. 'If I can talk to Diana, and you promise this will help not only me, but all the girls they have working for them, then yes, we'll help.'

Brendan pulled his phone from his pocket and called Diana, putting it on loudspeaker. It rang three times, then she answered.

'Brendan, is everything okay?'

'Diana. I have someone here who wants to speak to you, and before you hang up, it's not the father of your son.' He handed Elena the phone.

She switched to Romanian.

Brendan could understand and speak Romanian on a decent level, but her words were mumbled, with a local dialect, so the words he was able to pick up were few and far between. Her expression revealed the tone of the conversation more than her words did. Her eyes began to shine. She blinked, and a tear ran down each cheek. The conversation was short, but it wasn't a catch up.

She handed the phone back to Brendan and nodded her head, wiping her eyes. 'Okay, what do you want me to do?'

Brendan took the phone and shoved it in his pocket. 'Tonight, nothing. Just act like everything is normal. If Dimitru asks, tell him you eventually got me to loosen up and have some fun with you.' He took his phone out again, unlocked it, and handed it back to her. 'Here, type your number in.'

She took the phone, her hands shaking. He watched as she blinked repeatedly, trying to blink the tears out. 'Here.' She handed the phone back to him.

'You've got a lovely name. Elena.'

'What happens now?'

'We stay up here for a while, then we go down looking more relaxed than we did when we came in. Do you know anything about his operations other than this place?'

'I know the police officers who are coming here are very influential people. They're taking payments off Dimitru to allow him to run his little scams. The officers come here every week and help themselves to whatever free women there are available.'

How long has this been going on?'

'Long time.'

'Does this place have security cameras?'

She looked at him, unsure what the question was.

'CCTV?' He pointed to the corner of the room. 'Camera.'

'Just the entrance.'

'Do you know how to copy the video from tonight? Of the officers who come here for some fun?'

She nodded. 'Yes.' She stood up, turned, and faced him. She straddled him. 'I'd still like to show you a fun time.' She leaned in to kiss him, but he turned his head to the right, her lips landing on his cheek.

'I'm sorry.' He turned and looked into her eyes. 'Believe me, you're very beautiful and I'd love to have you, but I have a girlfriend. And I can't cheat on her.' His eyes darted from her left to right eye. 'But believe me, you're a very beautiful lady.' He kissed her on the cheek. 'You deserve to meet a nice man. Don't spend your life having sex and selling your body for some very dirty men who deserve nothing but to have their dicks cut off.'

She laughed, nodding her head. She looked at him, stroking his face. 'You're a good man, Brendan.' She kissed him again on the cheek. 'Maybe one day I will meet my prince.'

'You will,' he said. 'But first we need to start by getting you and all the other ladies like you out of this terrible life.'

'How do we do this?'

'Just you worry about capturing the video of the police officers, and I will take care of the rest. But you must pretend that nothing is going on. Just act like we had amazing sex and Dimitru will be none the wiser.'

# Chapter Thirty-Six

BRENDAN TOOK A SHOWER in the en-suite. Elena had offered to rub him down, but he reminded her that that, too, would have been an intimate thing, and something only a loved one should do. He realised a lot of these women had perhaps never experienced a normal intimate relationship and didn't know what was and wasn't acceptable behaviour.

He took his time, knowing the longer he spent in the room, the more believable it would look to Dimitru.

Feeling refreshed and cleansed, Brendan stepped out of the shower, gun in his hand. Regardless of the conversation he'd just had, and the trust he had that Elena truly wanted to get out of there, he still felt it important to keep his weapon within reach in case someone decided to give him problems.

He set the weapon down on the toilet's cistern and stepped in front of the mirror. Wiping steam from the glass, he looked at himself: bare chested, slightly pink. He stood and looked at himself for a moment, gazing into his own eyes. Looking for the person he thought he was – a troubled lad from Belfast. Brendan Cleary, who'd gotten into trouble more times than he'd like to count. That person was gone. The man before him had matured, and that troubled lad wouldn't even stand in the shadows of the person he now was.

A knock came at the door. 'Brendan, your phone has been ringing. Many times.' Elena's voice came through.

'Come on in.' He turned to face the door.

She opened the door, slowly peaking her head in.

'It's okay, I'm covered up,' he laughed, pointing at the towel wrapped around his waist, covering his bottom half. 'There's no point in being shy now.'

She stepped in, her eyes fixed on his chest. 'Someone called Lorna.' She walked across the room, still focused on his chest. 'I didn't want to answer it in the event it was the lady of your heart.' She handed him the phone. 'Is this the woman?'

'Yes.' He unlocked the phone. Three missed calls. He called her back.

'Brendan, are you okay?' Lorna sounded worried, a highly-strung tone ringing through.

'Yes,' he said. 'Are you? What's with all the missed calls?'

'I just wanted to tell you I've spoken to our friend in England. She's on her way over tomorrow.'

'Good, we might be able to get our hands on some CCTV from this place that will very kindly incriminate the local PSNI.'

'From there?'

'Yes, they have security cameras at the front door. We're getting a visit from a couple of peelers who regularly come around for some group sex and blowjobs. They're on their way around soon.'

'This is exactly what she'll need; this'll be all over the media if she gets her hands on it.'

'How are the other two?'

'Teodoro has pretty much moved into the gym. And Diana, well, you can imagine how she's been feeling.'

'And you?'

'Sweetie.' Lorna spoke in a sarcastic tone, being overly playful with her words. 'It's so sweet of you to ask,' she laughed. 'I'll be better when you come back.'

'I'll be home later this evening.' He looked at Elena, who was looking quite out-of-place. Perhaps she wasn't used to being in a room with someone and not having to do whatever they wanted. 'I'll call you later. Dimitru's in good form tonight, I'm excited to see what he shows me.'

'You take care. You have your gun, Brendan?'

'Of course.'

'Okay, talk to you later.'

Brendan set the phone down on the table. He looked at Elena. 'You must have a million questions running through your head right now.' She nodded. 'Go to my wallet; it's in my jacket pocket. Take whatever money there is in it.'

'Dimitru told me not to charge you. You were to get whatever you wanted, for free.'

'Well then, Dimitru doesn't have to know. Keep it for yourself, and there will be plenty more where that came from.'

'Are you sure?'

'Yes, go on, take it.' Brendan turned and looked at himself in the mirror again. 'The next few days are going to be very different for you guys.' He turned and looked at her. 'But it'll be for the best.'

'Thank you.' She turned to leave the room, pulling the door closed on her way out, but she stopped and popped her head back in. 'One question?'

He looked at her.

'Why are you doing this?'

'Let's just say I know what it's like to be taken advantage of by those more powerful.' He looked at her again. She looked at him, her eyebrows touching, her eyes tiny slits. She went to say something but stopped herself and closed the door.

He turned and looked at himself again. 'You better know what the fuck you're doing, Brendan,' he warned himself. 'Can't be getting any of these people into trouble.'

After getting dried and dressed, Brendan stepped back into the room. Elena was sitting on the edge of the bed, a wad of notes clasped tightly in her hand. She had that weak, vulnerable look, her shoulders slumped forward, her knees pointing inward, touching.

Brendan walked over and sat down next to her. 'You okay?'

'If I get caught even talking to you about this, you know what he will do to me?'

'That's why we've got to pretend nothing is wrong. Everything is normal, okay?'

She looked back down at the notes, now crushed in her fists. 'Okay.' She stood up and looked at her watch. 'It is almost seven. The police clients will be arriving soon. We better go down.'

'No,' Brendan said, sounding forceful. He stood up, looking at her. 'The local police must not see my face. We need to make sure they're all in their rooms before I leave.'

As Brendan said this, he received a text. It was from Dimitru.

*How are you getting on up there, you horny bastard? I knew you weren't that much in love with the lovely English bit. It was certain you wouldn't pass up an opportunity to shag our little Romanian gem.*

Brendan handed Elena the phone. 'You see the type of person you're working for.'

She read the text, then mumbled something in Romanian. Brendan couldn't make out what it was. She looked up at him and handed him back the phone. 'What I said means he'll die like a squealing pig.'

Brendan took the phone back and smiled at her. 'I kind of got the meaning.' The phone buzzed again. He looked at it. Dimitru again.

*If you're not too weak at the knees, you can tag along with me, see some of our operations.*

Brendan replied.

*I'm happy to tag along, but I can't be seen by those peelers when they arrive. They're not a big fan of me and my family.*

*Okay. Stay up there until they're getting seen to, then I'll call you to come down. They've just arrived.*

Brendan dropped his phone back into his pocket and looked at Elena. She still had that lost puppy look in her eyes. 'It'll be okay, I promise.'

She stroked his face with the back of her hand. 'I hope so.'

# Chapter Twenty-Seven

TEN MINUTES LATER, at seven twenty-five, the text from Dimitru came through. As if in synch, Brendan could hear the rowdy voices from the three members of the local police service, trudging up the stairs. Brendan walked closer to the door, listening, recognising one of the voices. One of the dirtiest cops in the city. Brendan had dealt with him in the past. Desmond Montgomery.

As he listened to them laughing and joking, he turned and looked at the now increasingly anxious Elena. Her expression spoke volumes about her current state of mind.

'Hey,' Brendan said. She looked at him. 'I need you to stay calm, can you do that?'

She nodded. 'I can.'

'Good.'

The laughter outside the room faded away.

'Where will they be going?'

She looked up at the ceiling. 'They get the big rooms, on the next floor.'

Steps could be heard from above.

'Right, that's us, then.' Brendan placed his hand on the door handle.

She grabbed his arm. 'Please help us get away.' Her hand trembled.

'Christ, what have them bastards done to you?'

'Just promise me this will all stop.'

He shut the door again and stepped in closer to her. 'I promise everything will be okay.'

She smiled at him, then nodded. 'Okay.'

He turned and opened the door.

They made their way down the hallway. Music could be heard playing from the rooms up on the next floor. Turning onto the stairway, Brendan saw Dimitru standing at the bottom, on the phone. His face was a light red complexion, with moisture causing his skin to glisten in the artificial light. Continuous rubbing of his nose and sniffing made him look on edge.

He looked up at Brendan and Elena, grinning. 'You had fun then?'

Brendan looked back at her, smirking. She smiled back at him, not taking any notice of her employer at the bottom of the stairs.

Dimitru laughed. 'I knew you were a dog, Brendan Cleary.' Dimitru slapped him across the back as he got to the bottom of the stairs. 'She's hard to say no to, isn't she?'

'Very hard,' Brendan said.

'Let's go, we have a meeting in one hour.'

'Who's the meeting with?'

'Just the team. Some of them are a bit nervous about the arrival of the boss man.' He looked at Elena, then back at Brendan.

'Why?' Brendan said. 'He's a mean bastard, this boss man?'

Dimtru looked across at Elena again, then laughed. 'He's the craziest guy I've ever met. Even calling him that would get you butchered.' He slapped Brendan across the shoulder. 'But the boss is a businessman first, and you've already proven that you can be financially valuable to us.' He looked across at Elena, who now draped over Brendan's shoulder. 'She likes you, my friend. Maybe you'll be back for her again.'

Brendan looked at her. 'I'll definitely be back for her.' He turned and looked at Dimitru, his smile dropping. 'But first, let's tend to your business.' He turned to Elena again. 'Was lovely to meet you.' He kissed Elena on the cheek, then looked into her eyes. 'I'll see you again soon, okay?'

She smiled. 'I look forward to it.'

Brendan turned and led the way down the hall towards the front door.

The night was cool. A damp smell lingered following the earlier rain. He led the way to the car. Before he got in, he scanned the area. He looked at the door; it hadn't been tampered with. He dropped to the ground, into a press-up position, and activated the torch on his Samsung. He cast the light across the engine, and all around the bottom of the car. Satisfied nothing had been fitted to it, he got back to his feet.

Dimitru was standing at the passenger's door, looking across the roof at Brendan. 'You're paranoid.'

'Don't take it personally.' Brendan unlocked the car and got in.

Dimitru dropped himself into the passenger seat. 'I don't.' He pulled his phone out, looking at it to see what had caused the melody. 'Good. They're all there.' He looked at Brendan. 'We're going to an old barn, just over the cave hill. You know the Seven Mile Straight Road? You can get to it by passing Ballysillan, and continuing up the country roads over the...'

'I know the road,' Brendan interrupted. He put the car in gear and pulled off a speedy U-turn, taking them back onto the Cliftonville Road. They headed north. He put the window down as Dimitru lit up another cigarette. 'You should really consider giving them up. If you want to live long.'

'I love smoking,' Dimitru protested. 'I will smoke even after it kills me.'

Brendan laughed. He could still find the levity in Dimitru's insanity.

The Range Rover negotiated the hills and windy roads with ease. Five miles along the road, after passing a half-dozen farm houses, Dimitru indicated for Brendan to take the second right, down a quiet, hidden country lane—an unmarked single-track that came to a dead end on approach to a rusted fence that stood as the grounds' perimeter.

'You wanted this to be private,' Brendan said, guiding the car through the gates, into the carpark. 'Well done, you definitely achieved that.' He reverse parked in the bay with the straightest run towards the gate.

There were five cars: two white Mercedes, a grey Audi, and two black BMWs. All lined up in the corner of the carpark.

Brendan put the car in neutral and regarded the other vehicles. 'Is this a big meeting?'

'You could say that.' Dimitru turned and looked at Brendan. 'You of all people will love this, Brendan.' He opened the door and got out. 'I've got another nice surprise for you.'

Brendan shut the engine off and got out. 'You're full of surprises.' He checked that his pistol was still in its holster, under his arm.

Dimitru laughed, as he always did after Brendan said something. 'You're the most valuable guy the family has come across, and we want to repay the favour to you.' Dimitru led the way towards the warehouse entrance. Brendan followed.

Brendan's senses sharpened. His eyes scanned the area. Was he walking into a trap, or was he just being paranoid? Either way, he needed to go on with it. He couldn't turn back.

There was an awkward silence as the two of them progressed across the carpark. As they got to the entrance, voices could be heard. The tone of the noise was high pitched, good energy. Dimitru shouted "police" in Romanian, then followed it up with his usual laughter. A large silhouette was drawn across the front door's stained glass. The door opened and Andrei appeared. He shook Dimitru's hand, then offered the same courtesy to Brendan. Brendan responded to keep the peace, regardless of how he truly felt about him.

'Is everyone here?' Dimitru said, stepping inside.

Brendan followed him in. Andrei closed the door and locked it.

'Everyone is here, boss,' another guy shouted from the dated reception desk. He sat in the chair, his feet up on the desk, relaxing.

'Brendan, meet Peter, my younger brother,' Dimitru said, making his way through the reception area towards the office to the back of it.

Brendan looked at Peter on the way past the reception desk. 'Pleasure.'

'Pleasure is all ours.' Peter spoke mockingly.

In the office there was a group of five, all sitting together. One of them was the other doorman Brendan had floored in the Red Brick. He looked at Brendan, then looked away. The laughter and chatter in the room fell into silence as Dimitru took the seat behind the desk, like a king seated on the throne.

'Brendan, you've already met Alexandru,' Dimitru said, looking at the one with whom Brendan had had the altercation. He pointed at the man immediately to his right. 'This is Adrian.' He then pointed to a group of two who were sitting on the sofa, smoking cigars. 'Meet Marian, and Marius.' He swivelled around in his chair and pointed at the overweight guy plopped on a stool. 'This is my number one cousin – Cristian.'

Brendan looked at each of them. 'Pleasure.'

Cristian stood up and trudged his way around the desk, offering his hand to Brendan. 'For your help in London, thank you.'

Brendan accepted and shook his hand.

Alexandru stood up next, towering over Brendan. Brendan's instinct was to plaster him before the giant got his chance to do something, but instead, Alexandru imitated Cristian.

Brendan accepted.

'Does he know about our little surprise?' Alexandru said, looking at Dimitru.

'Just about to tell him.' Dimitru stood up, walking over to the filing cabinet. He pulled out a brown folder, turned, and tossed it down on the desk, sending it sliding across.

'What is this?' Brendan walked over to the desk and picked it up.

'Your surprise.' Dimitru sat back down and pulled open the drawer to his left, pulling out a bottle of whiskey and a glass.

Brendan sat down opposite Dimitru, feeling all eyes in the room on him. He opened the folder. An inch-thick cluster of printed documents. The front page had the address in the Shankill Road. Brendan flicked through the documents. There were a number of properties and none of them popped out at him, until he spotted the outside of the café he'd been to for breakfast that morning. He pulled it out, looked at it, then at Dimitru. 'What the fuck is this?'

'That's your Aunty Mary's business, isn't it?'

Brendan glared across the desk at him.

'I'm not watching your family, Brendan. I have no interest. Why would I?'

'Then why these?'

'Friends of your old buddy Johnty Burrows asked us to keep an eye on them and wait for a moment to attack. You upset a lot of people when poor old Johnty died.'

'So why haven't you passed the information on to them? I'm guessing your little deal with the UDA won't be very healthy if you decide to go against them.'

'Because I have a better proposition for you, Brendan.' Dimitru took a drink from his whiskey and swallowed it, gasping as he looked at the side of the glass. 'Irish whiskey is the best.' He looked at Alexandru and grinned. Then he looked back at Brendan. 'We're about to put the protestant paramilitaries out of business in Belfast. We have locations of their arms. We have locations of the most powerful people in the organisation and have set up a meeting with our boss back home and the bosses of the UDA. Once that is done, once the UDA cease to be a threat, we will then run these depressing streets of Belfast.'

Brendan looked down at the documents, then back up at Dimitru.

'These sons of bitches want to hurt your family, Brendan. We want to repay the favour to you, for what you did for us in London. Like I said, I think we will have a very lucrative relationship. We can dispose of these paramilitaries, keep your family alive, and get very, very rich.' He looked around the room.

Brendan didn't know how to respond. He lied. 'I want to know exactly who ordered you to collect this information.'

'Yes. Yes. Of course.' Dimitru finished his glass and poured another. 'When we have them, I will make sure you're there to see us finish them.' He took another drink. 'You can even end their lives if you want to.'

'We're going to bring a shit storm to Belfast,' Cristian said, his expression and tone emotionless.

'A fucking Irish massacre,' Marius laughed.

Brendan looked at Marius, forcing a sarcastic smile. 'You're all fucking crazy. You start killing people, you'll put them on alert, and others will know you're coming for them.'

'Not if you do it all at once,' Cristian said.

'Yes,' Dimitru agreed. 'We put them all in one room and exterminate them all at the same time.'

The enormity of the situation was becoming clear to Brendan. Belfast was about to witness it's greatest massacre in a generation. He now had to decide whether and how was he going to approach this. He knew one thing – he'd made a promise to Elena, and he was going to keep it. 'How do you plan on bringing all these guys into one room together?'

'Mr Dalca has a long-standing tie with the head of the UDA here in Belfast. This is the reason the UDA believe the boss is coming here. But of course, as you know, the real reason is...'

'To see me and how I can grow his empire.'

'You see Brendan, the leaders of the UDA will come together out of respect for Dalca's efforts to come here. Therefore, they'll all assemble in one place, believing this is a friendly exchange. Then you enter, and we serve the people up who are watching your family, and in return, you go into business with us. Once we take over Belfast, the next place will be England, then...' He downed his whiskey. 'Who knows!'

'You said you have information on all major crime syndicates around the world?' Alexandru asked.

Brendan nodded. 'Lorna was very high up in British Intelligence.'

'Well, that's why you're still breathing after your little stunt in the Red Brick,' Alexandru said.

Brendan turned, looking directly at Alexandru. 'I'm still breathing because you weren't capable of causing me any harm.' Brendan spoke sharply and to the point. He looked at Dimitru, then back at Alexandru. 'Don't ever forget that.'

There was a tense silence.

Dimitru laughed, standing up. 'That's exactly why I know we're going to get on very well.' He walked around the table, taking centre stage in the room. 'Now, Mr Dalca is arriving tomorrow night. He's arrived in London this evening. Tomorrow night, we'll be treating him to a nice evening with the beautiful ladies of Clifton House, then we'll spend the evening getting acquainted.' He looked at Brendan. 'You will have an opportunity to sit down with him and discuss further your plans to make us all very rich.'

There was a collective cheer from the others. Brendan looked at them all, smirking. They all looked happy with what was about to become their future—or what they *believed* was about to become their future. But Brendan did not care about their future, he was more concerned about the poor girls who had suffered at their and their customers' hands. And Teodoro. The young lad whose next few years could mould him into either someone the world could do without, or someone the world could benefit from.

'So tonight, we will introduce Brendan to our world. Show him exactly what we've already got,' Dimitru said. 'But first, we toast. To our new friend. And a beautiful new relationship.'

Everyone in the room stood up, raised their beverages in the air, and looked at Brendan as if in salute.

'To new ventures.' Dimitru held his glass out in front of him, smiling at Brendan. Then he downed the drink. The others followed his example. 'This is going to be something big. I feel it.'

Brendan looked around the room at them all, smiling. 'Me, too.'

# Chapter Twenty-Eight

HEADING BACK TOWARDS Belfast, Brendan led the entourage of six cars. Dimitru had produced the bag of cocaine and was dipping the tip of his baby finger in, as if it were a kid's sour dip. He was in high spirits, like he'd just found a winning lottery ticket. He'd felt obliged to share with Brendan his memories of good times back in Romania and London, as well as his hopes and dreams for the future. The information Brendan and Lorna possessed was lucrative data for any criminal hoping to take over the game

Brendan was eager to see an end to them all. Dimitru was a man who'd just found his cash cow, and Brendan was about to take it away from him and then some. He didn't only want to hurt the local criminal network but cripple it. And if he could bring down any local corrupt officials, then he'd be even happier. Cutting the head off the snake is only useful if you can remove anything and anyone that could be of assistance in bringing the serpent back to life, like certain corrupt cops who'd probably become accustomed to the benefits that had fallen their way.

'Tell me about the police who were at Clifton House this evening,' Brendan said as the vehicle crawled over the mountainous road overlooking the city. 'Are they on your payroll or on the UDA's?'

'They're employed by us,' Dimitru shouted. 'They paid us a visit when we first opened the house. They threatened to close us down. When we offered them a free chance to try the goods, they changed their minds and were more understanding and supportive of the business.' He sniggered. 'Human greed is never too far away, Brendan. It doesn't matter where in the world you are – Romania, Ireland, England, wherever, people are all the same.' He looked out the window. 'Some sweet ass, drugs and money can make even the most honest people become tainted.'

'Was it the officers who helped you find out where my family live?' Brendan quickly glanced at Dimitru as the steep drop came to a stop at a red light.

Dimitru nodded. 'I respect you, Brendan.' He lit up a cigarette. 'I know your entire story. Your father: The Ghost. You killing Johnty Burrows for talking shit about your grandfather the day he was buried.' He took a long draw of the cigarette. 'I know it all. And I respect everything you've had to deal with. So, I'm not going to lie to you. The three cops that were at Clifton House this evening were the ones who'd supplied us with the information about your family's location.'

Brendan didn't speak for a moment. His eyebrows met in the middle. His nostrils flared. His gaze was fixed on the traffic lights, waiting for them to turn green.

'What's going through that head of yours?'

'I want them to be at the meeting tomorrow, along with the rest of them.' Brendan put the car in gear and took off towards the city centre again. Dimitru didn't respond. Brendan quickly glanced at him. Dimitru's eyes were fixed on his phone. 'Did you hear that?'

Dimitru pulled his eyes away from the device. 'Yes. I'll see what I can do. I wonder can we stop off at my house again on our way into town? I want to check if my bitch wife has arrived home yet. I've not had any missed calls from her, or any texts at all. This is not like her at all. It's very strange.'

Brendan nodded and took the next turn off the road they were currently on, making his way towards Ballysillan. 'It might look a little dodgy if all these cars roll into that little street of yours.'

Dimitru pressed the phone to his ear and nodded to agree. 'I'll tell them to meet us at the docks. Pull over.'

Brendan indicated, then made his move, pulling over on the side of the road just beyond a bus stop. The five vehicles behind them had done the same. Dimitru jumped out, slamming the door behind him. Brendan watched in the rear-view mirror, then took the opportunity to check his phone. There were two missed calls and the same number of text messages. He unlocked the phone and went into the message box. One of the messages was from Lorna. The other was from Elena.

The message from Lorna was her checking in on him. He called her, keeping his eyes on the rear-view.

'Brendan, are you okay?' Lorna sounded worried.

'I'm fine. I met with the rest Dimitru's crew. They're planning a massacre. They're taking out the leaders of the UDA, all in one sitting.'

'Jesus Christ.'

'Yeah. That's why the big boss is coming over from Romania.'

'When does he arrive?'

'He's in London tonight. He's flying into Belfast tomorrow evening. I'll get a chance to spend the evening with him and the lovely ladies down at Clifton House.'

'Did you have fun down there?'

Brendan laughed. 'I had to go into a room with one of the girls. Elena is her name. She's going to help us.'

'Great. If she could fit some cameras into the rooms, then we could have the video footage sent out to every major news broadcast here and in England.'

'What about your friend?'

'She's in the mood to start chopping balls off,' Lorna said humorously, then slowed down, her voice lowering. 'Diana tells me there is a house where all the ladies live together. Six to a room, sharing beds. A real pigsty. We need to get them out of there as well.'

'Does she know where it is?'

'Yes. She doesn't know the name of the streets or post code. But she said if she's in Belfast, she can take me to it.'

'Think she'll want to come back here?'

'She said try and stop her.'

Brendan sniggered. 'Great.' He could see Dimitru making his way back to the car. 'I gotta go. I'll call you back soon.' He hung up just as Dimitru jumped back in again.

'They'll meet us down there.'

'Do you have access to the docks? No security issues?' Brendan said as he put the car in gear, continuing up the road.

'All taken care of, Brendan. We have friends on the pay-roll everywhere and dockside security is no different. And it's the best place for us to store our stuff.' He laughed, sounding like he was getting one up on local law enforcement.

'Really, you think so?'

'Well, it's the last place anyone would ever think to look for anything illegal. So yes.' Dimitru trailed off, looking at his phone again. 'Where is this bitch? She's starting to piss me off.'

'Who?' Brendan knew exactly who he was referring to.

'My wife. She's not answering any of my calls.'

'She'll not be too far, I'm sure.'

Brendan turned right onto the Ballysillan Road and let the car build up momentum as gravity pulled it down the hill. He turned left into the street, parking directly outside the house. It was still in darkness.

'Fuck it, let's not waste time, she's obviously not here.' Dimitru put the window down and lit up another cigarette. 'Just take us to the docks.' He fixed his mobile to the dashboard cradle and activated Google Maps. He punched in a post code and address. 'Take us here.'

The next fifteen minutes in the car were quiet. Dimitru's mind was elsewhere, perhaps wondering where his wife and son had gone. He spent the entire journey, from his house right down to Heron View Road, with his eyes fixed on his phone screen. Brendan laughed when he pulled the car in through the gates of the warehouse. A sandwich production firm. But what was more intriguing was the building right next to it: a nationwide security company. And operating their little business directly next to such a company proved Dimitru was either stupid and reckless, or he had a level of tenacity that could work well for him, or against him.

Brendan pulled the car up next to Alexandru's black BMW. The five other cars were parked and empty.

Brendan shut off the engine and looked at Dimitru. 'That's a bold move.'

'What?' Dimitru looked at him, his eyes narrowed.

Brendan nodded his chin in the direction of the neighbouring factory. 'Or do you have them on the payroll, too?'

'We have many people on our payroll, Brendan.' Dimitru flung the door open and got out. 'When we take over this depressing city, it will simply be a formality.'

Brendan followed him out. Slamming the door shut, he didn't speak, his mouth closed, his ears on open. He followed Dimitru towards the side of the warehouse, along a narrow-paved pathway that led around to the back. Faded orange street lighting was their only assistance to see where they were going, until they approached the back; a bright white light illuminated the area, a goods in bay, marked but worn.

'The goods are sandwiches, or something else?' Brendan laughed, pointing at the white marking he was walking over.

'Sandwiches don't pay enough,' Dimitru said, leading the way in through the huge rolling door that was raised almost to the roof.

As they entered the warehouse, the others were busy shifting wooden crates around. Alexandru was behind the wheel of a forklift, moving a stack of crates to the far end of the warehouse, closer to the offices.

'There aren't sandwiches in there,' Brendan said.

Both made their way across the cold warehouse. The sound of wooden crates being cracked open with crowbars sent echoes bouncing off the four walls. When Marius pulled out an automatic weapon, Brendan's eyebrows raised. 'You're certainly planning to make a lot of noise.'

'We mean business,' Dimitru said, still looking at his phone.

'Are you going to keep your eyes on your phone until she calls?' Brendan snapped. 'You can't let your woman distract you from what you're doing.'

Dimitru stopped in his tracks, looking directly at Brendan, his eyes almost cutting a hole through him.

'Get your head together before you get us all fucking killed. Or make a mess of these big plans of yours.' Brendan was pushing Dimitru.

Dimitru forced his phone into his pocket and pulled out his cigarettes.

'And you smoke far too many of those things, too,' Brendan complained.

'Fuck you,' Dimitru sniggered, making his way towards the toilets.

Brendan walked over to the crates that were now open. Looking inside, he found a cluster of handguns. He reached in and lifted one out.

'We have bigger weapons in this one over here,' Cristian shouted, tapping on the crate Alexandru had just shuffled across the floor.

Brendan wiped his prints off the pistol and set it back in with the others.

As Brendan made his way towards Cristian, Dimitru's second in command pulled out an AK47 and pointed it at him. Brendan continued towards him. 'I could blow your head off right now,' Cristian laughed.

'You could, but you're not as dumb as you look,' Brendan said as he approached him, taking the weapon off him.

'You'll get yours one day, Mr Above It All.'

'That I don't doubt,' Brendan spoke out of the side of his mouth, dismissively addressing the Romanian. He inspected the gun, looking at it up and down. He grunted and handed it back over again.

'Stop toying around and come in here,' Dimitru shouted from the door leading into the offices.

As they all entered the office, Brendan regarded the cluster of monitors on top of the filing cabinet behind the desk. Dimitru was crouched down on his honkers, his head inside the boxy safe that sat in the corner. He pulled out a stack of documents and stood up straight. He chucked them down on the desk, sliding them across towards Brendan.

Brendan grabbed them. 'What are these?' He sat on the edge of the desk and opened them. A compilation of printed photos of three PSNI officers. Two of them in uniform. The third, who looked like he was in charge, was dressed in a three-piece suit. Brendan skimmed through the photos, images of the officers receiving their benefits in the privacy of the bedrooms of Clifton House. Many of the photos showed the boss of the three officers being tied up by a lady and being whipped.

Brendan smirked and looked up at Dimitru. 'This could be very embarrassing for the local police service.'

'Keep going,' Dimitru said, pouring more cocaine out onto the desk.

Brendan continued to flick through the documents. Copies of text messages and emails discussed the search for and whereabouts of the Cleary family. The emails came from the Assistant Chief Constable for the Police Service of Northern Ireland.

'Dirty bastards.' Brendan gazed at the documents.

'Yes, they are,' Dimitru said. He pulled a bank card from his wallet, chopping through the cocaine. 'I own these bastards.' He stood up, dragging an inch thick, six-inch-long line away from the pile. Pulling a twenty-pound note from his wallet, he rolled it up and crouched down. The line disappeared up the roll into his left nostril. He straightened himself up, glaring at Brendan with his glassy eyes. 'I own the fucking law enforcement. With your help, I'll own the entire criminal network, too. And there won't be a fucking thing anyone will be able to do about it.' He laughed. 'I can make you very rich, Brendan.' He looked over Brendan's shoulder. 'We're going to have a lot of fun.'

Brendan stood up off the table, throwing the documents down on the desk. 'You need to go easy on that shite before it rots your nose and your brain.'

Dimitru laughed, then sat back down in his chair. 'That's why I love you, Brendan. There is no bullshitting with you. You tell it how it is.'

'It'll get you killed one day,'Alexandru said, barging his shoulders into Brendan's as he passed him around the desk. He lifted the rolled note and helped himself to a line.

'Alexandru, Brendan is our friend,' Dimitru said humorously.

'That's right,' Cristian said, joining Alexandru alongside Dimitru.

Brendan watched as they all helped themselves to the white stuff. He looked at the monitors. Walking closer to them, he spotted Elena in one of the rooms of Clifton House, being tied up by one of the punters. From the distance, the camera couldn't give a clear view of her face, but it looked as if she were crying. Brendan thought of that being Lorna. His gut wrenched, his jaws clenched.

'Having a little sneak peek of the show are we?' Dimitru said. He stood up and joined Brendan at the monitors. 'Yes, I knew she would be popular among the customers.' He laughed, putting his arm around Brendan. 'I'm glad you got to have her sweet little pussy first.' He pulled Brendan in closer in a brotherly embrace.

'She was a good fuck,' Brendan lied, wanting to end Dimitru's life there and then. 'So what time will Dalca be arriving tomorrow?'

'His flight lands in the city airport around seven in the evening.' Dimitru turned and went back to his desk, helping himself to another line. He sat down again. 'So, the plan is to treat him to a nice evening at Clifton House, then we'll go for a drink. You two can get acquainted, talk to him about your business plans. Then later we'll be having our meeting with heads of the UDA.'

'Where is the meeting taking place?' Brendan asked.

'The little barn we were at earlier,' Cristian said.

'You must have a strong stomach, to see what we've got planned,' Alexandru laughed. 'It might scare you.'

Brendan looked at him and smirked. 'Don't worry about me.'

'Yes, don't worry about him.' Dimitru sprung up and walked around the desk, acting restless. 'This guy can more than look after himself.' He slapped Brendan across the upper arm. 'Now that you've seen our operations, let's go for a drive. I want to talk with you in private before we end the night.'

'I can't be out too late, I'm having dinner with Lorna.'

Dimitru turned to the others. 'Make sure everything is ready for tomorrow. I don't want any fuckups.' He pulled the door open and left the room.

Brendan followed, through the foyer and back out into the airy warehouse. He regarded the stack of crates as they made their way towards the door. 'You won't need all that tomorrow night.'

'We won't,' Dimitru said, pulling his phone from his pocket. 'Bitch still hasn't replied.' He stopped as Brendan caught up. He looked at the crates. 'But it's better to have them and not need them, than to need them and not have them.' He made a call and continued towards the exit.

Brendan unlocked the car and they got in. He started the engine. 'Anywhere in particular you want to go?'

Dimitru dropped the window. 'Just a drive. Didn't want to talk to you in front of the rest of the guys.'

'Why? They're your crew. Why do you need to keep things from them?'

'I don't. Alexandru is a loose cannon. He hasn't forgiven you for that little stunt you pulled in the pub. I love him, but for some reason I can't talk him around about you.'

'Let him come speak to me then. He and I can sort it out between the two of us.'

'We both know how that would end.' Dimitru flicked his cigarette butt out of the window, closing the window again. 'I'm just telling you to watch your back around him.'

'Thanks,' Brendan said. 'Appreciate it.'

'Good, now show me what this piece of shite car can do, then take me home. If my bitch wife isn't there, then internet porn will just have to be my company for the night.'

Brendan laughed and shook his head.

# Chapter Twenty-Nine

BRENDAN ARRIVED BACK at Donegal shortly after ten-thirty. It was dark, quiet and peaceful. As he got out of the car, he questioned why he didn't spend more time in this location. Belfast was where he'd spent most of his years, but this was a different world. Peace and quiet. Tranquil. But he thought about how bored he would have become staying here. He'd always been more interested in being with his mates, running the streets of West Belfast. Perhaps being away from his friends every summer, when his father had taken him away for his training, was what caused that longing to spend more time with his peers. But now, after the mayhem that had become his life, this environment was more welcoming in his overly aroused state—constantly on the run from some very powerful people, unable to switch off the fear of being caught or killed. He guessed he now knew how it felt to be his late father.

As he shut the car door, he could hear mumbles coming from around the side of the house. Instead of going in the front door, he followed the voices, taking him to the back finding Lorna and Diana sat at the garden table next to the pool. The pool lights caused the garden to glow indigo in the night.

Brendan cleared his throat as he came within twenty feet of them. Both of their heads shot around, perhaps unsure who it was.

'You scared the shit out of me,' Lorna gasped, clasping her pistol. She set it back down on the table. 'We weren't expecting you back for another few hours.'

'I got tired of listening to their bullshit.' Brendan sat down at the table, reaching over to a sliver tray, lifting the moka pot, checking if there was anything left inside. There was. He poured himself a cup, but it was cold.

'I'll go and make some more,' Lorna said, but before she got up, Diana shot up from her seat and grabbed the tray.

'I'll make the coffee.' Diana smiled, although still sounding nervous. 'I want to check on Teodoro anyway.' She turned and made her way towards the house.

'Is she okay?' Brendan threw his thumb in Diana's direction.

'What do you think?' Lorna said. She lifted a grape from a fruit bowl sat in the middle of the table. She threw it into her mouth and sat forward. 'So?'

'Dimitru's a piece of shit.'

'We've already established that.'

Brendan smirked. 'True.' He sat forward and took a grape, imitating Lorna. 'They've been watching my family. My Aunt Mary, at her business on the Antrim Road.'

'Your father's sister?'

He nodded. 'Dimitru claims the UDA had asked them to look up the Cleary clan.'

'Doesn't sound like the work of the UDA.'

'It doesn't, regardless of what my mother's brother Ivan thought of my father, they never would have fucked with a guy's family.'

'Ivan?'

'The bastard that hated his little sister for marrying my father and giving birth to a wee shit like me.'

'He's still in the UDA?'

'Christ, he helped form it in the early seventies.'

'That's right, I remember you telling me this before.' She sat back in her chair. 'So, what are Dimitru's plans?'

'He plans a massacre. Take out all the big players in the UDA—perhaps my uncle Ivan will be amongst them—and take over the entire criminal network in Belfast.'

'And when does this massacre take place?'

'Tomorrow night or the next day.' Brendan grabbed another grape and tossed it into his mouth, sitting back in his chair. 'Mr Dalca, the head of the Romanian family, is in London tonight. He's visiting his men over there. Then tomorrow evening he lands in Belfast. I'll get a chance to meet with him. Dimitru wants me to talk over what we can do to make him very rich with our little business proposition.'

'So, taking over Belfast will be a little trial run, then it'll be on to other patches.' Lorna sat forward again. She looked at him, shaking her head. 'What did you see tonight?'

'They have an arms depot on the docks.' He laughed, sitting forward again. 'Right next to the local security firm. They've got a lot of people in their pocket. I know where they've got dirt on the cops, including the Assistant Chief Constable. Some very incriminating stuff. Dimitru's gathered dirt on the police to hold against them. He's not stupid.'

'People in his position rarely are,' Lorna said. 'The foot soldiers – dumb as a bucket of shrimp. But the bosses can't afford to be. They're very cunning. Or they perish. It's that simple.'

'He's definitely that,' Brendan agreed, watching Diana approach with the coffee. 'But he's not walking away from this.'

'So, what's the plan for tomorrow?' Diana said, setting the tray down and taking her seat.

Brendan grabbed the moka pot and poured three coffees. 'Tomorrow, I need you to stay away from Dimitru until this is all done.' Brendan looked at her. 'Can I trust you to stay away, and keep that eager son of yours who's itching to hurt someone?'

'I'm coming back to Belfast to help the other girls, but I'll stay away from him. And let me worry about Teodoro,' Diana said, looking over the rim of her cup at Brendan.

'You'll need me to stay close, but not too close,' Lorna said. 'If something goes wrong, you'll need me around. If we're together we're no use to each other. If I'm too far, I'm useless.'

Brendan nodded. 'I'll just be getting acquainted with Dalca. I'll find out exactly where the meeting is being held. Then during the meeting, where they plan on carrying out the massacre, you can get the girls that work for them.' Brendan looked at Diana. 'Elena and the rest.' He took a sip of his coffee. 'How many of them are there?'

'About thirty girls in Belfast,' Diana said. 'There are loads more in London.'

'Well, we can get them some point down the line,' Lorna said.

Brendan downed his coffee and stood up. 'I'm going for a run before going to sleep. May as well make use of this place and its location.'

AFTER HIS RUN, BRENDAN entered the house, soaked to the bone. His clothes were drenched from the inside out. He pulled his hoodie and t-shirt off as he climbed the stairs, heading to the bathroom. He couldn't get them off fast enough, almost as if the garments were on fire, but the t-shirt was glued to his torso like another layer of skin. As he got to the bedroom, he could hear the TV from inside.

Lorna was lying on the bed, watching the widescreen mounted on the wall facing her. The news was on. She looked at him, her eyes heavy, barely open, but even through the tiny slits, she looked happy to see him. 'I was dosing off there.'

'I'm just going for a shower. Anything interesting on the news?'

'Same old nonsense.' She sat up, pointing the remote control, switching the TV off.

'I'm just jumping in the shower; be out in a few minutes. Go on to sleep.'

She rolled off the bed, slowly straightening herself up. 'I actually fancy a cup of hot chocolate. Do you fancy one?'

Brendan laughed. 'That's random. But yeah, why not?' He pulled off his tracksuit bottoms and grabbed a fresh towel from the wardrobe.

He ran the shower at a low temperature, trying to slow down his heart rate and drop his temperature back to normal. He'd spent the last few minutes of the run in a sprint, which always finished the job.

Switching on the waterproof radio that was fixed to the tiled shelf, he got Radio FM Donegal. The night shift hadn't started yet and the station was on the last few songs of heavy metal. Metallica was now resounding throughout the bathroom. With his eyes closed, Brendan just stood under the showerhead, letting the water massage his neck.

He felt a sharp blast of cool air. As he opened his eyes, Lorna was stepping into the shower, pulling the door closed behind her. 'I wanted hot chocolate, but I actually want something else.' She stepped up to him, looking directly into his eyes. She kissed him, slowly walking him back towards the wall. He ran his fingers though her hair and spun her around, pinning her against the wall. Their kiss grew in intensity. He lifted her and she wrapped her legs around his waist.

# Chapter Thirty

BRENDAN'S ALARM WENT off at the usual time: five-thirty. He reached below the pillow for his phone, frantically wrestling with it to kill the sound. He was glad he'd managed another good night's sleep, not waking until the alarm. For a while, he'd been waking long before the device was due to wake him, so the initial shock of being woken by the device helped jumpstart him.

Once he'd silenced it, he left it on the bedside cabinet. He dropped his head down on the pillow. Still only semi-conscious, he was drifting back to sleep when Lorna rolled over from her side, resting her head on his chest.

'Morning,' she groaned.

He grunted in response.

'Your phone's flashing,' she mumbled.

'Let it flash.'

She reached over him, grabbing his phone. 'Passcode is 2019?'

He nodded, his eyes still closed.

'It's from Dimitru.' She cleared her throat. 'He's asking you to come to Belfast this evening. Pick him up at his house at six-thirty to go and pick up the boss man from the airport.'

'Fine.'

'You're really tired this morning,' she said, setting the phone back down on the bedside cabinet. 'This must be the best night's sleep you've had in a long time.'

'I know,' he said, sitting up. 'It feels great, too.'

'You must have a settled mind, sleeping here.' She sat up beside him. 'I wonder how Diana and Teodoro slept.'

'Not great, I'd imagine.' Brendan rotated his legs off the bed, setting his feet down on the rug which the four legs of the king-sized bed rested. He stood up slowly, stretching out his limbs as he rose. 'I'm going to use the gym; that'll wake me up. I'll see you soon.'

'I'll come with you.' She jumped off the bed with more spring in her step. 'It's been a while since we actually trained together.'

'I don't want to embarrass you,' he teased, flinging a bundled-up pair of socks at her.

She quickly caught it and launched it back at him. 'I'm too quick for you, Cleary.'

As they made their way down the stairs, they could see the light from the kitchen spilling out into the living room. Brendan went first; Lorna followed. He reached the doorway and looked in. Diana sat on one of the stools at the central island, hunched forward, her elbows slumped on the table.

'Could you not sleep?' Brendan said, approaching her.

She looked around at him. 'He's been calling me all night.'

Brendan and Lorna each took a stool on the opposite side of the island. 'He's threatening to kill me if I don't go back home to be his bitch wife slave, as he likes to call me.'

'You can't go back to him,' Lorna said. 'You can't possibly want to go back to him. Do you?'

'I want to cut the bastard's balls off,' she spat, pushing the phone away from her. 'At least he's upset that I've left. At least I know it's had some kind of negative effect on him.'

Nodding his head, Brendan agreed. 'Yes, and it's going to be easier to take him out if he's not of sound mind. If you're playing with his mind, then it means he won't be truly focussed.'

'He'll definitely be worried about who you've gone to, and who now knows about what he's been doing to you,' Lorna said. 'The bastard.'

'Not only that, but he'll be wondering who I might have told about our accounts.' She sniggered, shaking her head. 'He thought he was so fucking smart, giving me access to his money. That way I'd be the one questioned about the contents.'

Lorna looked at Brendan. 'Go and get the laptop.' She looked back at Diana. 'You can access the accounts and make a transfer.'

Brendan went into the living room and grabbed the laptop from the sofa. Returning to the kitchen, he saw that Diana was now in tears. He set the laptop down on the table and flipped it open, tapping in the password then gave it to Diana.

'Have you slept at all?' he said as he went to the fridge.

'No.' Diana's answer was abrupt. She dragged the laptop closer to her and opened the browser.

Brendan brought back three bottles of water.

'I'll make some coffee,' Lorna said, making her way towards the fridge. 'I'm going to do some omelettes as well.'

'I'm not hungry,' Diana snapped. She accessed one of her bank accounts.

'You need to eat,' Brendan protested.

She swivelled the screen around for him to see. 'I'll eat when he's dead.'

Brendan looked closer at the screen. The balance was a staggering four million pounds. He looked at Diana. 'How many girls suffer at his hands?'

'Quite a few.'

'Well, you can divide this money out among you all.' Brendan turned the screen back around to her. 'See it as a little compensation for the shit you've all been put through.'

'This is only one account,' Diana said. 'There's much more.'

'Then that means much more compensation for you all,' Lorna called from the cooker. 'I'll make you some breakfast. If you don't want it, we'll share it between us.' She looked at Brendan. 'Your eyes are usually bigger than your belly.'

'Make some for Teodoro, too,' Brendan shouted.

Diana sniggered. 'He'll eat everything in the fridge if you let him.'

'With the amount of energy I've seen him burn off in the gym, it wouldn't surprise me.' Brendan stood up. 'I'll go and see if he wants me to teach him a few things in the gym this morning.'

'Maybe he can teach *you* a thing or two,' Lorna said, cracking eggs into a mixing bowl.

'Probably,' Brendan said, making his way through the living room and up the stairs towards Teodoro's room. He knocked on the door. Unexpectedly, Teodoro pulled the door open within seconds, dressed in a white t-shirt and navy jogging bottoms.

'You going somewhere?' Brendan said.

'I'm going to make use of that gym of yours.'

'Great. Lorna's making some breakfast first.'

# Chapter Thirty-One

AT THREE-THIRTY IN the afternoon, Brendan had a shower and checked his father's pistol, the one that had earned the late Damien Cleary the title of "The Ghost". The weapon had been given to Brendan in Milan by the second-in-command and son of the head of the Botticelli family, whom Brendan had helped get out of Italy in return for help saving Lorna.

As he sat on the bed and took the weapon apart, a ritual before going into something dangerous, he was visited by Teodoro.

The kid popped his head in the door. 'Can I come in?'

Brendan looked at him, nodded, then continued what he was doing.

'Is it broken?' Teodoro came in and sat on the desk chair, wheeling himself across the room, closer to Brendan. 'How'd you break it?'

Brendan smirked. 'It's not broken. I'm just cleaning it.' He began piecing it back together again. 'A tiny speck of dirt on this at the wrong time, and I might not come back here to teach you some more skills.'

'Dimitru always had guns in our house. But they were bigger. Like machine guns.'

'I couldn't walk into a bar, or wherever he plans on taking the boss, with a machine gun hidden in my coat.' He popped the last bullet into the magazine and slammed it into place. He looked at Teodoro. 'Are you okay?'

'I want to come to Belfast with you and see what you do.'

Brendan sighed, shaking his head. 'You really don't want any part of this, mate.' He stood up, putting on the holster. He fed the pistol into it's cradle and put his jacket on over the top. 'Trust me. You don't want his blood on your hands.' He grabbed his phone. 'Let's go and see the two ladies of the house.' He led the way out of the room and down the stairs. The news could be heard blaring from the TV in the kitchen.

'Why do I get the feeling this has something to do with us?' Brendan mumbled to himself. He entered the kitchen. Both Lorna and Diana were fixed on the TV.

Lorna's head swung around to Brendan and Teodoro. She turned back to the screen. 'Looks like the body count in London's rising. And there's been speculation that a turf war is breaking out.'

'More Romanian bodies?' Brendan stood behind Lorna, resting his hands on her shoulders.

'No. The Smith and Hyde clans, the two groups that have come to be known as modern-day Krays. A lot of their men have been found.' Lorna turned and gazed up at Brendan. 'They were all butchered.'

Brendan fixed his eyes on the screen, watching as the news reporter stood outside, delivering the programme.

*This appears to be a gangland style slaying. But with the savagery of these murders, this wasn't just a simple hit. This was a message, a clear message intended to instil fear. And it's safe to say that it will strike fear not only in the locals, but also other participants in this dark world. The question is, who did it?*

'Looks like Dimitru's boys in London are letting people know that they're ready to take over,' Lorna said.

'It's a good thing we're putting a stop to them, before it gets even bloodier,' Brendan said.

'Look, there's Uncle Andrei.' Teodoro pointed at the screen: a photo of a middle-aged man, wearing a black suit and sunglasses, getting out of a car. The reporter continued.

*This man's name is Andrei Dalca. He is said to be a prominent figure in the Romanian underground, seen in this photograph getting out of a car at London Gatwick. This appearance comes just days after members of the Romanian underground were found dead in a massacre of a similar style as the ones we are witnessing here today.*

Diana was fixed on the TV, her eyes almost popping out of their sockets. Brendan looked at her. She turned and looked at him. 'Be careful, Brendan. He is one very dangerous man. Ruthless.'

'I'll show him ruthless,' Brendan said.

'He doesn't travel alone,' Diana said. 'His men are very good at blending into the background, making it look as if he's on his own. But in fact, he'll be surrounded by many guards, all waiting to put a bullet in anyone who tries to attack him.'

Lorna stood up and walked towards the door. 'They'll not be the only ones blending into the background. I'll fucking show them.'

Brendan's phone rang. He looked at it. 'It's Dimitru. Everyone keep quiet.' He answered. 'Dimitru?'

'Have you been watching the TV?'

'Just seen Dalca.'

'We've got a rat among us.' He cleared his throat. 'What time can I expect to see you?'

'Hold on a second.' Brendan looked at Diana, then Lorna. 'You've just told me there's a fucking rat?'

'We know who it is. And they'll be joining us tonight. It'll be their last supper.'

'Who is it?'

'It's funny you should ask, because it's the one who spiked your and the lovely Lorna's drinks in the Red Brick.'

'How do you know he's been ratting on you?'

'Because he let something slip that he shouldn't have known,' Dimitru sniggered. 'Stupid bastard shouldn't have taken a drink. Loose lips sink ships.'

'I'll be at your house by six.'

'Can you make it five-thirty? We're picking Mr Dalca up from the airport at seven-thirty and I don't want to be late.'

Brendan looked at Diana, then Lorna. 'Well, it's his first time coming over. Hopefully it won't be his last. See you at five-thirty.' Brendan hung up and looked at Teodoro, then Diana. 'You guys alright?'

Neither of them spoke.

# Chapter Thirty-Two

SHORTLY AFTER THREE-thirty in the afternoon, Brendan left in the Range Rover. He set Dimitru's address in Google Maps, and the estimated time for arrival was around five. The sun was in the sky. The usual grey sky of Ireland had thankfully changed to a light shade of blue.

Brendan felt as if this drive, this tranquil experience, was simply the calm before the storm. His phone rang, and he patched it through the car's sound system.

'You're right behind me, what's wrong? Am I going too fast for you?' he joked, thinking it was Lorna.

'Brendan. This is Elena.'

'Are you okay?'

'Yes. I wanted to tell you that I have copied, or how do you say in English, burned the video footage onto a disk for you.'

'What's on it?'

'Footage of the three police officers from last night coming out of the room, looking quite unprofessional.'

Brendan smirked, looking at Lorna, following behind him in the other car.

'I also have footage of Dimitru coming and going. And footage of him taking drugs in the house.'

'Do you have anything of the police and Dimitru involved in any kind of friendly discussion?'

'Yes, in the downstairs living room from last night. This was when you and I were in the room together.' She cleared her throat. 'Dimitru had ordered the girls to look extra special for the arrival of some powerful guests that evening.'

'Can you get footage of events tonight?' Brendan put the window down, letting the fresh air in and around his face.

'Yes, I will.'

'Are you okay?'

'I'm fine.' Her tone rose. 'I'm giving attention to Mr Dalca this evening.' Her voice sounded positive, but forced, not authentic.

'See you soon. And Elena...' Brendan paused for a second. 'It's going to be okay. Don't worry.'

'See you later.' She hung up.

Brendan called Lorna.

'You're driving too slow,' she joked.

'I've just got off the phone to Elena. She said she has footage of Dimitru with the local police, getting nice and cosy in Clifton House.'

'Great. This is exactly what we need. Make these dirty bastards known for what they are.'

'Once we reach Belfast, go and visit Clifton House. Talk to Elena, while I take Dimitru to the airport.'

'Just be careful, Brendan. And don't you drive the car.' Lorna's voice deepened. 'You don't want any of them sitting behind you while you're at the wheel. Talk to you soon

Brendan arrived at Dimitru's house shortly after five. Lorna made her way to Clifton House. As he pulled up outside the house, Dimitru was just stepping out through the front door, as if he were anxiously waiting for Brendan.

As he marched across the garden path, Dimitru flicked a cigarette away and lit another. He was immaculately dressed. A navy suit, with an open-neck purple shirt, made him look as if he were making an effort for someone. His black hair was extra shiny. As he dropped himself into the passenger seat of the car, the wind carried with it an overpowering stench of cologne.

He slammed the door shut and lowered the window. Brendan regarded Dimitru's trembling hand as he raised the cigarette to his mouth.

'Are you nervous?' Brendan said causally, putting the car in gear and circling the street before driving back out onto the Ballysillian Road.

'Me?' Dimitru sniggered, dismissively shrugging off the question. 'I don't get nervous.'

'Why's your hand trembling, then?'

The expression on Dimitru's face was one of someone who wasn't used to being questioned. 'I'm fine.'

'I'm ditching this car. We need to use another one. One that can't be traced back to me, and which hasn't been fingered by this rat.'

'It's funny you should mention him, because it's his car we'll be using,' Dimitru sniggered. 'It was his pride and joy.'

'Was?'

'Well, he'll never be inside it again.'

'You've taken him already?'

Dimitru nodded. 'We've had to move the meeting forward a little bit.' He cleared his throat. 'Everything's happening tonight. And I think my bitch wife has been feeding him the information. She's disappeared, just as all this has come to light.'

Brendan's mind raced. Not knowing what to say, he didn't want his dancing vocal chords and internal dialogue giving away how he was feeling.

'You have a nice shiny new car waiting for us at Clifton House.'

'You can drive.' Brendan spoke sharply. 'I'm not your chauffeur.'

'I'm happy to. You feel the need to bring a gun with you?'

Brendan looked at Dimitru, briefly, then brought his eyes back to the road again. 'You say there's a rat in your organisation, so yes. If I get in a tight spot, I'll be shooting my way out of it.'

# Chapter Thirty-Three

GEORGE BEST BELFAST City Airport was quiet by the time they arrived. It was six-fifteen, and the majority of the vehicles left in the short stay car park were idling taxis waiting for the day's remaining flights.

Dimitru had taken the electric blue BMW 4 series, feeling good about the way he drove, driving recklessly, abusing the vehicle. Brendan sat in the back, watching the streets of Belfast in the evening fly by. Every detail passed by in a flash, like the memories and people who came and went from Brendan's life. From a young age, he'd gotten used to the fact that those closest to him would leave. His father leaving was something he'd accepted as the norm, and if the man who'd been his best mate, greatest critic and hardest trainer could leave him, Brendan didn't see why anyone else would stay. But Lorna. Lorna was different. He got the feeling she wasn't going anywhere.

'You're very thoughtful,' Dimitru said, reverse parking into one of the bays closest to the zebra crossing the arrivals passengers would cross.

'I guess I am.'

'You're wondering about the person who owns this car?'

'I couldn't give a shit about them. I'm more concerned about what he's been saying.'

'You mean has he told the UDA that the infamous Brendan Cleary has come home to roost?'

Brendan didn't answer; he kept his eyes on the terminal's exit. The man whom he now knew to be the head of the Romanian mafia had appeared from the inside and was now walking towards them. In spite of the fact there was no sun around, he was sporting a pair of sunglasses. He looked like one of those characters dragged straight out of an American gangster movie. He had the walk of a man drenched in confidence, a man with so much swagger it almost dripped off him. He stood around six-foot-five and was athletically built like Brendan. It was clear it wasn't just his position within the group that gave him confidence; it was also physical. He would be hard for a normal person to take down.

'Here comes Mr Dalca,' Dimitru shouted, tooting the horn. 'Now the fun's about to get started.'

Brendan ignored the comment. He kept his eyes on Dalca. And even from behind the shades, Brendan knew he was being watched. He had that smile, the sinister grin of someone who could cut your throat in front of you and watch the life drain from your eyes as you bleed out in their presence.

Dimitru jumped out of the car, popping the boot.

Brendan continued to keep his eyes on Dalca. It was as if he and Brendan were trying to stare each other down, and Brendan wasn't about to shift. Instead, the boss stopped directly outside Brendan's door, glaring in at him. He spoke in Romanian, perhaps unaware Brendan could speak the language.

'Who is this fucking guy? Does he want me to pop his eyes out before...'

Brendan opened the door and stepped out. Dalca's reaction to Brendan's fast and aggressive exit from the car was an indicator that the Romanian was not accustomed to people having the balls to act in such a cocky manner.

'Nice to finally meet you,' Brendan said in basic Romanian. 'Welcome to Ireland.' He offered his hand.

Dalca took off his shades and looked at Brendan, his hazel eyes darting from one of Brendan's eyes to the other, as if inspecting them, looking for a hint of deceit.

'My hand won't stay here much longer.' Brendan spoke with cold confidence, a sureness that he'd get away with it, given the fact he had information that was of benefit to the Romanians.

His hand was accepted. They both smiled at each other as if not trusting the other in the slightest.

'This is Brendan Cleary.' Dimitru interrupted the apparent stare-down between the two.

'Nice to meet you, Cleary,' Dalca said.

'It's Mr Cleary, or Brendan. Whichever you prefer.'

Dalca looked at Dimitru and exploded into a fit of laughter. 'He's confident. I can respect that.' He handed his bag to Dimitru and got in the front passenger seat.

Brendan got back into the car, directly behind him.

'So,' Dalca started. 'Why have you decided to come out of the woodwork and offer to help our organisation?'

'Because.' Brendan put the window down. 'As much as I despise your shitty underworld, I hate the UDA more for what they did to my family.'

'I think we should talk more in private,' Dalca said, as Dimitru jumped back in behind the wheel. 'I don't like being in places that I haven't had a chance to check for any listening devices.' He looked at Dimitru.

Dimitru nodded. 'Can't fucking trust anyone these days.'

'I hope where we are going is a place we can feel comfortable to talk freely?'

'Yes.' Dimitru put the car in gear. 'Not only freedom to speak, but plenty of sweet Romanian ass for us all to enjoy.' He lit up a cigarette as he drove out of the arrivals car park, merging onto the duel carriageway city-bound.

Brendan regarded Dimitru's hand, still trembling. He saw his glazed eyes in the reflection of the rear view, struggling to focus on the road ahead. It was clear that Dalca had the capacity to instil fear in the people who worked for him. Up until now, Dimitru had seemed like the man in charge, a person feared and respected. But now, around the new arrival, he was nothing more than a snivelling weasel.

'Have you spoken with UDA representatives?' Dalca asked Dimitru. 'I hope they're aware of the situation and that we need to move things along. I can't be here any longer than twenty-four hours.'

'I spoke to Ivan Moore today.'

Brendan's ears perked up. His eyes almost shot out of his head. Ivan Moore. His uncle. A man he hated with a passion, but his mother's brother all the same.

'Ivan is happy to meet tonight?' Dalca asked.

Dimitru nodded. 'They've been informed of the rat. They know we've got him. They want to be there during his interrogation. Then...' he laughed, looking over at Dalca, then back at Brendan. 'We will make them our new business proposition.'

'I trust everything is in place to make sure nobody can cause us any problems?' Dalca spoke with the tone of a condescending employer who wasn't fully confident in his staff's ability to adequately execute a task.

'No need to worry. Tonight is going to be an eventful evening in Belfast.' Dimitru looked at Brendan. 'And Brendan here is going to become the little gem of our organisation.'

Brendan nodded falsely, hoping that he and Lorna could somehow stop the massacre.

# Chapter Thirty-Four

THE STREET OUTSIDE Clifton House was lined with cars along both sides. The only space available was at the end of the road, the opposite end to where the house was located.

As Brendan got out, he realised how tall Dalca was—towering over him, causing a shadow. Brendan slammed the door closed and followed Dimitru as he led them towards the house. As they got to Clifton House, music could be heard blaring out of the bottom window. Brendan considered the place a little tacky, a poor way to treat such a beautiful Victorian era building.

As they approached the front door, it opened before Dimitru had a chance to lift the knocker. Elena stood dressed in a tight-fitting black dress that was both short in the leg and low in the cut. She smiled at Dimitru as he pulled her in for a kiss. Dalca entered after Dimitru, pulling Elena in for a hug. She looked past him, smirking at Brendan, her eyes glazed and enticing. He could see why she was the prized possession of the company. Her beauty was hard to match. Those full red lips and big brown eyes could capture the heart of many. And they would, if she had a chance at a proper life.

Brendan stepped inside, following Dimitru and Dalca into the living room. Dimitru indicated for Brendan to accompany him to the kitchen, away from any ears.

As Brendan stepped into the kitchen, the polite small talk between Dalca and Elena disappeared with the door closing. 'What's happening?' Brendan said.

'I'm thinking maybe you shouldn't be here when the UDA leaders arrive. We don't need anything going wrong.'

'You mean like them bastards having a problem with someone who has the Cleary surname, causing a fight before you have a chance to drug and butcher them?'

'Exactly, Brendan.' Dimitru smiled.

Brendan looked at him, wanting to bounce his head off the kitchen sink. 'You're right. Where are you planning on carrying this out?' Brendan swallowed, realising the gravity of the ever-unfolding situation.

'You know the barn we went to?'

Brendan nodded. 'Thought so.'

'We plan on having them here, only briefly. A few drinks, maybe a slut or two, then we'll be making our move once the drugs begin to take effect.'

'Where are the rest of your men?'

'On their way here now.' Dimitru turned and poured out a drop of cocaine onto the kitchen top. He pulled out a note, rolling it up, taking a line. 'Alexandru is staying up there with the little rat.' He snorted, standing up straight, wiping his nose.

'Maybe you should go easy on that shite?' Brendan complained. 'Can you keep it to a minimum and not get us fucking killed? If these UDA men smell something off, the next thing they'll do is end it for everyone.'

Dimitru looked at Brendan.

'I'm simply doing this so I can get paid.' Brendan shrugged.

'And address the bastards that have gone after your family.'

Brendan felt like knocking every tooth out of Dimitru's head. His gut instinct told him Dimitru was the one who'd gone looking Brendan's aunt Mary. He clenched his jaws. 'Exactly.' He turned and looked through the door's window pane, into the living room. Dalca was sitting on the sofa. Elena was seated on his knee. 'From the moment you knew you had a rat, we were out of time. Every second we stand around talking shite is another moment when we could all be caught.' He looked back at Dimitru. 'Give me the key to the car. I want to go and have a little word with our friend. Maybe I can give him some encouragement, find out what he's said and who he's said it to.'

Dimitru handed Brendan the key.

Brendan looked at Dimitru, glaring at him, a stern look in his eye. 'You fuck this up, your life's over. We make it through this plan, you'll be richer and more powerful than your wildest dreams. Don't forget that.' He turned and walked back through the living room, giving Dalca nothing more than a civil nod of the head, then smiled at Elena. 'Mr Dalca, I've got to go. It was nice to meet you.'

'You, too, Brendan.'

He closed the door and walked along the hallway, listening to the laughter of Dimitru. Reaching the front door, he began removing the chains. Elena followed him out, hissing for him to stop.

'Where are you going?' she whispered, pulling on his sleeve, as if clinging for her life. 'I don't want you to leave me with them.'

Brendan opened the door. 'I've got to go, but after tonight, it'll all be over.' He pulled her in closer to him. 'Just stay strong for me, can you?'

She looked back down the hallway, then back at him. 'I trust you. Now you must not make me regret giving you that trust.'

Brendan stroked her cheek with the back of his hand. 'I'll not let you down.' He turned and made his way back to the car. Jumping into the driver's seat, he adjusted it. As he started the engine, Lorna called.

'Lorna, where are you?'

'I received a call from Diana. She's told me something very interesting, Brendan.'

'What?'

'Dimitru's head is even further up his arse than we originally thought. Dalca is about to join the other Irish corps in the massacre.'

'Why?' Brendan said as he put the car in gear and took off. 'I couldn't really care who kills who. Either they'll go to prison or they'll be dead. Either way, their lives as they know it are over.'

'She's also sent me the address of where the other Romanian girls live together. I'm going to check the place out tonight. If I can get them out of there, I will. She said she doesn't want to come back to Belfast. She wants to keep Teodoro away from it.'

'Looks like tomorrow, these poor girls get their lives back,' Brendan said, driving the car up the Cliftonville Road towards the city's outer limit.

For the rest of the journey Brendan was quiet, thoughtful. This country road, lined with lush green trees and winding roads, was one he'd taken many times. The view of Belfast was a sight to behold, and many times he'd found himself looking down over the city in which he'd grown up, drenched in a mixture of hatred and regret for having been born in such a depressing place, among backward people with nothing better to do than to insult the other side of the peaceline. But from this distance, from the top of the mountain, Brendan saw a city that had enough scars and bloodstains to last it a lifetime. It didn't need another massacre to hit the headlines.

The car rolled into the barn's entrance, crunching over tiny stones and dirt. Shutting off the engine, he stepped out, drawing his pistol. With the weapon resting by his side, Brendan made his way in through the deteriorated front door. He could hear thumps on the wall coming from the room behind the reception desk. As he approached, he recognised Alexandru speaking, sinister humour in his tone.

As Brendan stepped inside the room, the first thing he realised was that the rat had soiled himself, perhaps where he sat—in the chair, stripped and bound. He had multiple lacerations on his exposed skin. His right eye was swollen closed. His nose was swollen, stretching across the centre of his face.

Alexandru looked at Brendan. 'What do you think, Cleary?'

Brendan looked at the rat, then at Alexandru. 'Are you fucking stupid?'

Alexandru went to speak, but Brendan cut him off.

'Don't answer that, we already know the answer.'

Brendan looked at the rat, crying in the chair, his body slumped as if he didn't have the energy to sit up straight. 'Who and what have you told about this?'

'Fuck you.' The rat coughed, then spat blood on the ground just beyond Brendan's feet.

'You see, he deserves everything I'm going to give him.' Alexandru punched the rat on the back of the head. He walked over to a wooden table that had a collection of knives of different shapes and sizes. It was like a butcher's work station. He grabbed a cleaver and chopped it into the edge of the table. Then he walked back over to the rat. 'Dimitru has given me orders to keep you alive until later, but I can still remove some body parts.' He looked at Brendan.

'Put the cleaver down and stop being an animal. I don't want to see this shite.' Brendan looked at the rat, then back at Alexandru.

Alexandru grinned. 'Fuck you.' He raised his knife-wielding hand, but before he had a chance to swipe, Brendan shot him in the hand. Alexandru yelled, stumbling back.

Brendan raised the pistol above his line of sight, towards Alexandru's head. 'You're lucky it's not between your fucking eyes.'

'You've just signed your own death warrant.' Alexandru ran towards Brendan, swinging his right fist. Brendan stepped out of the way of the blow, allowing the giant's momentum to drive him into the wall.

Alexandru reached for his phone. Brendan kicked it out of his hand, sending it crashing to the ground. Alexandru swung a kick for Brendan; Brendan again stepped out of the way, following up with a counter punch that sent Alexandru stumbling into the table of knives. He grabbed one of the knives and ran at Brendan in a fit of rage, managing only two steps before Brendan put a second bullet between his eyes. Dropping to his knees, he was dead instantly.

Brendan stood over the corpse, watching the blood pool. The rat was now breathing heavily, as if gasping for his life.

'Fuck.' Brendan sighed, pulling his phone out of his pocket. He called Lorna. She answered almost immediately.

'Brendan, is everything okay?'

'We've run into a problem.'

# Chapter Thirty-Five

'WHY DOESN'T THAT SURPRISE me, Brendan?' Lorna spoke sarcastically, in an upbeat tone, as if to reassure him that nothing bad was going to happen. 'So, what's happened?'

Brendan listened as car doors could be heard slamming from the other end of the line. 'Alexandru. He's dead.'

'He's one of Dimitru's men?'

'One of the pair we met in the Red Brick when our drinks were spiked.'

'Where are you?'

'In an old abandoned barn a few miles outside the city.'

'Perfect place to carry out their little mission to cleanse Belfast.'

'Yes.'

'Who are you there with?'

'Just a good-for-nothing rat who was just about to become part of Alexandru's meat cleaver.'

'Who is he?'

'Remember the barman who spiked our drinks?'

'Piece of shit. Should have let Alexandru carry on.'

Brendan laughed, astonished. 'I swear you don't have the face for that mentality.'

'Guess I've just been exposed to the horrors of the world and become more accustomed to it.' She cleared her throat.

'Now, you've got a dead body at your feet. You need to make him disappear...'

'What am I, a fucking magician?'

'These Romanians are about to take out some of the most dangerous men in Belfast tonight. They need to believe you're on their side.' Lorna began to speak as if she were Brendan's commanding officer, needing him to listen very carefully, taking in every detail. 'Where are Dimitru and the others?'

'They're at Clifton House. They're meeting the UDA leaders there for a few drinks before coming here.'

'How much time do you have?'

'Dimitru said he'd call when they're on their way. He knows I can't be seen by any of the UDA men. They can't know I'm here.'

'You're right.'

Brendan looked at the rat. He was shaking from head to toe, clearly traumatised, but regardless of how much he was fearing for his life in that moment, he wasn't about to talk. If he was, he would have done so at the first sign of the kitchen utensils.

'Where are you?' Brendan asked.

'I'm at Diana's house.' She spoke humorously. 'I've been sent to grab her ginger cat.'

'Priorities,' Brendan joked.

'Are the local police...' Lorna was cut off by Brendan.

'Lorna, I've got to take this call, it's my aunty Mary. I'll call you straight back.' He hung up and took the other call. 'Mary, what's up?'

'Brendan, love, why the fuck have I got two Romanians standing here, kindly offering to help me lock up, keeping me inside?'

'What? Where are they now?'

'They're in the kitchen, helping themselves to the food. Cheeky bastards even asked me to cook something for them.'

Brendan looked down at Alexandru's body at his feet.

'They said they've been told to come and protect me. They seem to believe I'm in danger.' She laughed without humour. 'Brendan, love, why do I get the impression it isn't just a coincidence that this happens in the same week you just magically show up again?'

'Because it's not.' Brendan walked to the door, exiting the building out to where the car was parked. He opened the vehicle and jumped behind the wheel again, starting the engine. 'Everything's going to be okay, Mary. I'm doing a bit of work for them and they're just there to make sure you're...'

'Brendan, I wasn't fucking born yesterday, love. For Christ sake, I even wiped your daddy's arse once upon a time. So don't treat me like an idiot. What are you caught up in?'

'The Romanians are planning to take out the heads of the UDA tonight, and plan on taking over their business.'

'And you're helping them?'

'They think I am.' Brendan cleared his throat, lowering the window. 'I've told them I want to go into business with them, give them information about other organisations that Lorna's collected from MI5, in exchange for a cut of whatever money they make.'

'It's not a good way for them to do business, coming here.'

Brendan thought it was strange. He wasn't sure whether the Romanians were really there to protect Mary from the UDA or were there to use her as ransom. Either way, they shouldn't have brought her into it.

Looking in the rear-view mirror, he spotted what looked like the beginning of a rubbish dump.

'Mary, I'm sending Lorna over there. I'm going to clear up the mess over here, then I'll be on my way there, too.' He hung up the phone and called Lorna back.

'Brendan, what's wrong?'

'Two Romanians have just taken over my aunty Mary's shop on the Antrim Road. I don't know what they're fucking playing at, but the Romanian boss is going to regret sending them over there.'

'Is she okay?'

'She's tough. But still, can you go down there? I'm going to dispose of Alexandru's body, then I'll be on my way down.'

'Okay. Send me the address.'

Brendan hung up the phone, then jumped out of the car, slamming the door shut. He thumbed in the address and sent it to Lorna. He ran back inside the room. Scanning it, he looked for something with which to dispose of the body. Nothing. He went back outside. Running over to Alexandru's car, he lifted a rock and threw it into the front driver's side window. He reached inside and opened the door. Reaching across under the steering wheel towards the footwell, he pulled on a tiny plastic leaver, releasing the boot. He ran to the boot and searched for something useful. He found a collection of guns, ammunition, a sleeping bag and a role of plastic lining. Grabbing the sleeping bag and the plastic lining, he slammed the boot shut and went back inside.

The rat wasn't a threat; he was still bound, and from his body language, he was too exhausted to even try to break free. Brendan dropped the sleeping bag, then set the lining down, rolling it open alongside the body. He ran to the other side of the corpse, squatted down and rolled it onto the plastic. He rolled the dead weight across the room, wrapping more and more of it up with each roll. He then unzipped the sleeping bag and opened it. He rolled the body onto the sleeping bag and zipped it closed.

He went to lift the body but thought it stupid to end up with an injury moving a dead body, so he dragged it outside.

After dragging it fifty yards, he reached a ditch. He didn't care how out of view it was, he just needed it to be out of sight for the night. He'd be gone from Belfast in the next twenty-four hours anyway. He rolled it into the ditch and watched it slide, tumbling thirty feet into it's mass grave. He was sure there were going to be more before the night was over.

He ran back to the barn. A cleaning store separated the male and female toilets. He grabbed a mop and bucket and ran into the males', filling the bucket with water. Making his way back to the room, he poured some of the water over the blood and began collecting it with the mop.

After five minutes, the water was the same shade of red as the bucket. Brendan looked at the shiny floor with a hint of appraisal for his clean-up job.

He secured the room, made sure the rat wasn't going anywhere, then ran out, locking the door behind him.

As he got into the car, Dimitru called.

'Well, how's the little meeting going?' Brendan said. He connected the device through the car's sound system and took off.

'We're just discussing some possible business opportunities. How's the little rat? Is Alexandru having some fun with him?'

'Haven't been up there yet,' Brendan lied. 'I'm helping Lorna with something first. What time will you be arriving?'

'Change of plans.'

'What do you mean, change of plans?'

'It's best to keep our plans changing; it helps prevent anyone who's tracking us from staying on our tail.'

'Okay, so what is it this time?'

'We're finalising our meeting at the docks, the warehouse.'

'That's a courageous place to send out a message.'

'We plan on making the headlines with this one, Brendan. And with your help, we're going to make world news very soon. I'm going to make you very rich and powerful.'

'That's very kind of you,' Brendan said, a hint of sarcasm in his voice.

'See you at the docks tonight, at ten. The meeting has been arranged.'

'See you then.' Brendan hung up. He sent a quick text to Lorna, telling her he was on his way.

# Chapter Thirty-Six

ARRIVING OUTSIDE THE shop, Brendan spotted Lorna's car parked on the other end of the road, about one hundred yards from his location. She wasn't in it. He called her.

'Brendan,' Lorna said. 'Your aunt is fine.' She laughed. 'She'd put the fear into even Dalca.'

'Even my father wouldn't have messed with her.' Brendan got out and slammed the door shut. 'Are you inside?'

'Yes, I'll let you in.'

Brendan hung up and made his way towards the shop. As he approached the entrance, Lorna appeared from the inside. She quickly unlocked the door and opened it, shutting it again the moment Brendan stepped inside.

'What happened?' He looked at her, confused.

'I acted dumb, came banging on the door, and when they saw I was just an unarmed lady demanding to see Mary, they didn't suspect I was a threat, until one of them took a kitchen knife in the foot.'

Brendan pulled her in close to him. 'You're really sexy when you talk like that.' He kissed her, then broke away again. 'Where are they?'

'In the office.' She pointed over Brendan's shoulder.

They turned and made their way into the back room.

As Brendan entered the, the two Romanians were face down on the ground, their hands bound behind their backs.

Mary sat behind the desk, her shirt blouse ripped open, pinching her nose closed with a tissue.

'Are you okay, Mary?' Brendan said as he walked farther into the office, stepping over the two hostages. He touched the opening of her blouse. 'What did they do?'

Before she had a chance to respond, one of the two shouted. 'We were told to rough her up, make her afraid; that way she'd be more accommodating.'

Lorna sunk her foot into his side, then walked around him, stomping on his head, pushing it farther into the ground.

'Why did you come here?' Brendan said.

The other, who looked a lot like a thinner version of Dimitru, struggled, trying to break free from the cable ties. As he continued to struggle, he shouted through a gasp. 'Your bitch aunt is insurance.'

'For what?' Brendan said. 'Dimitru knows I'm helping him. What does he need insurance for?'

'Just in case you decide to go against him.'

Brendan looked at Lorna, then Mary. 'We need to get out of here. There could be more of them watching this place. If there are more outside, they'll be feeding it all back to Dimitru and this whole thing goes up in smoke.'

'What are you going to do, Brendan?' Mary said. 'This isn't a game, son. These bastards are animals. They'll chop you up with the rest of them and leave you to be found.'

Brendan shook his head. 'Not while they still believe I'm more valuable alive than dead.' He looked at Lorna. 'Can you take Mary to her house and get everything she needs?'

'Of course,' Lorna said. 'We can leave this pair of twats here.'

'I don't need to go anywhere,' Mary protested. 'If the bastards come anywhere near my house, it'll be the last thing they do.'

'Mary, just do it, please?' Brendan pleaded, but with a tone that sounded more like an order than a request.

'And where are you going?' she said.

'I'm going to go and watch the show. The UDA men will all be drugged and rendered useless by the time they get to the warehouse, so it'll only be the Romanians I need to worry about, and I think I'll have them covered.' He looked at his phone. 'I'll see you all in a few hours. I'm going to leave a nasty surprise for whoever walks into this warehouse tomorrow.' He rushed to the door, then looked back as he reached it. 'See you soon.'

As he stepped out of the shop, his heightened awareness of his surroundings would prove useful if he were being watched. He became conscious of the fact the pistol was still holstered below his armpit. He walked at a slow pace towards the car. Opening it, he jumped in and started the engine, taking off towards the docks.

The roads were quiet. He found himself taking in his surroundings with a newfound appreciation. Every detail. The old taxi depots on the Antrim Road, Saint Malachy's Secondary School where he attended, the rear of the Mater Hospital where he was born; somehow, his memories of these sites seemed more pleasant than they ever had before. Then there was the Orange Hall on Clifton Street – the very place where he and Lorna were brought together and forced to go on the run, covered in the assassinated blood of Lorna's old MI5 superior.

He smirked as he even managed to feel appreciation for that. Lorna. In spite of the life they'd been left with, he had her. And Lorna was more than enough to make it all worth it. To Brendan anyway.

He turned left off Clifton Street, onto the Westlink, the main artery that connects North, East, South and West Belfast. He headed east on the M3 towards the docks.

The docks were a vast opening, windy and cold, but at this time of night – deserted. The orange street lighting fell into the rear-view mirror every thirty yards, becoming somewhat hypnotising. He reached the location, being the first there. Taking an opportunity to scope the place out before the others arrived, he parked the car next to the reception doors and got out. Checking again that his late father's trusted pistol was still holstered, he made his way inside.

As he closed the front door, it was as if he'd just stepped into another world, a world that was currently at peace, and that was about to be shattered.

He stepped into the office and turned on the light. The room was tidy. Too tidy for what was about to take place. He noticed the family photo on the desk: Dimitru, Diana and a younger Teodoro. They looked happy. For a second, he felt guilty for being responsible for separating the family in the photo. It was as if he were doing the same to Teodoro as the British government had done to him when he was younger.

His phone rang. It was Elena.

'Elena, are you okay?'

'Yes, I'm alone now.' Her voice sounded weak, traumatised.

'Are you sure you're okay?'

'Yes. I am now that they have left.'

'Okay, good. Well, you'll not have to see them again. You should be glad. We're getting you all away from Belfast. Tonight.'

'Where are we supposed to go? We don't have much money.'

'Don't worry about the money, I'm going to help you with that.' Brendan walked over to the security monitors, watching a black transit drive past his car towards the rear of the building. 'Do you have transport?'

'Yes, we have enough cars to get away.'

'As long as you have enough cars, and fuel to get you to where I need you to go, you'll be fine. Don't worry about anything else.' He could hear the shutter door to the warehouse lift. 'I've got to go. I'm sending you help. My partner, she's very smart. You'll be safe with her.'

'The lucky lady who has captured your heart.' She giggled.

'Yes, she'll show you a safe place to stay until this all blows over. And don't worry. They will never find it.'

'Okay. Send me the address where we should meet her.'

'I'll see you soon. And, Elena...' Brendan paused for a moment. 'I keep my promises.'

'See you later.' She hung up.

Brendan quickly sent Lorna a text.

*Lorna, they've arrived at the docks. I've just spoken to Elena. She's going to get all the girls and leave. I've told them to*

*meet you. You can take them all back to the house in Donegal.*
*They'll be safe until we can send them back into the world. This*
*is about to get underway. I'll text you when this is all done.*

As Brendan left the room, Lorna called him.

'I can't talk,' he said, 'I'm heading out into the warehouse
now.'

'Brendan, you be careful,' Lorna said. 'The first sign that
something's not right in there, you get out. And keep your
distance.'

'I've got to go. I'll speak to you soon.' He hung up, then
sent a message for Elena to meet Lorna at the Apple Green
Service Station on the M2 northbound between Belfast and
Antrim.

As he stepped out into the airy warehouse, the sound of
screeching tires from the forklifts sent a feeling of urgency
through the air. The plant machinery was bringing one of the
crates of ammunition towards the van that had just arrived.
As Brendan got closer, he noticed the van was empty inside.
No hostages. He recognised Peter, Dimitru's brother, as the
one driving the forklift.

Brendan watched as the forklift lowered the crate onto
the back of the van. 'You moving that stuff somewhere?' he
shouted, making Peter jump.

'Christ, you scared the shit out of me.' He shut the engine off and stepped out. 'Nice to see you again – man with
the plan.' He spoke humorously, pulling his cigarettes from
his jeans pocket. He offered one to Brendan. Brendan refused, and Peter offered his hand instead as he lit one up for
himself.

Brendan accepted. 'Where are Dimitru and the others?'

'On their way.' He spoke through smoke-filled breath, making his way towards the van. 'We're moving house. These weapons can't be here any longer.' Peter reached into the van and pulled the side of the crate open. An AK47 assault rifle fell out. He raised it, looking down the sight, firing a mock shot. 'We've found a buyer for some of these guns, in London. But what they don't know is that, once they handed over their money, we'll take the guns back and make them all disappear.'

'You've all lost the fucking plot,' Brendan said.

'Thanks to the information you've supplied us with, there is going to be a lot more fucking plot losing.' He mocked Brendan, putting on a poor imitation of an Irish accent. He turned the gun on Brendan, raising the weapon.

Brendan gripped the end, lowering it again, and swung a kick at Peter's head, sending him to the ground. He intercepted the weapon and reversed the aggression, standing over Peter with the gun pointed right at him.

'You're lucky I don't put a bullet right through your *fucking* eye,' Brendan spoke through gritted teeth, as another two vans flew in through the large door, towards them.

Brendan turned his attention to the new arrivals. Dimitru was next to arrive in a white Mercedes, his smug grin plastered across his face, Dalca seated in the passenger seat.

Brendan walked over to the Merc, not paying much attention to the vans.

Dimitru jumped out.

'Everything going according to plan?' Brendan said.

'We've got everything *and* everyone,' Dimitru said, his eyes glazed.

The sound of one of the van's sliding doors being slammed shut snatched Brendan's attention. He spotted three men whom he'd known for years. One was, as he'd expected, his uncle Ivan—his mother's older brother, a bastard in Brendan's eyes. Ivan hated Brendan because of who his father was. But he was his mother's brother all the same, and Brendan wouldn't stand by and watch some foreigners taking over his home city while sending his uncle to see Brendan's mother sooner than he should.

'Brendan, you can have first touch on these men before we carry out the executions,' Dimitru said. Another six men, all bound and gagged, were dragged from the rear of the other van. Nine of the UDA's most influential members were about to be massacred and left to be found.

Dimitru stood beside Brendan, grinning proudly.

Brendan looked at him. 'You know if the leaders die, the others will just start up again and will come after you.'

'Not if they've got no weapons. It will take them too long to build up enough force to take us on. Instead they can come work for us; I'll be happy to accommodate them. And with the police on our side, there'll be no stopping us.'

'Where are they? I thought they were supposed to be at the meeting, too?'

'They're on their way. I told them I'd inform them when it's time to come in. I'm letting you have your fun with this scum first, then once you hand them over to us, we'll be done. You can go, and we'll finish the job.'

'And the message we send out here tonight, when people see what's left of these poor bastards, nobody will fuck with us,' Dalca said, standing beside Dimitru.

'You've got it all worked out, haven't you?' Brendan said sarcastically.

'Thanks to you.' Dalca smirked.

The nine UDA men all lay facedown, with their hands bound behind their backs.

Ivan woke, trying to struggle but getting nowhere. 'What the fuck is this?'

Before he had another chance to speak, Marius stomped on his head. 'Shut your fucking mouth, you Irish pig.' He pulled a knife out and crouched down. 'I fucking hate you Irish scum. I'm going to shut you up.' He pulled Ivan by the hair, lifting his head off the ground. He reached around to the front with the knife.

Brendan pulled his father's Desert Eagle from under his jacket. He pointed it and shot Marius in the side of the head, sending blood spraying against the side of the van. 'Anyone in here says they hate Irish people again, and our business deal goes down the drain. Is that fucking clear?' Brendan's heart was racing; his hand gripped the pistol extra tight to hide the shaking. He'd taken a big risk, but he'd gone solely on instinct, and it was either that or watch his mother's brother have his head severed like a fish.

He stood there, looking at all the Romanians: Adrian, Peter, Marian, and Cristian.

'You've got some balls,' Dalca said.

'I've got information that can make your current little empire look like a fucking joke,' Brendan said, holstering the weapon again. 'Which is why you haven't killed me yet. Now are we going to do this or not? Just get it over with; I know who sent them after my family anyway. My aunt Mary's safe now, she's been taken away.' He looked at Dimitru, whose attitude had taken a slight turn for the worse.

Dimitru cleared his throat. 'Okay.' He looked at his men, then pointed towards the centre of the warehouse. 'Place them all in the middle of the room. I want all their body parts removed but left close enough that they can still be identified.'

Cristian, Peter, Adrian and Marian started dragging the hostages across the floor by their bound ankles, all kicking and squealing like pigs, aware that they were about to meet their end. Brendan watched the sinister look on the face of Dimitru. Dalca also looked as if he were enjoying the display.

Dimitru put his hand around Brendan and walked with him towards the hostages. 'You sure you don't want to pull the trigger before we take the knives to them?'

Brendan stopped, ten feet from the nine. He struggled with what he should do. He knew had the UDA got their hands on him only a few days prior, he'd be dead. But this was different. This was evil. Barbaric. And regardless of what he thought personally about his uncle Ivan, he was still his mother's brother. She would be turning over in her grave if she knew the position her only son had gotten himself into.

'You know what?' Brendan said. 'These bastards would put the bullet in my head if it was the other way around.' He looked at Dimitru. 'I'll regret it if I don't. He pulled out his father's pistol, but Dimitru stopped him.

'Here, take this.' Dimitru took one of the rifles off Adrian and tossed it to Brendan.

Brendan caught it, looking it up and down. He felt his heart rate go up again. He stood there, on the spot. He felt as if his feet had been cemented to the ground. He knew if he hesitated, he'd be joining the other nine on the floor. He walked closer to the group, getting ready to fire. He took aim at the first one on the left-hand side of the row – his uncle. His mind raced. He took aim at the back of Ivan's head. One of the Romanians joked in his own language, not knowing Brendan could understand.

Brendan lowered his aim and looked around. 'Now what the fuck would you want me on camera doing this for?' He looked at Dimitru. Dimitru shook his head. Brendan was secretly grateful, because it took their attention off the execution. Brendan took aim at Dimitru. 'You're setting me up?' This time he spoke in Romanian.

'You're outnumbered, Brendan.' Brendan kept his aim on Dimitru as the sound of multiple guns clicking echoed throughout the warehouse. 'I own you, you piece of shit. And you're going to cooperate with us, or the rest of your dirty family will suffer a horrible end.'

Brendan backed away, creating more distance between himself and the guns pointed at him. He knew Dimitru wanted Brendan's intel more than he wanted him dead. With that, he believed he wasn't going to die there. 'Your two assholes who visited my aunt today? You won't be seeing them again. Alexandru? He's in a pit.' Brendan backed farther away, towards the corner where the vehicles were parked. The farther back he moved, the more guns came into his view. He knew he couldn't open fire on them; they would kill him if he tried to kill them.

'Police. Everyone freeze. Nobody move,' a voice shouted from behind Brendan, coming from the reception area. 'The building is surrounded.'

Brendan knew the Romanians weren't going to walk out of there in cuffs. They'd rather go out in a blaze. He was ten feet from one of the vans. He fired a shot in the air and dropped to the ground, rolling towards the van, continuing underneath it as the shooting began. A hail of bullets. He continued to roll through to the other side of the van. He jumped up and pulled the driver's door open, throwing himself in, lying across the seat, the windows shattering, shards of glass coming down over him. His phone rang. It was Lorna.

'Lorna,' he shouted. 'Where are you?'

'Brendan. I knew something was going to go wrong. Is that gunfire in the background?'

'We've got a big problem. We're surrounded by the police.'

'It's a load of bollocks. I'm outside now. There's no police around. It's the bent cops from Clifton House; guess they're trying to get the upper hand on who's controlling who.'

Brendan hung up the phone. He crawled along the seat, finding the keys still in the ignition. He started the van. Not even looking where he was going, he rammed it in gear and stomped on the accelerator, the sound of gunfire still crackling through the air. He swerved the vehicle from side to side until he felt something collide with the bonnet. Peter ploughed face first into the windscreen, his lifeless eyes looking at Brendan. Brendan looked up. He was five feet away from the building's wall. In the rear view he could see the opening. He dropped it into reverse and stomped on the accelerator, sending the vehicle in the opposite direction. Peter's body rolled off.

The vehicle lost control following the sound of an air explosion. It ploughed into the wall. There was a momentary silence. Then the sound of guns being reloaded. Brendan looked through the front driver's seat into the back. He'd chosen the van that was loaded with weapons. He climbed through into the back. Lifting the lid off a crate, he pulled out one of the rifles. He removed the magazine to check it was full, then slid it back in.

Brendan didn't know which way they were coming, but he knew if they didn't want him alive, he'd be dead already. The van's sliding door flew open. He put two bullets into Adrian's chest.

'Brendan.' Dimitru's voice was crisp and clear, as if the last few minutes had sobered him up. 'We can all walk out of here alive. You can work with us, we can make you very rich, as originally planned, or you can die here. Either way, you're not leaving here without us.'

Brendan stood up from his crouched position. Unable to fully stand up in the back of the van, he stepped into the light of the open door through which he'd shot Adrian. A collection of bodies scattered around the warehouse. The UDA men were all still lying on the ground, bound. None of them had been shot.

'I knew those bastard cops were going to try something. So, I had some of our London friends follow them.' Dimitru stepped closer to the van.

Brendan stepped out, looking at Adrian.

'Don't worry about him,' Dimitru said, casually putting another bullet in his chest. 'He knew what he was getting in-to.'

Brendan raised the AK, pointing it at Dimitru. 'So did you.'

Dimitru paid little attention to the gun. He put a cigarette in his mouth. 'As you can see, even Mr Dalca has taken a bullet. Now, I run everything. You and I can become very powerful, Brendan.'

Brendan looked at the three members of the local police service, all lying in a pool of their own blood. 'You know the police will find you.' Brendan lowered his weapon. 'You didn't really think this all through, did you?' he sniggered.

'Oh, I did.' Dimitru pointed in the direction of the nine UDA men. 'This has been planned for a long time.' He walked towards Brendan's uncle Ivan and the others. 'Their fingerprints are on all of these guns. They will be set up for this mass murder as an arms deal gone wrong. My good friend – the Assistant Chief Constable – has already been made aware.'

'And most of your men have died because of this stunt.' For a second time, Brendan looked at the selection of national and foreign national bodies around the area. 'You've got nobody left.'

Dimitru looked at Brendan. His eye twitched. 'The rest of my men are on their way in, with your bitch English...'

Dimitru took a shoot in the shoulder.

Brendan looked across the warehouse. Lorna was coming in. He put a bullet in Dimitru's leg, dropping him to the ground. Brendan stood over him, pressing the barrel of the gun into his face.

'Am I always going to have to save your sorry ass?' Lorna kissed Brendan on the cheek.

Brendan glanced at her, smiling. 'I do think you're my guardian angel.' He looked back down at Dimitru. 'Have you got some cable ties?'

Lorna nodded her head. She looked up at the UDA men, still facedown on the concrete. 'What are we doing about them?'

Brendan was about to answer.

'Before you say anything, your aunt Mary told me your uncle Ivan warned her about the Romanians.'

'I knew it wasn't their style.' Brendan looked at Dimitru, then over at the UDA men. 'This isn't for them to take the heat.'

'Here.' Lorna handed him a knife. 'They'll need to go into hiding for a while.'

Brendan walked over to the group, cutting each of them free.

Ivan stood up, towering over Brendan, looking around the warehouse.

'Well, Ivan.' Brendan spoke with little more than a civil tone. 'I wish I could say it's lovely to see you.'

'Why didn't you shoot us? You had the chance.'

'My mother would be cross with me.' Brendan smirked. 'And I guess I own you one. Even though Mary can handle herself.'

Ivan smirked and offered Brendan his hand.

Brendan accepted it.

'There's still people in Belfast that want you dead. I can't stop them all.'

'Wouldn't expect you to.' Brendan turned and made his way back towards Lorna. He turned and looked at Ivan, who was looking at all the bodies. 'You need to get out of here, Ivan. You don't want to get caught up in this.'

'I don't want the same level of notoriety as my pain-in-the ass nephew,' Ivan said. 'I'd appreciate it if you would let me deal with the Romanians.'

Brendan looked at Lorna. 'Did Elena get all the girls away?'

'They're all safe,' Lorna said.

Brendan turned and shouted at Ivan. 'They're all yours.' He turned and put his arm around Lorna. 'Let's go and get these girls sorted, then we can disappear.'

They stepped into the reception area. Making their way through the front entrance, Brendan spotted his father's black Audi fly into the carpark.

'Christ, that's Diana.' Brendan turned and ran back out into the warehouse. The sound of the Audi's tires screeching sent an echo throughout. It all happened so fast. The car raced into the warehouse and skidded right beside Dimitru, who was now being beaten by the UDA.

Diana jumped out of the driver's seat, gun pointed at the group. Brendan shouted for her to stop. Pulling his gun from it's holster he sprinted across the warehouse as one of Ivan's men pointed an AK at her. Brendan shot him in the leg and fired another shot at Diana's feet, stopping her in her tracks.

'Get back in the fucking car, Diana. Now!' Brendan shouted. He ran to her, grabbing her by the arm, dragging her back to the car. 'Ivan, take your men and get the fuck out of here, now,' Brendan shouted, firing another shot in the air. He pulled the rear door open and shoved Diana into the back. 'I fucking told you not to come here.' He slammed the door closed. He jumped into the driver's seat and put it in gear.

'We can't leave without Teodoro,' Diana shouted.

'Where is he?'

She pointed through the windscreen. Teodoro was creeping up behind the vans, a gun in his hand.

Brendan jumped out just as Teodoro jumped out from behind the van, face-to-face with his father, who was now beaten to a pulp.

'Teodoro don't do it,' Brendan shouted. 'He's not worth it.'

'Go on, you little piece of shit, shoot your own father then,' Dimitru screamed as he walked towards Teodoro.

Teodoro pointed the gun at his father, his hand trembling, only ten feet between the two.

'Well, are you going to pull the trigger or not?' Dimitru shouted.

Teodoro froze. Then lowered his weapon and broke down, falling to his knees, sobbing. Brendan walked over to Teodoro, picking him up.

'Hold on a second, Brendan Cleary,' one of the UDA men shouted. The sound of a gun clicked, followed by a second, then a third. 'We can't let you leave.'

'You should have shot us when you had the chance,' another said.

'Put your guns down and let him go,' Ivan ordered.

'Fuck you, Ivan,' the third one with a gun on Brendan said. 'He's not walking away from here alive.'

'The fuck he isn't,' Ivan said, stepping out in front of the three. 'I'm still your commanding officer. I gave you an order, now put the fucking guns down...' He paused for a second. They all looked at him. 'Now!'

One by one, the three lowered their weapons.

With his back to Brendan, still facing his men, Ivan shouted, 'We're even, Brendan. Now fuck off before I change my mind.'

Brendan grabbed Teodoro by the scruff and dragged him back to the car. Lorna had jumped into the driver's seat. The car sped off, leaving the carnage behind.

'Where's your friend?' Brendan looked at Lorna. 'Has she made it over?'

'Haven't heard from her,' Lorna said, guiding the car along the thirty miles per hour speed zone. The other business units passed by, left in the past along with the scene that was just about to become world news.

'Let's just get back to Donegal.' Brendan sat back in the seat, dropping his head onto the headrest.

'Where are the girls?' Diana asked.

'Where going to meet them now,' Lorna said as she turned onto the motorway.

Nothing else was said. The wind whipping by the open windows and the car building up speed was all that was heard.

Brendan closed his eyes, thinking about his mother. He didn't care much for his uncle, and with Ivan, the feeling was mutual. But they both loved the same woman. One as a son, the other as a brother.

# Chapter Thirty-Seven

AFTER MEETING WITH the Romanian girls at the meeting point, the entourage of six vehicles made their way to Donegal, arriving at the estate a little after two in the morning. While most of the girls were tired and eventually fell asleep, curled up in sleeping bags on the living room floor, Brendan, Lorna, Diana and Elena sat around the open fire, watching the logs burn.

Diana clung to Elena, as if she'd just been reunited with a long-lost loved one. Lorna lay with her head on Brendan's lap. None of them spoke. It was as if they were all hypnotised by the flames, causing shadows to dance up the wall, stretching along the ceiling.

There was a feeling of uncertainty, a terror-filled silence throughout the room. The world would be turning it's eyes to Belfast once again for all the wrong reasons. More bloodshed. More families ruined. All those who now lay dead in the sandwich manufactures on Heron View Road at Belfast docks had families – Mothers, fathers, brothers, sisters, sons and daughters. The people who perished would have left behind an unbearable aftermath for the innocent members of their own households.

The many local UDA-linked families that the massacre would have ripped apart had been replaced by the families of the dead Romanians.

The sex slaves that Brendan and Lorna had taken away from the horrific lives they'd been forced into would hopefully be able to walk away, and perhaps build new lives for themselves. They'd remember the Irishman and English lady simply as the *Good Samaritans* who couldn't stand by and watch those less fortunate suffer.

Brendan's attention was snatched away from the roaring fire by the cries from one of the girls, shouting in her sleep, repeating asking them to stop.

Brendan looked at Lorna. Lorna looked at him.

'We've done a good thing, Brendan,' Lorna said, her glazed eyes looking up at him as she continued to lie on his lap.

He stroked her face. 'I know.'

'What about your contact from England?' Diana asked. She looked at Lorna. 'The activist.'

Lorna sighed, shaking her head. 'I don't know.' She sat up and grabbed her phone that lay by her feet. Opening the device, she sighed again. 'Nothing. I've tried calling her, but the phone's disconnected.'

'Try and get some sleep.' Brendan stood up, stretching out his limbs.

'Where are you going?' Lorna said.

'I'm going to sit out in the garden.'

'Are you okay?'

'Just want some fresh air.' He crouched down and kissed Lorna on the forehead. 'Go to bed. I'll be up soon.'

Brendan jumped awake as he felt someone shake him. He looked around, Diana was smiling at him.

'You slept out here all night,' she laughed. 'You must have been tired.'

He sat up, feeling his neck strained. Realising he'd fallen asleep on the garden chair, and had slept through his alarm call, he squinted as he looked at her. 'Are you okay? Have a seat.'

He tapped on the edge of the seat as he rotated his legs off and placed his feet on the ground.

She sat down beside him, both facing the same way, looking across the garden toward the ocean. She nudged him with her shoulder. 'Thank you.'

He looked at her and nudged her back. 'Don't mention it.' He looked back out to sea. 'What are your plans now?'

'I don't know. Stay away from Belfast, that's for sure.'

'Well, you can all stay here for as long as you need. This house needs to be lived in anyway. And you've got plenty of room. Use this as your base. Get your hands on the money you have access to and use it give yourself and everyone else in there a new start in life.' He turned and pointed at the pool house. 'And there's a big gym in there to keep Teodoro entertained.' He looked back at her. Her eyes glimmering, filling up like tiny glasses of water. 'You've got the rest of your life. Take the opportunity to bring your son up in a better home.' He stood up, took her by the hand and helped her up. She put her arm around him and they made their way back towards the house.

'What are you and Lorna going to do now?'

Brendan smirked. 'Who knows?'

*Hey guys, I would be extremely grateful if you would kindly leave a brief review. As you've reached the end of the book, I now see you as a faithful reader and I will enjoy having you come along on the next adventure with us. Reviews help my work get seen so more people can also enjoy the story. If you'd like to help, you can access the book's review page by clicking the following links:*

# Chapter One

BRENDAN AND LORNA SAT facing each other in the small family run cafe down a side street of Leicester's city centre. They'd been in England three days, and Brendan was already starting to relax. Away from Belfast. Away from Union Jacks and Tri-colours marking out the various danger zones of the city he called home. No mentions of IRA or UDA. No murals or portraits of dead paramilitaries who'd died fighting for their community. Brendan didn't want to see any of that ever again. He'd seen it all. His mother's father and two brothers were brigadiers in the Shankill Road UDA. His father's grandfather and uncle were long serving members of the Provisional IRA army council; calling the shots for the republican movement. Giving Brendan Cleary one of the most controversial names in this part of the world.

When Brendan came to realise that his family was so heavily involved in the troubles, he began to hate the surname. Ashamed. He was twenty-seven years of age and for the past ten years he'd lived with the knowledge that his family were responsible for so much destruction on the streets on Belfast.

Having been a rebellious teenager, he'd watched his friends on the Falls and Shankill roads being subjected to punishment beatings for joyriding in stolen cars. His best friend Mickey hung himself after being beaten so severely he'd lost his marbles.

Brendan had become the definition of a product of his environment: angry, hardened, an aggressive.

He'd watched his family get torn apart because of the division between the two sides. His mother became an alcoholic and his father was non existent – AWOL – disappeared. An unexpected chain of events in Belfast caused him to re-evaluate himself. The love of a woman – a stranger – was pivotal to all this.

Lorna Woodward: a twenty-nine-year-old British agent had Brendan's only support. And him her's.

Upon discovering a corrupt government in both Ireland and Britain, Brendan and Lorna now faced a life on the run with nobody to turn to. They were real a life bonny and Clyde. Just a little less psychotic than the infamous American couple.

'What are you staring at?' Lorna nudged Brendan with her elbow, causing him to flinch, hitting his still full-to-the-brim flat white that he'd let go cold.

He snatched up a napkin and dabbed the ring of coffee, then the bottom of his grey ceramic cup before placing it against his lips and taking a swig. 'Lukewarm coffee, almost as bad as warm piss!' He crunched up his face to show his disgust. 'Look at that pair of twats over there.' He gestured out the window to where two men were handing a bag to a young boy on a bicycle. The lad wasn't a day over thirteen and looked like he hadn't eaten a proper meal in weeks.

'Litttle shit should be in school,' Lorna said. 'Not out here on a dope run for his bum parents.'

'That's if he even has parents,' Brendan finished the rest of his coffee. 'Let's go.'

They got up and left the shop.

Stepping out into the rain they watched as the boy peddled towards the pub at the end of the street.

'Come on,' Brendan said, taking Lorna by the hand. She put her umbrella up for them. As they approached the run down pub that looked like a bulldozer would be just as relative as a refurbishment, a tall thin guy in his middle to late thirties stood with his hands inside the pockets of his Adidas tracksuit bottoms. He had one foot on the ground and the other against the shop window which he was leaning against. He looked up for a split second at Brendan and Lorna, only long enough for the two to see his eyes, glazed over and struggling to focus.

'Any spare change, mate?'

Brendan stopped and emptied his pocket, giving the guy about seven quid in shrapnel. 'Thank you, brother,' the guy cupped the coins in both hands as if Brendan had just given him a lifeline.

'Get yourself some food with that, mate.'

'You're Irish? My grandfather was Irish. I love Ireland.'

'If you grew up in Belfast, you'd probably think differently.' Brendan laughed as they made their way towards the door of the Leicester Arms.

'You know he's just going to buy more drink or drugs with that?' Lorna said, as Brendan held the door open for her.

'But that's one less person who'll die on the streets tonight.'

He followed Lorna inside. The dimly lit pub was complete with varnished tables, chairs with burgundy coloured cushions, navy walls with brass railings about waist height and a faded blue carpet that had stained patches sporadically throughout.

Three elderly men sat propped up on the bar stools, probably spending their pension, enjoying their retirement.

'What can I get you guys?' The lady behind the bar asked. She had chin-length mousy brown hair and mahogany coloured eyes. A white blouse that promoted her feminine curves in all the right places.

'Diet coke for me,' Lorna said.

'Same for me,' Brendan said. 'What time do you start serving food?'

'We can put it on now for you,' she reached under the bar and pulled out two cardboard folded menus. 'Have a look at...'

'I already know what I'm after,' Brendan said. 'All day breakfast, large.'

'I'll have the same,' Lorna said.

'It'll be around twenty minutes. That'll be fourteen pound fifty, please.'

Brendan pulled his bank card out and handed it to her.

'Thanks. Where in Ireland are you from?'

'Belfast,' Brendan said. 'You ever been?'

'No, never. Would love to go. Mind if I use the contactless?' She looked at him, he waved his hand dismissively, giving her the green light. She swiped his card and ripped the receipt from the machine. 'Maybe one day I'll go,' she smiled and handed Brendan his card and receipt.

A group of three men came into the pub, making their presence known with the volume of their laughter.

'Why don't you just ask for her number?' Lorna said, getting up from the stool and making her way towards the seating area at the back of the room.

Brendan laughed and followed her. He looked back at the lady behind the bar who was still looking at him. He smiled. And she smiled back. Their view of each other became blocked by one of the three rowdy men. The man turned around and looked at Brendan. His look was one of disapproval for the brief interaction between the two. Brendan assumed he was her boyfriend and thought nothing else of it.

Lorna grinned at Brendan as he sat down beside her. 'You like her.' She nodded in the direction of the bar.

'I only have eyes for you,' he nudged her back then kissed her on the cheek. Then came an uproar of laughter coming from the group at the bar. Brendan looked towards them. The one who looked like the bar lady's boyfriend was still looking over at him. A smug grin written across his face.

Brendan held his stare. A few throats were heard clearing and the laughter from the rest slowly faded away until there was nothing left but the clinks of cups and cutlery from the kitchen.

'Don't start, Brendan,' Lorna said. 'We haven't even had breakfast yet.'

Lorna's words passed through Brendan's right ear and straight out his left. 'I guess we've met the local hard man, then.' Brendan said, as his phone began to ring.

'Who the hell could that be?'

He answered it. They both laughed when was a woman with Indian accent, telling Brendan he may be eligible for compensation after an accident Brendan and Lorna weren't aware of.

At least the call had taken Brendan's attention off the so-called hard man at the bar.

'Are you positive he comes in here?' Brendan looked at Lorna who was on her laptop searching through files she'd saved from her former post as an upcoming agent for her majorities forces. Her MI5 badge gave her exclusive access to the criminal world that plagued the UK. This was now what Brendan and Lorna were devoted to cleaning up.

'The Leicester Arms, this is his hangout,' she slapped a few fingertips on her keypad and turned the laptop around for him to have a look at the image. An image of a short thin man, with a false tan and a blue Leicester City football top on. His white smile sat directly below his Rayban sunglasses. His perfectly styled hair told Brendan the guy spent more time in the tanning and beauty parlours than he did in full-time employment. 'Handsome devil isn't he,' Lorna joked.

'This is him?' Brendan said. 'This is Leicester's drug kingpin and god of the local underworld?'

'He might not look dangerous, but believe me he is, and he's had many people brutally tortured and killed. He never gets his hands dirty or allows himself to have a direct link to anyone he doesn't know for a very long time. He's very smart.'

'He won't be when we're done with him.'

'Alright, tough guy.' Lorna looked at Brendan then back over at the group of hard men at the bar. 'How are we going to take down this gang, then?'

'I've got to get close to him, gain his trust.'

'Brendan, I've already told you, he's not stupid. If he doesn't know you, he'll not even give you a second thought.' She pushed a strand of hair behing her ear. 'You'll not even get a handshake from him.'

'Want to bet?' Brendan sounded confident, looking over at the three men that were acting like they owned the bar. He looked at them as if he'd just found a precious stone. 'You think those three are acting as if they can do what they want?'

Lorna looked over at them. 'Yeah, they're acting like they're untouchable, like they've...'

'Got some heavy back up from someone influential?' Brendan gestured back at the screen. 'Like they're in tight with our tangoed friend here?'

'Brendan, those guys probably work for the guy who works for the guy, that reports to...' Lorna gestured at the lap-top screen. 'This guy.'

'I'm going to ask for a job,' Brendan said, as the bar lady came over with their breakfast. 'After this.' She set their plates down. 'Thanks.' He smiled at her, she smiled back, turned and walked away. She turned and smiled at him again as she walked away.

Lorna cleared her throat, breaking Brendan out of his stare. He looked at her and she gestured towards the group again who were now all staring at him. The smug grins on their faces had disappeared and been replaced by expressions of three angry pit bulls.

'That's enough eye-balling my missus, pal,' the man shouted over, finally disclosing the relationship between the two.

Brendan was about to react to him, Lorna kicked his foot below the table.

'Sorry, mate,' Brendan shouted back, putting his hand up in a sign of peace to the three. He looked at Lorna. 'You happy now?'

Lorna looked at Brendan, sucking a greasy mushroom into her mouth. She nodded and smiled at him. Brendan heard the group of three laugh among themselves, feeling his neck redden in anger. He looked back at Lorna who was dipping a sausage into her egg yolk. 'Let them have their little laugh. She grinned and looked up at him. 'We'll have the last laugh,' she put the sausage in her mouth and winked at him. 'Now eat your breakfast. Perhaps their boss will make an appearance.'

They both sat quietly, listening to the group of three laughing, reminiscing their recent trip to Amsterdam. How they got "fucked up" and were made to wash their cocks before shagging the hookers. Brendan and Lorna both struggled not to laugh when they heard this, had they burst out laughing it was liable to indicate their ability to hear them. They didn't want to throw away a valuable opportunity to pick up some information on the waves.

What the group talked about next was something that caused their ears to perk up. One of them mentioned "the big boss" going to his house in the costa del sol for a week and was due to return from the Spanish resort with news about the organisation. Upon his return he was holding a *cleansing* meeting for his organisation and was planning on cutting away the dead wood. One of the three was nervous about what this mean for him. Clearly, he was the weak link in the chain and wasn't confident in his employment being extended at that meeting. Or was he involved in something he shouldn't be. Whatever it was, he wasn't looking forward to it.

'I'd like to be a part of that meeting as a new recruit for when the boss man comes back,' Brendan said. 'Who do I need to impress in order to get an invitation to this meeting? You know these streets better than I do.'

'You need to do two things, one: make them like you,' Lorna said, as she stood up and hung her bad over her shoulder. 'And two: make one of them replaceable so that you can step in as the likely candidate.'

'Where are you going?'

'Powder my nose.'

He watched as she made her way across the bar towards the females. The music got louder. Local charts were playing. Brendan looked up at the bar, there was now a guy in a white shirt and bow tie leaning across the bar chatting up the bar lady. Brendan grinned to himself, almost feeling like he could read his new friend's mind, he looked around at their table. The three were all looking at the guy chatting up the lady. Brendan looked back up at the bar, the well-dressed guy had straightened himself up and made his way to the front door. His sheer size said he could probably wrap all three of his new friends around his little finger, but if

these guys were part of an organisation, the doorman probably wouldn't have had the balls to do anything. Brendan, on
the other hand, well, he'd dealt with the IRA and the UDA
in the past, groups that would look at a Leicester gangster as
nothing but the shit on the bottom of their shoe.

Brendan looked down at his hand, noticing he'd
clenched his fist, as if his sub-conscious was preparing him
for something. He looked at his phone, a new bulletin had
talked about Ireland and the mass shooting that had taken
place at the docks. The hunt was still on for the culprits.

Brendan watched as Lorna made her way back from the
ladies. She was grinning, looking directly at him. Just as
Brendan was about to ask her what was the smug grin for, the
building's evacuation alarm went off. Everyone in the pub
was directed to calmly make their way out to the assembly
point in the car park.

'What did you do that for,' Brendan asked.

'I'm giving us all a little opportunity to get to know each
other.' She pulled lipstick from her bag and ran the scarlet
coloured stick across her lips. 'Let's go.' She popped it back
into her bag and led the way through the sea of wooden tables and chairs.

Brendan stood up and followed her towards the front
door. The doorman made his way into the pub. The girl behind the bar shouted to him to check the females.

'You okay, babe?' Brendan and Lorna's new friend shouted as he followed Brendan out through the doors.

'Probably just a false alarm,' she replied as she, too, followed them out. Accompanied by two chefs, a cleaner and

the manager who'd been scratching his ass in his office, probably watching the TV.

The assembly point was in the pubs carpark. The homeless guy that Brendan had given money to on their way in was now vibrating on a more positive vibration with a bottle of cider in his hand, clearly being entertained by the drama that was unfolding. They all stood in the gravel covered carpark at the end of the city block. A run-down look in contrast to the high end, vibrant part of the city called the Highcross Shopping Centre.

Brendan stood with his hands in his pockets, still being stalked by the bar lady's eyes. He looked back at her. She had those wide green eyes that you could fall in to. She was a gem for sure, and this local hardman would have his mind reeling at the thought of her going with someone else. Especially given the fact that she was so flirtatious.

'Who was smoking in the females?' The doorman shouted from the side exit. The group of ten men and women all looked more interested in getting back inside than giving a shit about who'd set the alarm off.

'Sorry, that was me,' Lorna said. 'It's a bad habit, I'm sorry.'

'Okay, you're barred.' The doorman said. 'The rest of you can go back in again.'

'What do mean barred, fuck you, fat neck, I've just ordered food.'

'Tough, you should have though of that before you went for a smoke.' He looked even more smug when the manager came through the side fire exit with another three doormen.

'You stupid cunt,' the manager snatched the cigarette butt off the doorman and threw it at Lorna. Brendan swiped the butt away and stepped in front of Lorna.

'What did you just call her?'

Before Brendan could say another word, the manager was surrounded by the door staff. 'Piss off now, mate, you're both done here.'

'Do yourself a favour, pal,' Brendan's new mate sounded like he was passing on valuable advice. 'Piss off, and don't come back, yeah?'

'What are you, this cunt's secret protection,' Brendan spoke calmly. 'We've paid for our food, and we're not going anywhere before we get it.'

'Clearly, your Irish accent means you don't know who the fuck we are,' the manager said. 'For that, I'm going to give you a pass for that, and let...'

'I don't give a shit who you are,' Brendan stepped closer to him.

Two of the door men lunged forward towards Brendan. Brendan used one their momentum to throw him headfirst in to a wall. The second grabbed Brendan but Lorna kicked him in the balls from behind. The third doorman grabbed Lorna but Brendan bearhugged him from behind. He lifted the giant rugby player sized guy and threw him into the red Vauxhall Corsa that was parked next to the fire exit.

'You've got some balls, Irish!' The manager said. He looked at the Brendan's first mate of the day, nodded his head, gesturing in Brendan and Lorna's direction.

The guy looked at Brendan. Then he looked at his two mates. He then looked at the three door men who were standing bunched together, all of them reluctant to go in for a round two.

'This is your door security?' Brendan mocked the three.

'You'd do well, to leave now, mate,' the manager said, he pulled his phone out to take a photo of the two, but before he raised the device to point it, Brendan swung a roundhouse kick, sending his phone out of his hand.

'I'm calling the police,' the bar lady shouted. 'All this over a fucking smoke in the toilets,' she looked at Brendan and Lorna. 'You two, fuck off, now. Come back later when these dicks aren't here.' She looked at the door staff. 'You three are fucking useless.'

'You come back here, and you'll be shot, you hear me? You'll be fucking shot,' the rugby player sized bouncer made another run for Brendan. Brendan spun in a circle, lifting his leg and kicking the rugby player in the side of the face, knocking him out before he hit the ground.

Lorna pulled Brendan away, 'come on, Brendan. We'll come back later. For a refund.'

Brendan put his hood up and linked arms with Lorna as they made their way to the other side of the street. They repeatedly glanced over their shoulders, making sure they weren't followed.

Getting to the Highcross Shopping Centre, they went to the third floor car park, to section A5 to where their BMW 6 Series was parked. The heavily tinted windows allowed them to stay anonymous.

As Lorna jumped into the driver's seat, she started the engine and laughed. 'You get who the manager was?'

'I guess you're going to tell me, but I can have a good guess... He's someone I want to impress?'

Lorna looked at him a nodded, grinning. 'Well be back later.'

# Chapter Two

AFTER AN EARLIER THAN usual McDonalds and a drive out into the lush Leicestershire countryside, Brendan and Lorna returned to their hotel, set in the suburban area of North Leicester, convenient – only a short drive from the city centre. They decided to change into more formal attire and planned to make use of the millions left to Brendan by his late father. He joked about himself being like Bruce Wayne. Left with millions. Money he didn't care about, but what he did give a shit about was making the lives of criminals around the world hell, and if the money could support that, then he'd found good use for not only his life, but for the money he was in possession of.

After a shower, and sprucing themselves up, Brendan and Lorna left their hotel room, with nothing but a bank card and a small handgun that Lorna kept in her purse. Brendan didn't want to waste bullets on the small fish. Why would he be interested in wasting his time with the scum that worked on the streets when his and Lorna's time was better suited for the heads of the local menaces.

Passing through the foyer, they were greeted and wished a lovely evening by the receptionist, and then the night porter as they made their way towards across the front door. Brendan drove this time. Lorna directed him while playing around on her phone.

'What's got your attention?' Brendan asked, as he pulled onto the A6 duel carriageway city bound. The time was shortly after six and the evening traffic was beginning to thin out.

'I think it's not just the English gangsters we need to be thinking about.' She looked at Brendan. 'I'm reading a local news report that talks about there being an influx of Italians in the Leicester area. Not only Italians, but drugs and weapons that appear to have come from Italian shores.'

'Our recent trip to Italy has come back to haunt us already?'

'We'll soon find out.' She put her phone in her purse and put the window down. 'If Italians have muscled in on the local gangs, then it brings the level of sophistication, and brutality of the criminal world to a new level. But right now, I just want my money back.' She laughed. 'I was looking forward to that fry today too.'

'I'm wondering who out of that group of three clowns we can use to get close to that group.'

'Don't think about it too much, just let it come naturally.'

The next fifteen minutes were spent in relative silence. Stopping at a red light almost every two hundred yards would have been enough to put the most patient of people in a bad mood.

King Street on the city centre was a residential area, mostly catering for students of the local De Mumfert University. This meant, most of the residents didn't have cars. What was more frightening to students than having to pay a parking fee? Brendan had plenty of spaces to choose from.

And after parking the car, they made their way towards the Leicester Arms to get their money back from the breakfast they'd ordered that morning.

'Is it too late for a fry?' Lorna joked.

'Never too late for a fry,' Brendan laughed; locking the car he zipped his jacket closed. He was about to follow Loran who'd already crossed the street and created an impatient distance. 'What?' he looked at her as she pointed towards the back of the car.

'You want to go in here holding nothing but your cock in your hand?'

He laughed. 'I'm pretty sure I can handle them with my hands.' He popped the boot open. In the middle of the boot was a backpack. It would have passed for a school bag, but the contents of the bag were certainly not that of school materials. Two handguns, nestling in their leather shoulder holsters. Brendan had confidence that the magazines had more than compressed air in them, but he pocketed fresh mags just to be safe. He unzipped his jacket and tossed one of the holsters over his left shoulder. He mirrored with the opposite arm and holster. He threw his jacket back on and zipped it closed, crossing the road to join Lorna.

'Let's go, tough guy.' She linked arms with him. 'You're a softy really, Brendan Cleary. I've seen your soft side.'

He laughed off the comment. 'When?' He slipped his hand into his trouser pockets.

They used the local internet and sat nav services, making their journey quicker. Rounding a corner, they had fifty feet and about ten pedestrians between them and the door. There was one guy on the door and he was chatting to a group of three women. They were obviously flirting with the six-and-a-half-foot bodybuilder. He had a tan that certainly didn't come from standing on the streets of an English city. Perhaps he was one of the not so nice Italians who'd moved from their southern Europe coasts to the cooler climate of Britain.

As Brendan and Lorna got within ten feet, the accented door man was certainly Italian, or at least of that region. And the local ladies clearly found it attractive. They were not ejected from the pub, yet they'd found more entertainment chatting to the foreigner than going inside. And what was better for Brendan and Lorna, the Italian seemed to be enjoying the attention, certainly enough to not give Brendan and Lorna a second glance. He even held the door open for them in.

Brendan entered first, followed by Lorna. The warm air hitting their faces was a welcomed feature to the venue. The overpowering stench of stale beer and the sticky floors as they headed towards the bar was not. Brendan looked back a Lorna and smiled. She blew him a kiss. It was almost as if the two were enjoying the buzz. As he got closer to the bar, he seen the same lady serving. She caught Brendan's eye almost as fast as he caught hers. She smiled and held his gaze right up until he reached the bar.

'You've got balls, Irishman. I'll give you that.'

'And you've got money belonging to us,' Lorna said. 'Now cough up.'

The bar lady smiled at Lorna, but her expression was not half as welcoming as the one she gave to Brendan. 'How about I get you both a drink, then I'll go and get you your refund. Either that or we can try again tomorrow?'

'Thought we were barred? How's the boss man going to feel about that?' Brendan said.

'You pissed him off, that's for sure. But he respects people with balls. And you pair,' her eyes darted from Brendan and Lorna. 'Did make our door staff look like a bunch of pussies today.'

'I'll have a sparkling water, please,' Lorna said.

'White coffee.' Brendan added.

'Grab a seat over there, I'll bring them over to you. Louise is the name by the way,' she reached her hand over the counter, first towards Lorna.

'Lorna,' Lorna shook her hand.

'And you?' Louise reached in Brendan's direction. 'Brendan.'

'Lovely to meet you both.'

They both turned and zig zagged through the free spaces on the pub floor in the direction of their seats, taking the same seats as they had earlier. Brendan took his phone out and took a photo of Lorna.

'What are you doing?' She smiled awkwardly.

'I wanted to see a real-life picture of a jealous expression.' He laughed out loud and pulled her in close to him. He kissed, but as he moved in, he spotted someone coming up behind her. 'We may have a problem,' he whispered in her ear. He pulled her around to his side of the table.

They both stood together, shoulder to shoulder as the three guys they'd met today approached.

'Thought you two would have learned your lesson this morning.' The one who acted like Louise's boyfriend said. The other two just stood on either side of him, serious expressions on their faces. Brendan looked at the one he'd sussed as the trio's weakest link and broke his stare almost instantly.

Lorna sat down. Brendan did the same. Both of them emanating a quiet confidence. Which was at least recognised by the group.

'We're just here for a drink,' Lorna said as she pulled her phone out and took a picture of Brendan, grinning at him, paying more attention to Brendan's silly expression towards her than the three onlookers. She looked back at the three. 'Now fuck off.'

Brendan smiled at them, then turned his attention to Lorna. 'What was that photo for?'

'I wanted to see a real example of a pissed off expression.'

He laughed a looked at the three. 'You heard her, fuck off.'

The leader of the three was about to step in closer to them when Louise interrupted.

'Look, we don't want any trouble with you. We understand we may have tread on your toes this morning, but we were tired and hungry,' Brendan said.

The nervous one of the three finally looked as if he had a mind of his own. He stepped in closer and gestured to Brendan. 'He reminds me of Jonty Moore Jr. The accent. The hardman untouchable act. It's funny, in a cute kind of way.'

Brendan stood back up again. And the guy stepped back again, with the other two acting as his bodyguards. 'What do you know about Jonty Moore Jr?' He looked at the three who all looked like they were ready to pounce.

'Just that when he and his dad came to the meet the boss, they brought with them the same swagger and cockiness as you have.' The leader of the group said. 'But the difference between you and him, is that his name brings with it the notoriety.' He looked at Lorna then the other two. 'You on the other hand,' he stepped up to Brendan. 'Who the fuck are you?'

As much as Brendan wanted to plaster the guy all over the bar, mixing in his mates with him, he now felt he had a reason to back down and, do what his father always taught him, be smart and plan the next move.

'You three, fuck off and let the two of them have their drinks. This morning was just a misunderstanding. And he's done us a favour by highlighting how shit our door security is.'

They all managed to laugh.

'That's it,' the one who highlighted Johnty Moore Jr said. 'You're part of the Irish MMA scene and want people to know that.' He nudged Louise with his elbow. 'We've got a local tough guy wanting to make a name for himself. Maybe he wants a job.'

'Well, we both know I could spread your scrawny ass around this room without much bother.'

Louise grabbed the little mouthpiece and the turned him around.' Fuck off and stop starting shit and then hiding behind their back. You start more shit than enough.' She turned around and smiled at Brendan and Lorna. 'You two enjoy your drinks. If you need anything let me know.'

They watched as she left and went back to the bar, weaving in and out of the human traffic.

'You know Johnty Moore and his son of the same name?' Brendan took a drink.

'I do. I've worked with British intelligence for a few years and the bastard's name cropped up more times than I would have liked.' Lorna lifted her drink and looked inside the glass first before taking a drink. 'But we were under the impression that Johnty had went into exile in Scotland.'

'Maybe he's decided to come down here. Maybe Scotland is too close to his old culture.' Brendan looked around the pub. The venue was full of people who were having a normal social. A mixture of young and old. The older crowd perhaps desperately trying to hold onto their youth. The younger ones more reckless and adventurous. They'd be the ones that would be easy pickings for the local drug dealers. He took another drink of his coffee and smiled at Louise as she fixed her eyes on him as she pretended to wipe down the top of the bar.

'You know she's only trying to sweeten you up,' Lorna said, sounding bitter. 'She could have any guy in here, why'd she give a shit about you?'

Brendan laughed. 'Why don't you go and ask her.' He nudged her. Both their attention got dragged away to the other corner of the room where a guy had fallen off his stool for trying, and failing, to hug one of his mates. There were always the ones in a club that would end up getting kicked out by the bouncers and it looked if it was going to be that group.

'So,' Lorna brought Brendan's attention back to their table. 'What about this scumbag Johnty.'

Brendan looked at her, fighting to contain his expression. 'Do you really need me to tell you what I'm thinking or can you figure it out for yourself.'

'Maybe I just need some clarification.' She took another drink. 'You probably talked about to your friends how much you, or perhaps most people your age, would offer up to be given the whereabouts of someone who was responsible for some many innocent deaths in Belfast. Now, the most unlikely person in the world,' she gestured to the group of three who were still watching them from the bar. 'Just handed you a winning lottery ticket.' She finished her drink. 'And now, the only thing that's running through your head is – how do you go about cashing in.' She smiled at him. 'Did I miss anything?'

He leaned in and gave her a kiss on the cheek. 'You summed it up perfectly.' He stood up and fixed his jacket. 'I'll be back in a second. 'I'm going to go ask for a job.' She looked at him and blew him a kiss. He responded in kind. As he made his way towards the bar, the manager that they met this morning came to the till on Brendan's near side of the bar. He opened the drawer and started taking the cash out.

'Is it wise to do that with so many people around?' Brendan shouted across the bar to the manager who didn't even look at Brendan as he tipped the tray of notes and coins into a navy cloth pocket.

'Most people wouldn't have the balls to even attempt it, mate.' He slammed the cashdrawer closed and finally looked up at Brendan.

'You can't mean your security team gives you that confidence. After this morning we both know they aren't worth the shit wages you pay them.'

'You think you can do better?'

Brendan smiled.

'You're cocky, kid,' the manager shouted. 'What are you after?'

'A job.'

'Here,' the manager handed Brendan a twenty pound note. 'That's for missing out on the best fucking breakfast in Leicester this morning.'

Brendan refused the money. 'Give it charity. What about the job?'

'Come back tomorrow, then we'll talk.'

Brendan turned and spotted the guy who looked like Louise's boyfriend sitting down in Brendan's seat. He was talking to Lorna but looking at Brendan at the same time. If Brendan didn't know any better, he'd think he was trying to wind him up. The guy clearly didn't know that Lorna had impeccable taste and, in her eyes, she was way out the guy's league. Brendan turned back to the manager and told him they'd be back in the morning.

He walked back to Lorna, she was looking at her new friend, but he maintained his stare on Brendan. Brendan got within five feet of the table and the guy jumped up from the seat. He put his hand out to shake Brendan's. Brendan responded in kind.

The guy pulled Brendan in close and whispered in his ear. 'She's fit, mate, watch her close.' Still maintaining the tight handshake, he squeezed Brendan's hand, as if trying to cut off the blood supply. 'Was nice knowing you. Pity we couldn't have got to know each other a bit better.' He spoke sarcastically.

'I'll be back in the morning. The boss man is meeting me about a job.' Brendan smiled smugly, as if replacing the other guy's who's facial expression had now dropped. 'See you tomorrow if you'll be here.' He looked at Lorna and indicated that it was their que to leave.

# About the Author

'I'm simply a guy who wanted to write his partner a book in her language, it's just got way out of hand!'

P.M. Heron was born in Belfast and spent the first 27 years of his life on Irish soil before moving to Loughborough, England to finish his study in sports management. He completed his degree in May 2012, which was, to say the least, an inspiring time to be in Loughborough. That summer, the university hosted Team Japan and Team GB for the 2012 Olympic Games in London.

At that time, he met his partner who came to England from Italy also to study sports management. Quite a summer to remember. Obviously graduating wasn't too bad either!

Later that year, he decided to teach himself to speak Italian. As a way for him to practice what he had learned, he began writing in his work diary - in Italian - and this was how he discovered a love for writing.

In March 2015, he decided to write his partner a book - in Italian - for their 3rd anniversary.

So, after 6 months, he managed to finish that book: a story titled "La Storia Della Mia Vita" which is Italian for "The Story Of My Life".

So, he fell in love with writing but didn't know how to continue. Until Sunday 11th October 2015, while talking to a friend in a leisure centre which he had been managing at the time, he came up with the idea for his first fictional series. It's simply snowballed from there!

Read more at pmheronauthor.com.

.

Printed in Great Britain
by Amazon

18430608R00202